Neill William

Autobiography of William Neill: With a Selection from His Sermons

Neill William

Autobiography of William Neill: With a Selection from His Sermons

ISBN/EAN: 9783337156435

Printed in Europe, USA, Canada, Australia, Japan

Cover: Foto ©Raphael Reischuk / pixelio.de

More available books at **www.hansebooks.com**

Yours truly W. Neill.

AUTOBIOGRAPHY

OF

WILLIAM NEILL, D.D.

WITH A

Selection from his Sermons.

BY THE

Rev. J. H. JONES, D. D.,

PASTOR OF THE SIXTH PRESBYTERIAN CHURCH, PHILADELPHIA.

PHILADELPHIA:

PRESBYTERIAN BOARD OF PUBLICATION,

821 CHESTNUT STREET.

1861.

PREFATORY NOTE.

————•◆•————

THE reason for preparing this Narrative is thus given by the author himself: it is "to note down and arrange some recollections of my past life, for the gratification of my children and other friends when I am gone; and also for the purpose of celebrating the goodness of Divine Providence towards one who was exposed, from early childhood, to the hardships of orphanage, and the temptations of the world; and who, without earthly guardian vested with authority, was left to follow the propensities of a wayward and depraved heart. Truly *a Father of the fatherless and a Judge of the widows, is God in his holy habitation.*"

It will be the common regret and disappointment of the readers that it is so short; that one whose life had been so useful, and so long, should have written no more of what he had known, and felt, and done, which surviving friends would gladly read. The small service which we render, in preparnig it for the press, is done at the suggestion made by our friend not many days before his death. It came into our hands in the well prepared state, as respects the composition and arrangement of facts, in which it is given to the reader. Not a few are yet living, who had the privilege of enjoying his ministry, who will read the Sermons of their lamented pastor and friend with scarcely less interest than they have read his Life. As the narrative was suspended by the writer a few years before his death, we have appended the discourse preached in commemoration of his life and character, in which are mentioned the most important events of the latter part of his life to its close. It is an inadequate tribute of affectionate respect to a loved and honored predecessor in the same pulpit, where his memory is still fragrant.

CONTENTS.

———◆◆◆———

AUTOBIOGRAPHY.

I BEGIN to note down and arrange some recollections of my past life, for the gratification of my children and other friends when I am gone; and also, for the purpose of celebrating the goodness of Divine Providence towards one who was exposed, from early childhood, to the hardships of orphanage, and the temptations of the world, and who, without earthly guardian vested with authority, was left to follow the propensities of a wayward and depraved heart. Truly, "a Father of the fatherless, and a Judge of the widows, is God, in his holy habitation."

My parents were born and raised in Chestnut Level, Lancaster county, Pennsylvania. All that I know of them is from report, as I have no recollection . of either of them. My father, William Neill, or Neel, (as the family then spelt the name,) was of Irish descent, and my mother, Jane Snodgrass, if I am rightly informed, was, by at least one branch of her parentage, of Scottish lineage; so that the family, like many of the early settlers of Pennsylvania, were denominated Scotch-Irish.

When on a visit to my Chestnut Level relatives,

1

some years ago, I was shown the spot where my father's residence once stood. It was marked by a shapeless pile of stone, in a field, as if to remind the traveller of the transitory nature of his earthly abode. "We have here no continuing city, but we look for one, which hath foundations, whose builder and maker is God." In the year 1775, if I mistake not, the family including four children, Dorcas, Mary, John, and Jane, removed to the west of the State, Allegheny county, where my father purchased two farms, one on each side of the Monongahela river, a few miles from Pittsburgh, then called Fort Pitt. The family lived on the place southwest of the river, two or three miles from what is now called McKeesport, and eight miles from Pittsburgh; there my youngest sister Margaret and myself were born—she in the year 1776, and I in the spring of 1778 or '79; the 25th of April was fixed on as the day, although there is some uncertainty about the year and day, owing to a deficiency in the record, for those were troublous times. It was in the midst of our Revolutionary struggle. The hostile Indians were committing frequent and fearful depredations—destroying property, and murdering the inhabitants all along our frontiers. They usually made their way into the white settlements in small parties, under cover of night and the forests; and, perpetrating their deeds of plunder and blood, retreated to their lurking-places before a sufficient force could be rallied to arrest them. The chief reliance of the people for safety was on their fire-arms and block-houses, a rude kind of forts constructed of logs, and capable of being defended by a few armed men in the inside. On any alarm of an Indian incursion the women and children repaired to these fortresses with all speed, while the men went in pursuit of the enemy.

To the barbarity of one of these marauding parties of savages my father fell a victim. The circumstances in brief, as I have gathered them from credible tradition, were these. In the spring of 1779 or 1780, he, with my mother and my brother, then a lad of some eight or nine years, and myself, an infant of a year old, together with my uncle, John Neill, and a part of his family, passed over to the farm on the opposite side of the river, eight miles from the ordinary residence of the family, in order to put in a spring crop. While there, another brother, Adam, from Lancaster county, arrived on a visit, and with the intention of moving his family out in case he liked the country. The next morning after his brother's arrival, my father and he went out to look after their horses, and were both shot down and scalped by the Indians, within sight of the house. The other brother, John, upon hearing the report of the guns, suspecting what had happened, took his rifle, and ran in the direction of the sound, exclaiming, "There they are—turn out, turn out!" This involuntary exclamation, it has always been thought, was the means, in the hand of a kind Providence, of saving those who were in the house from being massacred. The savages, taking the alarm, fled to a neighbour's of the name of Marshall, at some distance, murdered three of his sons, and after an unsuccessful attempt to set fire to his house, escaped from the neighbourhood with their scalps and other booty, unmolested and in bloody triumph. My mother, carrying me in her arms, fled with the rest of the family party to the block-house, distant about a mile, crossing several high fences in the way. My murdered father and uncle were buried in one grave, and in each other's arms. Well do I remember the spot; for I have often looked upon it with pensive emotions. It is a hillock, formerly shaded by a clump of trees, near a fine spring, on what our family used to call the "Long Run Farm," from a small stream of that name which passes through it, two or three miles west of Long Run meeting-house, and the like distance south of the turnpike road, and about half-way between Pittsburgh and Greensburg. The place of my father's sepulchre is thus minutely designated, that if any of the relatives or descendants, in time to come, should wish to see it, they may know where it is to be found.

Upon the disastrous death of my father, the family broke up housekeeping, and the children were located among their friends. My mother's health, under the pressure of care and sorrow, declined rapidly. She survived my father, I think, but about three years. Her remains lie interred near the Lebanon Church, a few miles from the old homestead. I was now, at about four years of age, placed in the family of an uncle, Robert Snodgrass, three miles south of Pittsburgh, where I passed six years of my boyhood, in a manner by no means favourable to intellectual or moral improvement, doing light work on the farm, and attending a common country school, at the distance of two or three miles. I used to be terribly afraid of wolves, bears, and panthers, in passing to and from school, there being great numbers of those ferocious animals prowling about the rugged hills and dense forests in that part of the country. Deer, wild turkeys, pheasants, quails, and various other species of game, were also very abundant, and constituted an important item in the provisions of most tables.

My uncle lived remote from a place of public worship, Pittsburgh being the nearest place where the gospel was preached statedly; but the river being in the way, the family searcely ever went thither to attend worship. I remember my uncle and aunt went occasionally on horseback to a church, distant some four or five miles; but I have no recollection of having attended public worship while I was a member of the family, excepting now and then in the summer season, when there happened to be preaching at a farm-house, or in a neighbouring wood. Nor was there any regular attention to family religion; religious books were scarce, and there were no Sabbath-schools; so that, at ten years old, I was almost as ignorant of the doctrines of the Gospel, and of the duties which I owed to my Creator and Redeemer, as any tawny child of the forest.

At the age of ten or eleven, with consent of the parties concerned, I left my uncle, and went to my oldest sister's, Mrs. Sampson, in the Forks of Yough; but no one having authoritative control of me, I

1*

became a wandering, wayward, homeless orphan boy; and but for the unseen and unheeded guardianship of Divine Providence, I must have gone speedily to ruin. I lived now with one sister, and then with another; and, for a year or two, with my brother, who then owned and occupied the place where my father's bones rest. At length, having attended school so much as to be able to read, write, and use figures a little, I became a clerk in the store of John Dayly, a near neighbour of one of my sisters, and who proved a friend to me, as he was an example of industry and probity, and gave me some knowledge of the mercantile business, on a small scale. With this worthy man I remained but a short time, when, having reverted to my idle and migratory way of life, I received, by favour of Providence, an offer of a clerkship in the store of David White, a respectable young man, who had recently commenced business in Canonsburgh, Pennsylvania. This offer I promptly accepted, and its acceptance took me away from my near kindred, from whom I have been separated ever since, except occasional visits.

My father's earthly estate fell into careless hands, and was badly managed, so that it never amounted to much. We were all obliged, therefore, to be industrious, and practise economy. Let my children note this, and avoid indulging a discontented and murmuring spirit, if Providence shall see fit to keep them in straitened circumstances. Let them not make haste to be rich, but let them be industrious and honest, keeping their expenditures within their means; and may the lively oracle impress their hearts—"Godliness, with contentment, is great gain."

I went to Canonsburgh, as near as I can recollect, about the year 1795, pursuant to the offer before mentioned. There, though it was a religious atmosphere, and a place of good moral influences, I was at first thrown into company and a way of life not at all favourable to my spiritual interests. Mr. White was a gay young man, not remarkably attentive to his business, or to the conduct of those about him; in consequence of which habits he ultimately failed, and became poor. I was equally reckless—a child of nature, addicted to folly, and wholly destitute of the wisdom that is from above. But God soon laid his hand heavily, but, I trust, mercifully upon me. Attending a country dance, very common in those days, even around Canonsburgh, after being much heated by the engagements of the evening, I got wet, returning home at the midnight hour, and took a cold, which brought on a fever that threatened my life. This was the severest and longest illness I ever had; it lasted from six to eight weeks. During a part of the time I was deranged in mind, and unconscious of what was passing; but when my reason returned, I felt that I was in forlorn and awful circumstances; away from all my kindred, in a strange place, and in a small room, attended only by a young and inexperienced girl; wasting and sinking under a violent fever, induced by my own folly; apprehensive of death, but unprepared to die; my physician visiting me not oftener than once a week, for he lived at

Washington, seven miles distant, and I knew not whether there was any one resident nearer. I watched the setting sun through the window, day after day, and cried literally and bitterly unto the Lord for help, promising, with many tears, that if he would but raise me up, and give me space, I would repent, and live to his glory. He heard my cries, and raised me up. But, alas! for sick-bed resolutions! They are but the expressions of fear, and are seldom kept. Upon the restoration of health, I recovered in some degree my relish for folly and sin; but I was not left entirely to despise the chastening of the Lord, or to forget how terrific death appeared to me, when conscious that I was an impenitent and Christless sinner. I was more guarded and cautious than before, and occasionally paid some attention to religious duties; but it was some eighteen months or two years after this, before I took any decisive steps for the renunciation of my sinful ways, and the dedication of myself to God.

The Rev. Dr. McMillan preached stately two miles from town, and very frequently on the Sabbath evenings in the old Academy in the village. I began to attend pretty constantly upon his ministrations. He was a very faithful and alarming preacher, and aimed directly at the heart and conscience. Under his thundering voice and sound doctrine I have often been roused, terrified, and melted to tears. Sometimes he made me angry, and I felt tempted to quit hearing him; but, upon the whole, I began to find out, under his preaching, that I was a sinner, and that it was indeed a fearful thing to be in a state of condemnation with the wrath of God abiding on me. His manner was rough, and rather repulsive. I remember he passed me once, on his way to church, when I was engaged in shooting pigeons, (it was a fast-day, if I recollect rightly,) and addressing me in a stern manner, said: "It is an audacious and unseemly thing for a sinner on the broad road to hell, to be killing innocent birds by the way." Harsh as the remark was, it had some effect in convicting me of sin and danger.

When it became known that I was beginning to be thoughtful on the subject of religion, the pious students of the Academy took opportunities of conversing with me, and, by degrees, drew me into their society and to their prayer-meetings. This was of great service to me in my ignorance of divine things and under my incipient convictions. I now betook myself to secret prayer and the serious reading of the Bible, and was punctual in my attendance on public worship. I became, in a word, deeply concerned about the salvation of my soul, and soon made arrangements to quit the service of Mr. White and devote myself to study, with a view to the ministry, if I should become, hopefully, a subject of redeeming grace. This was an important movement, and it cost me some anxious thoughtfulness. My patrimony was small, quite inadequate, I knew, to the expense of a good education, and I had no wealthy relatives to look to for aid; yet, after serious deliberation, I resolved, with a sort of vague trust in Divine Providence, to make the attempt, and proceed as far as I could. Accordingly I entered the Academy and opened my Latin Grammar, if my memory serves me well, in the year 1797. But as yet, I had no satisfactory evidence of a change of heart. My solicitude on the subject, however, continued, and, of course, I sought the society of the pious, and threw myself in the way of good influences; "following on," as it is expressed in Scripture, " to know the Lord"—seeking him in the ways of his appointment as opportunities offered. I began to relish religious services, and to esteem the Sabbath a blessing, and the courts of God's house amiable. With these feelings I often walked eight or ten miles to be present on sacramental occasions, in neighbouring congregations, which were generally very solemn, and in which the exercises were usually continued for several days in succession.

It was on one of those blissful occasions that, I humbly hope, I was enabled to commit my soul to Christ, renouncing all confidence in the flesh, and acquiescing joyfully in the glorious gospel plan of salvation by free grace. I do not attach undue importance, I trust, to time and place in the matter of conversion; but there is a *time*, and there is a *place*, when and where the regenerate soul is born into the kingdom, and there are some cases so strongly marked in relation to both, that they can never be forgotten. It is a great change; it is from darkness to light, from enmity to love, from a state of death in sin to that of spiritual life and peace with God, through our Lord Jesus Christ. Such a change, with some of its attendants or associations of time, place, and means, will be very likely to be had in grateful remembrance. But I would be far from making these circumstances, striking as they are in some instances, essential to all cases of genuine conversion. God is not confined to specific modes or means in his work of mercy; but we may humbly tell what he has done for our souls, and should remember, if we can, where, and when, and by what means he rescued us from impending ruin. However different may have been the experience of others, I, for one, cannot soon forget the circumstances in which the Lord appeared in the plenitude of his gracious power to my soul, and, as I trust, changed my mournful state. It was on a tranquil summer's evening, away from human view, in the closet of a dense wood, at the eventide hour for secret devotion, after attendance on the services of the sanctuary, and while Divine truth was yet bearing down upon conscience, alone with God, I felt guilty, and confessed that

"If my soul were sent to hell,
God's righteous law approved it well."

My heart was burdened. I was without strength, and yet without excuse; means were inefficient, the arm of human power was withered, and could not be stretched forth without Divine aid. What could guilty helplessness do, but cry for mercy? There was the throne of grace, and thence there seemed to issue a voice fraught with good tidings of great joy, "My grace is sufficient for thee;" "My strength is perfected in weakness;" "Come unto me, all ye that labour and are heavy laden, and I will give you rest." It is enough. The word is with power and in demonstration of the Spirit. The deaf ear is unstopped, the dark mind enlightened, the will subdued, the heart softened, and the whole soul sweetly won over to God, on his own terms, and "Christ is all, and in all." Can all this be a delusion? I think not. The individual may be deceived, for "the heart is deceitful above all things, and desperately wicked." We should look well to our experience, testing it by the word of truth, which liveth and abideth for ever. Nor is regeneration to be regarded as releasing us from the obligation of "giving all diligence to make our calling and election sure." It is but the commencement of the Christian warfare. We are to watch and pray, and labour in our Lord's vineyard, pressing onward toward the mark, for the prize of our high calling of God in Christ Jesus. The conscious debtor to free grace, will, as opportunity serves, keep the Redeemer's commandments.

Thus it was, in some humble degree, with the subject of this narrative. Though his feelings have been variable, and his failings great, he has never entirely relinquished his hope in God. I am what I am, in regard to Christian attainments, and official faithfulness. My sole dependence for usefulness, acceptance, and heaven, is the mercy of God, through the merits and mediation of Christ; and I humbly hope, that He who has called me by his grace, will keep me by his power, through faith unto salvation.

Reader, I ask you very seriously, not whether your experience tallies with that just narrated, but whether you have indeed experienced "the renewing of the Holy Ghost, and the washing of regeneration." And you should not rest easy till you can answer the question in the affirmative; for you know who has said, "Except a man be born of water and of the Spirit, he cannot enter into the kingdom of God."

I was admitted to the communion of the Presbyterian church in immediate connection with the church of Chartiers, Washington county, then under the pastoral care of the Rev. Dr. John McMillan. And now I pursued my studies with more diligence, and, as I trust, from better motives than before. I was a member of the Academy about two years and a half. My time was spent very agreeably, and not altogether unprofitably. The society of the pious students was delightful; and there were families whose dwellings were Bethels, where we often met for prayer, and praise, and religious conference. There was as much of the primitive spirit of Christianity among us as I have ever witnessed since. Upon the occurrence of slight alienations between the brethren, we were in the habit of making mutual concessions, and going, together with our difficulties, to the throne of grace. We "kept the unity of the Spirit in the bond of peace." It was quite a common practice with us, in taking our morning and evening walks, to go two and two together, to some sequestered spot, and there to unite in prayer. These were refreshing exercises,

2

and exceedingly favourable to our proficiency in study, and growth in grace.

In the autumn of 1800, I took leave of Canonsburg, for the College of New Jersey, at Princeton, in company with my friend and fellow-student, John Boggs. We equipped for the journey on horseback, intending to sell the nags on our arrival, which we did. A little incident which occurred on the way may be mentioned as illustrating the happy influence of the habit of acknowledging God in all events. We were to call on Boggs's father, who resided some distance off the direct route, in the edge of Virginia, not far from Martinsburg. Crossing the Potomac river, a little before sunset, and finding, on inquiry, that the distance was greater than we expected, we became apprehensive that we should not be able to reach Mr. Boggs's that night; and, although our pathway was a blind one, we determined to proceed as far as possible. Night fell upon us; our dim path utterly failed, and we found ourselves in a dense forest, in profound darkness. What was to be done? Must we stay in the bush over night? No; our horses would suffer or be lost, and we were not accustomed to such exposure. We resolved, therefore, (call it fanaticism, or what you will,) to look to God, and do what we could to get forward. Drawing our horses' heads close together, we united in prayer for Divine guidance and protection. Our minds became composed; we took courage, and pressed onward through a pathless wilderness, leaving our animals to pick their own way; for it was impossible for us, in such circumstances, to

judge of the points of the compass. We had not proceeded far, when the barking of a dog gave signs that
we were approaching a human habitation. It was a
gladsome sound, and we said, "The Lord hath heard
the voice of our supplication." Whether it was so in
faet, or not, it was pleasant and proper for us to
ascribe our deliverance to Him whose tender mercies
are over all his ereatures, and whose ear is ever open
to our cries. Upon reaching the spot, we found there
was no room for us; but receiving direetions to a
place called Bath, I think, some miles ahead, wo
pressed forward, and found quarters for the remainder
of the night. Our aeeommodations were rough, but
we were thankful for them; and at an early hour the
next day, we arrived at the dwelling of my companion's father, where we were reçeived and entertained
for several days, with every mark of cordiality and
kindness.

Resuming our journey eollege-ward, we arrived at
Princeton just at the opening of the winter session.
It was a time of bustle; and the scene was new, and
rather appalling to us green boys, from beyond the
mountains. However, we endeavoured to mind our
own business—appeared before that formidable body,
"the Faculty;" delivered our letters; and were
examined, and admitted—Boggs, as he was ahead
of me in preparatory studies, to the Junior class;
and I into the Sophomore, for which I was hardly
prepared. My age and apparent sedateness, I believe, turned the scale in my favour with the good
President and Professors. The Rev. Dr. Samuel

S. Smith was then President. I think there were but two Professors—Dr. John Maclean, (father of the present Vice-President,) Professor of Mathematics, Chemistry, &c., and the venerable William Thomson, Professor of Languages—with two Tutors, viz. Benjamin B. Hopkins and Cyrus Riggs.

Boggs and I were assigned a room together in College, and we were mutually helpful to each other in our studies, and in our endeavours to maintain a Christian spirit and deportment. But our principles and the strength of our attachment to Christ were put pretty severely to the test. Many of the students were dissipated and shockingly profane, and there were very few professors of religion then in the Institution. We kept up weekly prayer-meetings, however, and had the usual privileges of public worship on the Sabbath; but we had to bear a heavy cross, and watch unto prayer assiduously against conformity to the world. College is a fiery furnace to piety, and where there is not a predominance of Christian influence, a place of imminent peril to the morals and souls of reckless and inexperienced youth.

My own means of support being inadequate, I, like many others, was admitted, through the recommendation of friends, to a participation in the interest of the "Leslie Fund" of the College, (a noble endowment established by a benevolent gentleman of that name,) without which I could not have met the expenses of my collegiate course. To that fund I am indebted to this day; I acknowledge the obligation, and it would give me pleasure to pay back all that I drew from it, if I felt able. Hitherto it has not seemed convenient to do so; and whether, with my large family, and the poor flock which I am now serving, very much at my own charges, I shall ever feel able to discharge the obligation, is extremely doubtful. If any of my children should find themselves, by favour of Providence, in easy circumstances, after I am gone, I should wish them to refund the principal at least, so that the benefits of the endowment may be extended to as many, and be continued as long as possible. Such charities, wisely administered, are blessings to the world, and may be reckoned among the pleasant fruits of civilization and Christianity, especially of the latter.

My first winter in college was not pleasant on several accounts. I had entered a class for which I was not well prepared, and, of course, had to study more closely than was either agreeable or safe in regard to health and good spirits. However, by dint of application, sitting up late, and rising early, and denying myself more than was meet of out-door exercise, I succeeded in making up my deficiencies, and obtained a pretty erect standing in my class, which I kept to the end of my course. But that which annoyed me most was the riotous conduct and gross intemperate habits of a large proportion of the students. Not only were the ordinary mischievous tricks of idle, unprincipled boys, practised nightly, but there were plots and insurrectionary movements at which the orderly and conscientious were obliged, by an over-

2*

whelming and menacing majority, to connive, and sometimes, seemingly, to approve of. I was once so far involved as to be present, though silent and inactive, at a disorderly meeting. I have always reproached myself for it since; I ought to have resisted and protested against sin, had it even been unto blood. This is one of the grievous evils incident to a public education, where a large number of young men are housed together, and the major part are of profligate manners. The well-disposed, especially if they be timid, are sometimes oppressed and actually coerced into sin, in violation of their consciences. Our disorders came to a crisis, or rather resulted in a fearful catastrophe, early in the spring, (March, 1802,) viz. the destruction of the College edifice, except the thick stone walls, by fire, together with a valuable library, the gatherings of many years. It was a tremendous conflagration; the fire was applied in the belfry, by the servant, no doubt, who rang the bell for dinner, at the instigation of a club of abandoned youth. The supposed ringleader in this foul affair was from the State of New York; he left the place soon after the deed was perpetrated, lived several years encompassed by clouds of suspicion, and died a worthless man. By the munificence of its friends the College was soon repaired, and we had better order. I became more reconciled to college life, as I got used to the course of study, and proved the truth of the maxim, "*Labor vincit omnia.*" Finding myself able by diligence to redeem time from class studies, I added considerably to my small means of support by giving private instruction to such students as had certain studies to make up in order to gain a full standing in their classes. There are many ways in which an indigent youth may help himself in getting an education, if he be diligent and moderate in his expenditures. During my senior year my private tuition fees amounted to more than a hundred dollars.

Having completed the ordinary course of college studies, I was graduated in September, 1803, and immediately chosen a tutor, which office I accepted and held for two years. And now the question of a profession for life came up, and was to be settled. From the time when I thought I first tasted that the Lord is gracious, I had kept the gospel ministry in view as the work to which I felt most inclined, and in which I supposed I could best glorify God and promote the good of mankind. As Providence had thrown no obstacle in my way, and as my preference for that sacred office was clear and decided, I determined upon it, and set myself to seek it by an appropriate course of study, trusting that as I had found grace to believe the gospel for myself, so I should obtain mercy to be faithful in proclaiming it to my fellow-sinners.

The Rev. Dr. Henry Kollock was then pastor of the Presbyterian church in Princeton, and volunteered his services, as a teacher of theology, to as many as chose to attend on his instructions. Of this privilege I availed myself, so far as was consistent with my duties as tutor. The office of a tutor was, at that time, very laborious, so that with official duties and theological pursuits, I was fully occupied; hands,

head, and heart. My health would have failed under
the pressure, but for the care that I took to pass all
the brief intervals of study in healthful exercise out
of doors, and in social visits. With my colleagues
in the tutorship and fellow-students, John Johnson,
Andrew Thompson, Alfred Ely, John M. Bradford,
and Selah Woodhull, I took sweet counsel. We kept
mutual watch of each other, and dwelt together in
delightful unity. Walking was our chief exercise,
and it is upon the whole, the safest and best that
students can take. Campus amusements are generally pursued with too much violence and rivalry, to
be useful either to body or mind. There were a few
families of my acquaintance about Princeton that I
visited frequently, and with great pleasure and profit,
particularly Colonel Beatty's, and the Van Dykes,
John and Matthew. In these hospitable mansions I
spent many an agreeable Saturday afternoon, and
always returned from such friendly visits, to sober
and responsible labours with renewed vigour.

At the end of two years, I resigned the tutor's
office, having resided in the College in all, five years,
three as an undergraduate, and two as a tutor. This
was an interesting portion of my life. Truly, Nassau
Hall is my *Alma Mater.* I am a member of the
"Whig Society," and Whig Hall is, to this day, one
of the most endeared and cherished spots in my
remembrance, about that venerable seat of learning.
Her present prosperous condition is, to me, as to all
her faithful sons, a source of high gratification. She
owes her good repute, and wide sphere of honourable

usefulness, chiefly to the Christian influence that has, from the days of our fathers, clustered about her; and particularly, to the deep interest taken in her welfare by Christians of the Presbyterian Church. She is, at present, officered by good men, capable, faithful, and true; may their successors, to the latest generation, be men like-minded!

In the autumn of 1805, the 2d or 3d of October, having passed the usual trial, for the purpose, I was licensed to preach the gospel, by the Presbytery of New Brunswick. My text was, "God forbid that I should glory, save in the cross of our Lord Jesus Christ, by whom the world is crucified unto me, and I unto the world." *Thirty-one years ago last fall!* Alas, how little I have done for the glory of my dear and adorable Master since then! Had I my ministerial life to live over again, would I not spend it to better purpose? Perhaps not; but I think I would endeavour to live nearer to, and depend more entirely upon, the Divine source of all evangelical efficiency. But the thirty-one years of opportunity are gone, and registered in God's book of remembrance, where they will be found, in evidence for or against me, when called to give an account of my stewardship. O! when I go up to the final judgment, may I obtain mercy of the Lord, and be found to have been made accepted in the Beloved!

On the fifth day of October, 1805, I was married to Elizabeth, second daughter of Matthew Van Dyke, near Princeton, New Jersey. Having some weeks previous to my licensure received an invitation to

Cooperstown, New York, to preach in the place then recently resigned by the Rev. Isaac Lewis, we set off immediately for Whitesboro', where my wife's sister, Mrs. Carnahan, resided, and whose husband, the Rev. James Carnahan, now Dr. Carnahan, and President of Princeton College, was pastor of the united Presbyterian churches of Utica and Whitesboro'. Leaving Mrs. Neill at her sister's, I repaired to Cooperstown, the first scene of my labours in word and doctrine. In the course of the next summer, I received a call from the congregation, which, being accepted, I was ordained to the work of the sacred ministry, and installed pastor of the church in that place, by the Presbytery of Oneida, November, 1806. This was to me a new and solemn undertaking; the exercises on the occasion were deeply affecting to my mind; I felt that I was accepting a charge for which I was in myself quite incompetent; but having learned, in some measure, where my life-springs lay, I accepted the charge, not without fear and trembling, but with hope, saying, "our sufficiency is of God."

The field to be cultivated here was large, and gave promise of much fruit; but great labour, it was manifest, must be expended on it. The church had been but recently formed, and it was the only church of any denomination within several miles around; the people were a good deal scattered, and there was a demand for much visitation and frequent preaching in the neighbourhood; and to one who was but slenderly furnished for the work, it was no slight service to prepare and deliver two, and often three sermons on the Sabbath, and lecture once or more every week in some of the surrounding settlements, besides attending funerals, and performing other pastoral duties, in a widely extended congregation. But by giving myself unreservedly and exclusively to the duties of the holy vocation, with the counsel and assistance of a pious and excellent session, the gospel had free course, and there was a gradual, quiet, and encouraging ingathering of souls to the visible kingdom, and, as we hoped, to the fold of the Chief Shepherd. Hitherto the people had not enjoyed the convenience of a suitable place for public worship, but held their meetings on the Sabbath in an Academy, which soon became too contracted for their accommodation. Within eighteen months or two years after my coming among them, they erected and completed, in a neat style, a church edifice which would accommodate eight or nine hundred persons. I purchased a comfortable dwelling for a small price, and we lived happily, and had all the necessaries, and some of the conveniences of life, on a salary of six hundred dollars a year.

In Cooperstown my two first children were born, viz., William Van Dyke and Elizabeth. The place was, in many respects, a very desirable residence. The cheapness of living, the good taste, social disposition, industrious and correct habits of the inhabitants were strong recommendations. The village is beautifully located at the outlet of Lake Otsego, the source of one of the main branches of the Susquehanna, the noblest river of Pennsylvania. The town was projected by Judge Cooper, the then owner of the soil, and the father of Cooper the well-known American novelist. This said novelist was, for a time, a private pupil of mine. He was rather wayward, cordially disliked hard study, especially of the abstract sciences; was extravagantly fond of reading novels and amusing tales. He became a fine writer—describes admirably—is quite at home in rural scenes and the incidents of a seafaring life. In Cooperstown and the romantic region around it, he laid the scene of his best novel, "The Pioneers." His Judge Temple in this work personates his father. The Judge possessed some charming traits of character; he was of simple, easy manners, very social, friendly, and hospitable. I shared largely in his kindness and hospitality while in his neighbourhood. His princely mansion stood at the head of a long, wide avenue, facing the lake, in the midst of ornamental and fruit trees. It is now, I think, torn away, and replaced by a more splendid dwelling, occupied, if I am rightly informed by his son, James Fennimore, the only surviving son. His daughter, Mrs. Pomeroy, and her excellent husband, are among my most esteemed friends. Otsego lake is a beautiful sheet of water, nine miles long from north to south, and averaging a mile in width, bounded by lofty and rugged hills on the east and west. It contains fine white perch of a large size, and what the people there call lake-fish, still larger; but they keep in deep water, and are difficult to catch. The valley below, and most of the land on the small water courses, is very fertile, and some of it highly cultivated. Upon the whole, Cooperstown is a delightful place, much improved since my time there. I left it with regret, and scarcely more than half my own consent.

In the summer of 1809, I received a call from the First Presbyterian Church in the city of Albany, to succeed the Rev. Dr. John B. Romeyn as their pastor. This brought before me a question of serious import. The call appeared to be unanimous. The meeting at which it was prepared had been moderated by the Rev. Dr. Nott, their former minister, who accompanied it with a letter expressive of his opinion and wish that it should be accepted. I held it under advisement for some weeks, looking upon the people of my charge, every time I met them, with tender emotions, and sometimes with a tearful eye. At length I resolved to accept,' with permission, and accordingly resigned my charge, under the sanction of the Presbytery, and removed to Albany in September, 1809. In taking this step, I yielded to considerations which, I fear, have, in many instances, too much influence on such occasions, such as a more ample support, a wider field of usefulness, &c. It may be, pride and ambition had something to do in the change. Had I remained in Cooperstown contentedly, and been faithful, bread would have been given, and water made sure to me and my household, and I should probably have been as useful and happy as I have been, with all the movements I have made. My first pastoral charge had engaged my first pastoral affections, and had given me strong proof of their

confidence and kind regards; and the parting scene
was really a painful one. I preached them a farewell
sermon from the text, 2 Cor. xiii. 11: "Finally,
brethren, farewell; be perfect, be of good comfort,
be of one mind, live in peace; and the God of love
and peace will be with you." The house was a
Bochim, and no one wept more bitterly than did the
preacher.

Never shall I forget the feelings that struggled in
my breast, as we ascended the long hill, from the
bank of the incipient Susquehanna, while the smooth
lake and tranquil village faded and diminished away
from our lingering, retrospective view. Why, said I
to myself, sunder such endeared and sacred ties? But
the relation is dissolved, and we must go forward and
abide the consequences. That which is done, cannot
be undone. Man deviseth his way, but the Lord
directeth his steps, and often overrules our wrong-
doings for good. But if we do wrong, we shall suffer
for it. "See that ye walk circumspectly; not as
fools, but as wise, redeeming the time." "Be ye,
therefore, not unwise, but understanding what the
will of the Lord is."

We had been settled in Albany but a few weeks,
when God laid his afflictive hand heavily upon us, in
mercy; and, as I trust, for the purpose of fatherly
chastisement. Mrs. Neill was taken ill, and after a
short but severe and unyielding sickness, died, November 12, 1809, and left me in charge of two infants,
the youngest but five months old. This seemed at
the time grievous; but grace accompanied the rod,

and made the stroke comparatively easy and sup-
portable. "I know, O Lord, that in faithfulness
thou hast afflicted me." The funeral was all arranged
and the expenses of it borne by the congregation.
The mortal remains were laid to rest in the burying-
ground belonging to the church, where they are
covered by a tomb, bearing an inscription taken from
Watts, with dates and a brief memorial. She was
amiable and exemplary in all the relations of life;
gave evidence, while living, of faith in Christ, and
died peacefully, and in hope of a glorious resurrection
unto everlasting life and blessedness, through the
merits of the redeeming Saviour.

I was very fortunate in procuring Mabel Abbey,
then resident in East Hartford, Connecticut, to keep
house for me, and take care of my children; which
duties she performed to my entire satisfaction, and
much to her own credit. She is still in my family;
and should she survive me, I commend her to the care
and kind attentions of the widow or children I may
leave behind me, to cherish and protect her in sickness and old age, as her circumstances shall require.
She has accumulated a little fund, by yearly savings
from the fruits of her industry, which makes her quite
easy and independent as to the means of support for
the remainder of life.

My situation in Albany was, in most respects, a
pleasant and comfortable one. The salary, at first
seventeen hundred and fifty dollars, was subsequently,
when the expense of living was increased by the war
with Great Britain, raised to two thousand. This was

an ample support. There were, moreover, frequent gratuitous expressions of remembrance; and marriage-fees constituted, by usage, an important perquisite. I remember that on one New-year's occasion, a few of my people presented me with a gift of seven hundred and fifty dollars in cash; and this present led me into the only speculation of any consequence that I ever perpetrated, and which did fail most egregiously. I never before had possession of so much money for which I had no immediate use, and wished to invest this handsome gratuity for the benefit of my family at a future time. Money was then flush, and real estate rose suddenly to a factitious and enormous pitch. The provident council of the city took occasion to sell out, at auction, a great many city lots on the outskirts of the town, on credit, to be paid for by easy instalments, taking care to fix a quit-rent of three dollars on each lot per annum, *ad infinitum* as to time. This, with the other usual taxes, made these *to-be*-valuable spots of ground, for the most part in the bush, a mile or two from the Hudson river, very expensive property. But it was a mania; the city was going to spread westward rapidly, and purchasers were soon to realize their own, with usury. By the advice of friends, in whose judgment I had full confidence, I ventured, with scores of others, and bought seven lots, lying side by side, and stretching from street to street—an acre of ground. I cleared and fenced it, paid instalments, interest, and rent, as they fell due. But the bubble soon burst; the said lots, and all such property, fell at the close of the war to little or no value. Upon calculation, I found my seven hundred and fifty had cost me some eighteen hundred dollars. I offered to surrender them to the corporation on their own terms; but no. At length, sick of paying rent, I tried to give them away; and even on these terms, years passed before I could get them off my hands. It is not long since I succeeded in getting rid of them, literally for nothing; having paid dear indeed for wit enough to have no more to do with hazardous investments. It seems a pity that the generous New-year's present had not been better managed. But thus it was; and perhaps the disappointment was designed by Providence for good. Had this my first adventure succeeded, I might have been induced to try others of a similar character, to the detriment of my own spiritual interests and of the success of the ministry.

As a field for ministerial usefulness, no place in the country seemed at that time to possess more advantages than Albany. There was then but the one Presbyterian church in the city, and as it was the seat of justice and legislation for the State, the congregation was large, and in all respects highly respectable and interesting. It comprised men of the first standing in society for intelligence and piety. It required constant vigilance and exertion to satisfy the just and reasonable demands of such a charge. I did what I could, with Divine assistance, and God smiled upon the effort, so that my labour was not in vain in the Lord; but I felt that it was peculiarly

3*

trying to be the successor of such men as Nott and Romeyn.

Soon after my settlement I instituted a Bible-class, one of the first that was formed in the United States, and before my removal I had the pleasure to witness the happiest fruits from this mode of instructing the youth of my charge. The members of the Bible-class very generally became hopefully subjects of renewing grace, and connected themselves in communion with the church. We had accessions to the communion, less or more, on every sacramental occasion, and frequent seasons of refreshing from the presence of the Lord, but no strongly marked revivals of religion during my time.

In the rapid growth and prosperity of the city, our congregation increased, so that our place of worship became too strait for us. There was manifestly a want of more Presbyterian room. This being seen and acknowledged by all concerned, a united effort was made, in which a few comparatively young and enterprising men took the lead, to erect an edifice for a second church. It was accomplished in a handsome style, and with great expedition. I officiated at the laying of the corner-stone, and preached at the dedication of the house to the worship of God. The Rev. John Chester, then of Hudson, was invited to take the pastoral charge of this new organization. He accepted the call, and was installed pastor of the Second Presbyterian Church, Albany, in the year 1813, if I mistake not. A portion of the eldership and communicants of the first church was

set off to form the nucleus of the second; and this was
done with good feeling and unbroken harmony. I
have often looked back to this enlargement of the
borders of our Zion with great satisfaction. Chester
was a man of a lovely spirit. There were no jealousies
between him and me, and no unhallowed strife, so far
as we knew, between our respective charges. We
both grew and prospered in peace and amity, under
the benignant smile of the Chief Shepherd. The new
church drew into its communion many persons that
had hitherto been unconnected with any denomination,
and the vacated pews in the first church were soon
filled by new comers; so that visible Presbyterianism
nearly doubled in strength during the seven years of
my stay in that city.

Not long after my settlement in Albany, the
"Board of Trustees of Union College" saw fit to con-
fer on me, partly, as I suppose, in compliment to the
respectable people of my charge, the honorary title of
D. D. This was altogether unexpected by me, and it
was a distinction to which I felt that I had no special
claim; but coming from such a source, I could but
accept it, and endeavour to fulfil the expectations of
those who conferred it. In regard to these factitious
distinctions among ministers of the gospel I am free
to say, after many years' observation, that they are at
least inexpedient and undesirable. They are often procured by undue influence, and bestowed without proper
discrimination; their tendency is to stir up jealousies
and invidious comparisons among brethren, and they
really seem to answer no valuable purpose. There

is less importance attached to them now in public
opinion, than some years back, and as the primitive
spirit gains ground, they will probably go into disuse.
They seem particularly unbecoming in our church,
where ministerial parity is a distinctive characteristic.
Besides, there is certainly a meaning in our Saviour's
counsel, "Be not ye called Rabbi; for one is your
Master, even Christ, and all ye are brethren."

In the year 1812, our Theological Seminary at
Princeton, New Jersey, was founded. In this enterprise I took a lively interest, and my people contributed liberally towards its endowment, as they have
done ever since for its support. I visited several
other congregations, at different times, to solicit
aid for it, and collected and paid into its treasury, as
near as I can now ascertain, from twelve to thirteen
thousand dollars, from first to last. I have had the
pleasure of being a member of its Board of Direc-
tors from its foundation, with the exception of a year
or two, when my re-election failed, in a warm contest
for the mastery in its government between the Old
and New-schoolmen—a distinction that has sprung up
among us and troubled us not a little of late years.
The Institution is now under the control of the Old-
school, and favoured, as it is, with the services of an
able and devoted set of Professors, five in all, it is a
bulwark in our Zion, and likely to prove a rich blessing to the American church. For soundness in the
faith, and for efficiency in promoting intelligence,
zeal, and piety among the rising ministry, it stands
first and highest among the numerous similar institu-

tions in our country. May a gracious Providence save it from being perverted amidst the distractions and contentions of our divided and unhappy church!

When the American Bible Society was formed, I was one of the delegates from Albany, to the convention that met in the city of New York, in May 1816, for the purpose of organizing it. Dr. Elias Boudinot, of Burlington, New Jersey, was its most munificent patron, and was elected its first President. I shall never forget the pertinent and pithy remarks of Dr. John M. Mason, on that occasion. In meeting some puny scruples that had been just uttered, in regard to the expediency of an organization, combining men of various and conflicting views in religion, he repeated the old adage, that "God never built a church, but the devil set about building a chapel," and added, that "his Satanic majesty was no doubt in the convention, self-commissioned, and ready with pen and inkpot, not to *ratify*, but to *blot out*, whatever might be passed in favour of the circulation of the Book—the Bible, of whose holy power he was extremely jealous." And as an instance of the license which a popular speaker has, to say what another may not say with impunity, he remarked in reference to our differences, on minor points of Christian belief and practice, that we had better let one another alone; for said he, "Although a wise man will bear to be rebuked, and that sharply, for a great and acknowledged moral delinquency, yet you may not tell him, even if it be true, that his nose wants wiping." This society is truly catholic in its constitution and aim.

It has done nobly, in preventing a famine of the word of God, not only in America, but in foreign lands. In the competition of voluntary associations, that have arisen within a few years, it has not received so large a share of public favour as it deserves. Divine Providence will put its resources and energies in requisition ere long, we trust, in filling the earth with the knowledge of the Lord.

On the 25th of February, 1811, I was married to Frances King, second daughter of General Joshua King, of Ridgefield, Connecticut. Our first child, Catharine, died in infancy, June 15th, 1812.

In reviewing this portion of my ministerial life, I find much, very much occasion for thankfulness, and and for humiliation, and self-condemnation. For thankfulness to the Author of all good for domestic happiness, ample means of support, and for a wide and fertile field of usefulness. In these respects, I had all that a minister of the gospel could reasonably and consistently desire. But O! what cause of self-abasement it is, to reflect how inadequately I appreciated my privileges, and how very imperfectly I improved my opportunities of doing good—how negligently and superficially the field assigned me was cultivated—how exceedingly I failed to "make full proof of the ministry," in winning souls to my dear, and ever blessed Master! I immured myself too much in my study, trying to make elaborate and acceptable discourses—often appeared in the pulpit with depressed spirits, and read my sermons too closely—was not enough among my people, visiting and preaching from house to house—had too much of the fear of man about me, in the declaration of God's truth—gave old sermons, with slight alterations, too often, a part of the day, to save the toil of writing new ones. I was not always so plain and urgent as an ambassador of Christ should be—did not agonize, and watch unto prayer, for the salvation of souls, as I ought to have done, under a sense of official responsibility to God. The remembrance of these and the like defects, is painful; but they are recounted for my own humiliation, and recorded as a warning to those who shall come after me in the sacred ministry. "Enter not into judgment, with thy servant, O Lord!" "Shouldst thou mark iniquity, O Lord, who could stand?"

In the summer of 1816, I received a call from the Sixth Presbyterian Church of Philadelphia to become their pastor. This was a new organization, that grew out of a secession of a portion of the members of the Third Church of that city, at the settlement of the Rev. E. S. Ely as pastor. The division was at first attended with bad feelings, hard speeches, and wrong-doing probably on both sides; but the difficulties were finally adjusted amicably, and those who chose to leave the old place of worship, with others who joined them in the enterprise, erected a neat and commodious church edifice on Spruce street near Sixth street. After serious consideration, I was induced to accept this call, and accordingly, upon being released from my Albany charge, I took leave of the congregation in a discourse from Heb. xiii. 8: "Jesus

Christ, the same yesterday, and to-day, and for ever"
—the immutability of Christ a source of consolation
to his people. Again I had occasion to feel the tenderness of the pastoral relation, and the pain attendant on its dissolution. In making this movement, I
was not influenced by the love of money, for the
salary offered was the same in amount as that which
I was receiving. But my health being delicate, some
advantage was anticipated from a removal southward,
and some relief was expected from close study, in the
use of a stock of written sermons on hand, which
could easily be adapted to a new scene. There was
something attractive, also, in the idea of being in-
strumental in gathering and training a large congregation, in a new house, in the midst of a dense population. Pennsylvania, also, was my native State, the
home of my kindred, the resting-place of my parents'
ashes, and intimately associated with my youthful
recollections and first religious impressions. These
and the like motives prevailed; but although they
seemed at the time to be good and sufficient, I must
confess, that I now regard them, on a serious review,
as of very questionable validity. The pastoral relation should not be dissolved without high and potent
reasons.

We removed to Philadelphia in the month of September, and I was installed early in November. The
people generously bore the expense of our removal,
and received us with every mark of kindness. I
entered upon their service in word and doctrine with
encouraging prospects, and, I trust, with renewed

resolution, by the grace of God, to devote all my feeble energies to the work of the ministry and the salvation of souls. Our congregation was at first small, and we filled up but slowly, amidst the strong competition of so many churches of the same denomination. But that which operated against our rapid growth more powerfully than perhaps any other cause, was the determination of the First Presbyterian Church to erect a spacious and elegant edifice for worship within a square of us. That people had hitherto worshipped on Market street near Second; but the business of the city crowding upon them, they sold out, and procured a location on Washington Square. They were then, as they are still, a numerous, respectable, and wealthy congregation; their pastor, the Rev. Dr. J. P. Wilson, was a man of talents, and held in high estimation; and, as it was expected that their new house would be tasteful and attractive, many families in the neighbourhood waited to see it completed, and eventually, finding the locality equally convenient, chose to connect themselves with the First Church rather than the Sixth; whereas, had the former been more remote, they would probably, as a matter of convenience, have joined us. We were not disposed to complain of this as a grievance, but we felt it to be a hindrance to our increase; and we verily thought that our beloved sister, of mature age and full strength, might have secured her own interests quite as well had she been a little more regardful of our infancy, and by selecting another locality allowed us more room for action and growth.

4

The good understanding between the two churches was not essentially disturbed by this occurrence, nor would the fact have been noticed in this narrative, were it not a matter of some importance, in the erection of new churches, to consult the convenience of the population, and avoid encroaching on each other's natural limits. The injunctions, "Look not every man on his own things, but every man also on the things of others"—"Study the things that make for peace, and things whereby one may edify another"—are applicable to congregations as well as to individuals.

During my time in Philadelphia, there was a good degree of harmony among the churches, and but little diversity of opinion on theological subjects among our ministers; yet there was not that free and frequent exchange of pulpits which seems to me desirable in the same denomination. By a free exchange on a part of the Sabbath, the people may enjoy, to some extent, the public labours of all the pastors, while acquaintance and good feeling are promoted, and united influence made more effective. Non-intercourse begets shyness and suspicion, tends to independency, weakens the ties that unite associated churches, and is altogether anti-Presbyterial. The venerable Dr. Wilson, mentioned above as pastor at the time of the First Church, was remarkably recluse in his habits, (feeble health was his apology,) made no social calls, seldom or never exchanged pulpits, and seemed reluctant to receive favours or attentions from his brethren, and, indeed, from any one, though ho was a man of courteous manners and a friendly heart.

I remember calling to see him once, when he was indisposed. He was sitting up, with pen in hand, and a huge folio of "The Fathers" open before him. After an agreeable interview of fifteen minutes, I made a movement to leave him; when, taking down a volume from a shelf near him, he wrote my name in it, saying, "I am going to give you this for coming to see me." Now, such a punctilious attention to the principle of a *quid pro quo*, even when, as in this case, connected with undoubted kindness, is unfavourable to social intercourse; for who would not hesitate to call often upon a friend that evinced a disposition to pay for his visits? The example of this good man, for he was esteemed by all who knew him, had some influence in limiting that freedom of intercourse which I like to see, and which I believe is friendly to the peace, and edification, and harmonious action, of churches holding to the same creed, and professedly aiming at the same thing.

In Philadelphia, as in Albany, I had a large and interesting Bible-class, composed chiefly of females; and the results of this mode of instructing the youth were here, also, happy and encouraging. In due course of time all, with a very few exceptions, were admitted to the communion of the church, and have since given good evidence that they received the truth in the love of it, and are governed by its divine authority. In conducting the exercises of the Bible-class, we followed no ¦system of questions, but read the portion of Scripture assigned with care, and then proposed such questions as seemed calculated to bring out the doctrines and practical lessons which it comprised distinctly—opening and closing the meetings with prayer and singing. It was my custom to catechize the children of the congregation once a month, assembled in the lecture-room for the purpose, and in the hearing of as many of the parents as could be induced to attend. The Assembly's Shorter Catechism was committed to memory by the children, and this was our text-book in my endeavours to make them acquainted with the truths and duties of the Christian religion.

Family visitation I attended to as fully as seemed practicable and consistent with domestic engagements. On this important branch of pastoral duty I have never been able to satisfy myself. The great difficulty is to get families together on week-days, and free, even for half an hour, from the ordinary interruptions of business and social calls. Visiting the sick and afflicted, I always found useful, and generally acceptable.

Soon after my settlement in Spruce street, we formed an association, composed of females, in aid of the Theological Seminary at Princeton, which we called "The Phœbean Society," after that Phœbe whom Paul the apostle mentions with commendation as a servant of the church at Cenchrea, and a succourer of himself and others engaged in the work of the ministry. This society has done, and is doing, nobly. It has contributed annually towards the support of indigent young men preparing for the ministry at that institution, with a zeal and liberality highly creditable to its members. They have for many years paid the interest of two scholarships, i. e., have sustained two students in succession, and from year to year, in that important part of their preparation for preaching the gospel. To one of their scholarships they were pleased to annex the name of the subject of this Memoir, and to the other, that of the Rev. Samuel G. Winchester, their present beloved pastor.

Ever since I have been in the ministry, I have endeavoured to train the people of my charge to habits of liberal attention to all evangelical enterprises, especially those which are immediately connected with, and controlled by, our own Church; and I have had the pleasure to know, from the records of the church, that the three congregations which I served for a time, have been uniformly exemplary in their regular and generous contributions to objects intimately connected with the general interests of the Redeemer's kingdom. Ministers may do much, and on them rests a serious responsibility in this matter: "Like priest, like people;" if a pastor is either too selfish or too timid to call upon his people for their prayers, and pecuniary aid in behalf of objects beyond their own immediate precincts, he contributes, indirectly at least, to make them stingy, selfish, and comparatively useless members of the visible body of Christ.

My situation in Philadelphia was very agreeable,

4*

and I trust my labours there were not altogether in vain in the Lord. We had peace and concord, and a gradual ingathering of souls, though we never had any special revivals of religion. The congregation was incumbered with a debt of some six thousand dollars, which made it rather difficult for them to meet their pecuniary engagements. I therefore voluntarily relinquished two hundred dollars a year of my salary, for the last two or three years of my time with them. We still had a comfortable living, though the family had now grown large. There were a few families among our people that presented us, from time to time, with acceptable and valuable tokens of remembrance, which lightened our necessary expenditures very considerably; and our excellent and esteemed family physician, Dr. Henry Neill, now a ruling elder in the First Church, attended us faithfully and assiduously, during the whole eight years of our residence in the city, without charge for his professional services. For this generous and laborious kindness I do still feel that we are deeply indebted to him.

In the summer of 1820, the infant, John Seip, son of the late Dr. Frederic Seip, of Natchez, Mississippi, was placed in my family and under my care, by a singular dispensation of Providence. The circumstances were these: Dr. Seip died at Natchez a little anterior to this date. Mrs. Seip, with John, her only child, came on to Philadelphia in very feeble health, and soon after her arrival, became very ill. Being desirous of leaving her child in a family where he would be likely to receive kind attention and be religiously educated, and getting some knowledge of me through an early acquaintance of hers, and a member of my church, she conceived a strong desire to leave John under my guardianship, to be raised in my family as one of my own children. I had never seen her, nor any of her family, and was from home at the time; but at her urgent request, her friend wrote to know whether I would accept the charge. I hesitated, but finally wrote home, that under the circumstances I could not refuse. On my return I found that the mother had deceased soon after the receipt of my letter, and that she had consigned John to my care, on such terms as should suit my judgment; there being property enough, and her brother, Dr. Andrew Macreary, of Natchez, being the executor of the estate and legal guardian of the child.

At my request, the compensation for the entire superintendence of the child was referred to three gentlemen, viz., Robert Ralston, Esq., General Cadwalader, and Rev. Dr. J. J. Janeway, who fixed it at two hundred and fifty dollars per annum. This was agreed to, and has not been altered since. John has grown up in the family as a tender plant; has been a pleasant boy, and is very dear to me and all the family. He is now nearly of age, and is coming into possession of a handsome estate. May God save him from the infatuating influence of outward wealth, and give him an interest in the imperishable riches of redeeming grace. I have done what I could for him. He knows what is right, and possesses an affectionate and amiable disposition; but he is as yet a child of nature. The Lord give him a new heart and a right spirit. O that his soul may be saved through the redemption that is in Christ! He has always treated me with filial piety and respect; and I have a pleasing confidence that he will not forget or neglect my children, if he survive me, when they shall become orphans, and when I shall have gone the way of all the earth. May no root of bitterness ever spring up to mar their friendly fellowship!

And now, before resigning the pastoral charge, for the third, and probably the last time, I will record briefly my views of the office and work of the Christian ministry. This office I of course regard as the most useful, the most desirable, and the most responsible that can be borne by man. Its design is to proclaim salvation to a ruined world, on the basis of the mediation of Jesus Christ, God's beloved and only begotten Son. Every minister of the gospel comes to men as an ambassador of Christ, to treat with them on the momentous subject of their reconciliation to God. The ground of hope is laid in the atoning blood and perfect, imputed righteousness of the Redeemer. The terms are easy, and well adapted to the helpless misery of sinners—"repent, and believe the gospel." The grand comprehensive means are the word and ministry of reconciliation. The efficient Agent is the Holy Spirit. The ambassador's book of instructions is the Bible, and his object twofold—the conversion of the wicked, and the edification of the pious; and in discharging the duties of his office, he is to apply the appropriate means with all his energy and skill, in humble and prayerful reliance on God for success.

The highest aim of this office is to save souls. Now God is pleased, through the preaching of the gospel, to save them that believe; and one saved soul is of more worth than the whole of the material creation. Hence we see that the office is the most useful; it is also the most desirable. That office is certainly the most desirable which affords the best opportunity of doing good. In this respect, no station will bear comparison with that of the minister of Christ. He has it in his power, under Divine favour, to promote the temporal and eternal interests of mankind in a degree that is indefinite and immeasurable. The office is highly desirable also, as regards the minister's own happiness. It brings him into close and constant intercourse with God, the Source of bliss, in looking to him for assistance, and giving him thanks for success. In a word, the ministerial relation has endearments and enjoyments connected with it, which are incomparable and indescribable. But this office is most responsible; interests are staked upon the faithful performance of its sacred functions, which surpass our most vigorous conceptions. No considerate man, therefore, would assume it, uncalled of God; nor will any one, when graciously inclined to it, undertake it in his own strength: "Our sufficiency is of God."

The work of the ministry, then, is good, pleasant, and weighty. The leading requisites for it are piety, aptness to teach, and intellectual culture. No man should venture to engage in this holy work, without a consciousness of love to Christ, and delight in his service; for how can we consistently recommend to our fellow-sinners a Saviour, whom we do not love and know to be precious and worthy of all confidence? Nor should a man rely altogether on his own judgment in regard to his fitness for this great work. He should take counsel, and submit himself to the scrutiny of others, entering upon the office, as did Timothy, through the laying on of the hands of the Presbytery. The motives that should impel a man to the faithful and diligent discharge of his ministerial obligations are the most cogent that can be imagined. Gratitude to the Redeemer, a concern for the glory of God, compassion for the souls of men, the pleasures of a conscience void of offence, and a desire to meet the approbation of our blessed Master in the day of judgment, urge us to be honest, active, impartial, and untiring in the execution of the duties of our stewardship.

In reviewing my life and labours as a minister of Christ, I find much reason to be humbled before God. Would that I had been more laborious, zealous, and urgent in my appeals to men's consciences. But opportunities once past and gone cannot be recalled; nor are regrets for neglected advantages of any avail, except as they lead to repentance and reformation. Let me, then, double my diligence for the little remnant of life that may remain to me; and may the next generation of preachers, warned by the lamented deficiencies of their predecessors, be careful to take time by the foreclock, and work with all their might, and with a burning zeal for God and souls, while the day lasts. "The night cometh, in which no man can work."

In the summer of 1824, I received an invitation to become the successor of Dr. John M. Mason, in the Presidency of Dickinson College, at Carlisle, Pennsylvania. This call was unsought and unexpected by me. After some consideration, I determined to decline; but on second thought, and further advice, I concluded to accept the offer, and accordingly resigned my pastoral charge, took leave of the people, and removed to Carlisle in September, 1824, having been pastor of the Sixth Church, Philadelphia, eight years. Without recounting the motives that actuated me in making this change, I would only say, that I am now, and have long been doubtful about the correctness of my decision. On review, the reasons that prevailed do not appear to me to have been strong and pressing. The substantial proofs of affectionate regard which I received from the people of Spruce street on leaving them, stirred up in my bosom tender and pensive feelings, as if I was going away from good friends and leaving a comfortable home. But the deed was done—the formal tie was dissolved. I was committed, and must away.

On entering upon my new scene of labour I found things in rather a low and unpromising plight. It is true that Dr. Mason's fame, together with the respectability of the Professors associated with him, had attracted public attention, and enlisted the favour

of the community in some degree in behalf of the
Institution. But the College had been closed for
a long time previously, and the Doctor's health did
not permit him to remain connected with it quite two
years, when the public confidence was again shaken
by his resignation. The funds were inadequate to
the support of the establishment, and when I went to
the place there were but from forty to fifty students
in the Institution. However, I resolved to identify
myself with its interests and do what I could, in con-
junction with the gentlemen who were on the ground
before me, for its thorough resuscitation and enlargement.

My first winter in Carlisle was peculiarly trying.
Amid the cares and duties of the College, I was
taken sick, and confined to my chamber six or eight
weeks. Well do I remember my feelings, as I lay
upon a sick bed, looking through the window upon
the dreariness of a hard and seemingly long winter. The recollection of past pleasures was painful and depressing to my spirit. The beloved and
affectionate flock that I had recently left; my pulpit,
my Bible-class, and our sweet communion seasons,
rushed upon my remembrance, and seemed to chide
me for having left my proper place through fickleness
and vain desires. All this may have been weakness,
or selfishness, or the want of courage; but I record
facts as they really were, that others may profit by
my errors, and learn to heed the good old maxim,
"Let well enough alone."

On the recovery of my wonted health I took

courage, determined to feel at home, and give myself fully and heartily to the duties of my station. A correspondence was opened with several Academies, and many congratulations and good promises were received. An annual allowance of $3000, for the term of seven years, from the State treasury, was obtained by dint of hard pleading and perseverance, by an act of the State legislature, in behalf of the College, on condition that a report of the state of the Institution should be laid before that body yearly, till the expiration of said term. This relieved our present necessities, and was beneficial in some respects, but it operated badly in the long run, as it impaired our independence, and consequently, relaxed our discipline, as will appear in the sequel.

We now went on prosperously; the classes filled up until we had about one hundred students, besides a flourishing preparatory school, which was as great a number as we could well accommodate. When I became connected with the Institution, there were three Professors, viz., Henry Vethake, Esq., Professor of Natural Philosophy and Mathematics; Rev. Joseph Spencer of the Protestant Episcopal Church, Professor of the Latin and Greek Languages; and Rev. Alexander McClellan of the Dutch Church, Professor of Moral Philosophy, Mental Science, and Rhetoric. In the course of a little time we had an accession of two more, viz., Dr. John Finley, Professor of Chemistry and Physiology, and the Rev. Lewis Mayers, of the German Reformed Church, Professor of German Literature. Thus the Faculty con-

5

sisted of six members, and the course of study was as
liberal and comprehensive as in most colleges of our
country.

The President was charged with the religious instruction of the young men in Natural Theology, the
Evidences of Christianity, and such Bible instruction
on the Sabbath as should be deemed suitable in such
an Institution. He was also expected to aid the
Professor of Languages, if necessary, and, in a word,
to take such part in the business of instruction as
should be found convenient and for the general interests of the College. This was a bad arrangement.
Every teacher in a public seminary of learning
should have his place and duties definitely assigned
by statute, so that he may know his responsibilities,
and not interfere with the appropriate duties of his
associates.

The sun of prosperity had not beamed upon us
long, when we began to feel the effects of certain
constitutional evils, which ultimately proved disastrous. These were—first, a participation of the
Board of Trustees in the exercise of discipline. The
Faculty could admonish, reduce to a lower class, or
suspend delinquents temporarily from the privileges
of the Institution; but they had not the right of
expelling a disorderly student without the sanction of
the Trustees. Of course, the subjects of discipline
were always disposed to make their appeal, directly
or indirectly, to the higher court; and from their
ex parte statements of their case, which they had
opportunities of making in the families of Trustees

resident in the borough, a sympathy was enlisted in their favour, and the authority of the Faculty was put in jeopardy. The Trustees, indeed, had too many meetings, and interfered too much (from good motives, doubtless,) with the internal police of the College. The government ought to be vested wholly in the President and Professors, and from their decisions there should be no appeal, except to the ultimate tribunal in all free States, public sentiment.

In the second place, the College was *too catholic.* It was open to the sons of parents of all religious persuasions, down to atheism itself. Consequently the wishes of parents must be consulted in regard to attendance on religious instruction, whether in class studies, or in the duties of the Sabbath. The students could not all be required to attend the lectures in the College chapel on the Lord's day; they were allowed to go to the churches in the village where they could be best suited, and if there was none of their persuasion, they were not obliged to attend any. It is easy to see how such an arrangement would operate. With many the Sabbath was a day of indolence and mischief. True, we had Bible-class exercises and Lectures on Biblical History in the College every Sabbath; but attendance on these services being voluntary, they were much neglected, and of very limited influence. Young men in whose education the principles of true religion form no part, may be expected to be insubordinate, immoral, and vicious; for religion is the basis—the only solid basis—of correct morals. Any institution for the training of youth, in the absence of religious principles, however extended and richly endowed it may be, is a great evil in the community.

In Dickinson College it was an object to have in the Faculty and in the Board of Trustees, men of different religious denominations. Hence we had, occasionally, jealousies, suspicions, and contests for the pre-eminence. On one occasion, in the election of Trustees, it so happened (whether by concert or not, was the question,) that the vacant seats were filled by gentlemen of one religious sect. This raised the hue and cry, sectarianism! religious domination! &c., and was used as a handle by which we were dragged before the Legislature of the State, where a tedious and vexatious investigation was had, without convicting anybody of misdemeanour, for there was no evidence; but the effect was to fix suspicion upon us, and raise a strong prejudice against us, from which we never recovered in my time.

A third evil, in our case, was *dependence on legislative aid*, created by the annuity mentioned before, and conditioned, as it was, on an annual report. This tended to unnerve discipline, as it constituted, in some sort, a high court of appeal from our doings, and opened upon us the mouths of fault-finders throughout the length and breadth of the Commonwealth. But for this dependence on, and responsibility to, the Legislature, we had not been arraigned on a vague and unfounded charge of sectarianism, and subjected to the injurious consequences that ensued. Let no institution of learning surrender its independence for the sake of money or popular favour. Better be poor and small, and win public patronage gradually by fidelity, zeal, and perseverance. The Legislature of the State, from the elements of which it is composed, is unfit to judge wisely in regard to the complicated business of instructing and governing youth. In the case of institutions endowed by the State, supervision is right and useful; but let it be vested in a smaller and less heterogeneous body, selected with due reference to the requisite qualifications for such an office.

In view of these facts, and after a good deal of observation and experience, I give it as my deliberate judgment: 1st. That in all seminaries of learning, great and small, the teachers should be the governors. 2d. That those seminaries, other things being equal, will do best for themselves, and best for the community, that are in the hands and under the control of some one denomination of Christians. The extreme of catholicism is practical atheism. The fear of impressing on the minds of youth sectarian views, tends powerfully to the exclusion of all religious influence from their hearts; and to educate our children without religion, is unfaithfulness to them, treachery to God, and ruin to the republic. 3d. That the less dependent schools and colleges are on State bounty, the better for them, and for the pupils, and for the cause of sound learning.

In a free country, it is perhaps best that institutions of science, and literature, and religion, like individuals, should rise into prosperity and repute by the

5*

excellence of their principles, and by their own well-directed efforts. Numerous schools and colleges, producing a generous competition, are preferable in our country to a few overflowing with pupils, and flushed into neglect of duty, or connivance at the idleness and immoralities of the youth consigned to their care. There is a propensity in colleges, as in other corporations, to monopolize and engross the business. This is inconsistent with republican principles, and inauspicious to the professed design—moral and intellectual culture. The more young men you collect together in one place, for the purpose of education, the more difficult it becomes to maintain order among them, and to do justice in the matter of instruction. The modest and weak are crowded into the background, and are often obliged to bear in silence the insolence of the bullies; they hide behind one another, tempt, and in some instances coerce each other into disorder and vice, which no supervision, however vigilant and active, can possibly prevent. What shameful outbreakings occur occasionally in our most crowded and popular institutions!

In Dickinson College, when our number was short of a hundred, we had a rebellion which it cost us no little trouble to quell, and which ultimately proved disastrous to the institution. The occasion was the suspension of a young man for insubordination to one of the Professors; the combustible materials took fire quickly, and the flame soon pervaded the whole mass. They insisted on the restoration of their fellow-student, alleging that the Professor was mainly in fault. They were of one mind, so far as we could judge, and came into the chapel, when called for worship, growling like mastiffs. Remonstrance, warning, and affectionate entreaty, were tried upon them in vain. They persisted, and it became necessary, for the maintenance of authority, to dismiss the whole of them, under censure, not to leave the town, but with an assurance that on the following day they would be re-admitted, if they chose, on reflection, to comply with the terms that should be proposed. Accordingly, most of them were restored, on acknowledging their fault and promising good behaviour for the future; but some half dozen held out pertinaciously, and we were obliged to suspend them. This brought on a correspondence with parents and guardians, that cost us weeks of painful labour; and by the partial representations of the affair that went abroad, a clamour was raised against us as tyrannical, &c.

We never recovered from the effects of this insurrection; indeed, one of its remote effects was that the whole Faculty left the College, and it was closed for several years. Not long since it was transferred to the Methodist Episcopal brethren, under whose management it seems to be rising, and bids fair to be useful. May the smiles of a propitious Providence rest upon it, and make it a blessing to the country and the world!

The winter of 1828–29 was a time of deep and various affliction with us. Besides the College troubles, my dear daughter, Maria, was gradually sinking under an incurable disease. She became ill early in

the autumn, and died on the 4th of April, 1829.
Evening after evening I passed in her sick chamber
with intense solicitude, endeavouring by reading, conversation, and prayer, to prepare her for the approaching issue. It was a mournful, but, I trust, an instructive school to me and to the family. She was aware
of her condition, and full of inquiries about death and
its consequences, which I answered as well as I could,
by reading to her select and appropriate passages of
Scripture. Her end was peaceful, and not without
hope. She was remarkably affectionate and intelligent, and of an interesting age. None but those who
have experienced the like, can conceive how painful it
was to part with her. But God took her, and sustained us under the bereavement; he is righteous, and
praised be his holy name! Her mortal remains
repose in the burial-ground of Carlisle. In August,
1829, my daughter, Elizabeth, was married to David
N. Mahon, M. D., of Carlisle.

After Commencement, the last of September, 1829,
my connection with the College being dissolved, I
accepted the office of Corresponding Secretary and
General Agent of the Board of Education of the Presbyterian Church, and entered immediately on the
duties of the station, my family remaining in Carlisle. In September, 1830, we removed back to Philadelphia, that being more central and convenient for
the business in which I was now engaged. The duty
of training young men for the work of the gospel
ministry, and of providing for the wants of the indigent, had long been felt, and had always received

some attention in our church; but the mode of accomplishing this desirable object, now adopted, was at that time new, and thought by many to be of doubtful issue. There were fears, prejudices, and rival institutions in the way, so that, during my connection with the Board, we did little more than consult the church, invite the coöperation of the Presbyteries, and prepare the way for a thorough prosecution of the important enterprise.

Every step was taken cautiously, and we proceeded on a small scale, watching the indications of Providence, and seeking the favour and united aid of our brethren. As the field opened before us, and the work accumulated upon our hands, finding that the duties were too heavy for my feeble health, I resigned the station, after occupying it about two years, in the autumn of 1831. The Rev. John Breckinridge was appointed my successor, and coming to the work with his eminent qualifications, and taking hold with a strong hand and a determinate purpose, the institution prospered, and is now doing, under favour of Divine Providence, great and good service to the cause of Christ. I am still a member of the Board, and feel a deep interest in its success. It is the natural ally of the Board of Missions, and constitutes one of the main springs of the evangelical action of our ecclesiastical body upon this fallen world. Being thus released from all local engagements, I accepted an invitation to Germantown, where I now write, to serve a feeble church of our connection, as a stated supply. Accordingly in September, 1831, we removed hither; and here we are surrounded with comforts, though in circumstances different from what we have been used to.

Two considerations operated mainly in bringing me to this place. 1st. I was anxious to resume the ministerial work as my sole employment. Germantown was the first place that offered; and though poor and unpromising, it was within the Lord's vineyard, and Providence seemed to say, Go. 2d. My dear and lamented friend, John S. Henry, Esq., whose family residence was here, expressed his earnest wish that I should come, promising a liberal contribution towards my support, which he more than fulfilled while he lived; for he died December 10th, 1835, deeply and extensively regretted.* The Domestic Missionary Board of the General Assembly have given from one hundred and fifty to two hundred dollars per annum, since I have been here, and several benevolent individuals have given something, so that with what the congregation find themselves able to do, from time to time, amounting perhaps to from two to three hundred dollars a year, together with my own small means, and good economy, we live comfortably. My son, William Van Dyke, is living in Virginia, married to a daughter of Dr. Thomas Triplett, Surgeon in the Navy. My younger children are going forward with their education, and I trust my labour is not in vain

---

* My youngest son I named for my dear friend, John S. Henry, whose death was a grievous affliction to his family, and an irreparable loss to us, and to the church. How mysterious are the ways of Providence!

in the Lord. "Godliness, with contentment, is great gain." We purpose remaining here till Divine Providence shall seem to us to say, "Arise and go hence." Our cup, since our residence here, has been a mixed one, but the predominant ingredient has been mercy.

Soon after our settlement in the place, the life of one of my daughters was threatened for many weeks; but by the blessing of God on the untiring attention and skilful treatment of our esteemed physician, Dr. Samuel Betton, she was restored to her usual health. Immediately on her recovery her mother began to decline in health, and after a lingering and progressive illness of eight or nine months, she died October 13th, 1832.

On the 15th day of April, 1835, I was married to Sarah S. Elmer, only daughter of Dr. Ebenezer Elmer, of Bridgeton, New Jersey.

The state of religion in this place, though lamentably low, has been apparently better this winter than usual. There has been for some months past a more than ordinary attendance on public worship. Our Sabbath-school is growing, and the cause of temperance is making some progress. I preach and visit pastorally about as much as I ever did, though in a much more limited field; am doing some good, I hope, by the distribution of religious tracts and papers; and we are looking and longing for a season of refreshing from the presence of the Lord. I sometimes think God has placed me here to test my attachment to the blessed Master's work, out of the way of being influenced by its temporal emoluments. Well, if it be so,

and I am enabled to stand the test, it is good to be
here. The lowest place in the kingdom is a post of
honour high enough for me; and I think I can hon-
estly say, that I do love the service of God in the
gospel of his Son, aside from the worldly advantages
and popular favour, which in some situations are
connected with it. Yet I may be deceived. Lord,
save me from every refuge of lies, and fix my heart
and hope on the deep, and broad, and firm foundation
of grace, which is laid in Christ, the anointed holy
King of Zion!

And now, praying that what has been written may
be useful when it comes to be read, if, indeed, it shall
ever see the light, and thanking God for the good
effect the review has had on my own mind, I arrest
the current of the humble narrative, on this second
day of February, 1837. If anything should occur
hereafter worthy of note, it can be added by another
hand, if mine should be suddenly and unexpectedly
rendered incapable of writing.

January 2d, 1840.—Three years ago, this day, I
began to write these memories, and having brought
the narrative down to February 2d, 1837, it was there
arrested, with the intention of resuming it, should my
life be spared. Now, at the opening of another year,
finding myself and family in comfortable circumstances, I raise my Ebenezer in honour of the Divine
mercy, and proceed to note down a few particulars
which occurred in the course of the last three years.

The year 1837 passed off quietly, and without any
events worthy of special note, but the next is memo-

rable. Early in the spring I took a lot of ground on rent, with the view of erecting a building on it, for the double purpose of a lecture-room and a young ladies' seminary. In this enterprise I received assistance from a few generous friends; the house was completed and in use by the beginning of winter. We worshipped in it on Wednesday evenings, and the school went into operation immediately with encouraging prospects; but, in the course of a year or eighteen months, we built a lecture-room adjoining the church edifice, and I transferred the school to a lady, who was to have purchased the house, but failing to do so, I changed it into a dwelling, and afterwards sold it at some discount.

September 18*th*, 1838.—My dear Elizabeth, wife of Dr. D. N. Mahon, of Carlisle, died. This was a painful stroke to us all, and a breach in our circle of loved ones which is irreparable. She was the only daughter of my first wife, and a woman of great worth, not only to her family and friends, but to the church of God, in whose prosperity she took a great interest.

In May of this year (1838,) occurred the great schism in our church, at the meeting of the General Assembly. The preceding Assembly had exscinded four Synods as incurably unsound. This act was disregarded by the Presbyteries concerned; but when their commissioners to the Assembly of this year presented their credentials and claimed seats, they were rejected; whereupon they retired and organized, claiming to be the Constitutional Assembly, commonly known since as the New-school body, though

6

clinging to the old style and title. What followed is well known, and by many on both sides was deeply lamented. Litigation, evil surmisings, and sad alienations, gave occasion to the enemies of Christ to reproach his cause, and served as a stumbling-block to many.

I always thought, and think now, that milder measures would have answered better, and been more for edification. True, discipline had been neglected, and serious evils had crept in among us, both in doctrine and order; but our system is recuperative, and would have recovered its energy in a few years, had its principles been applied by regular process. God is overruling our evil action, however, and both branches of the body may be regarded now as in a healthful and growing state. I prefer the Old-school, with all its faults; but the dividing-line, when drawn, threw very many dear disciples and noble churches on the other side.

The root of the evil was a Plan of Union, adopted in 1801, by our General Assembly and some of the New England associations, for the gathering in of churches in Western New York; which produced, in process of time, a mongrel style of discipline—a compromise between Presbyterian order and Congregationalism—well-meaning, but ill-judged. This compact was annulled on our part rather unceremoniously, which gave great offence. The New-school men clung to it, but of late they find it does not work well.

February 3d, 1853—at Philadelphia. I will now bring these notes to a close, if possible, before I stop.

In the autumn of 1842, we made arrangements to return to Philadelphia; and my friend, the Rev. Thomas B. Bradford, hearing of my intention to leave, signified his willingness to take the place. I introduced him; he preached, and was accepted unanimously as stated supply.

From the foregoing statement, it will be seen that I was eleven years stated supply at Germantown. And here it is natural to ask, What were the fruits of my labours during this period? Not great, indeed, but yet worthy of notice, to the praise of Divine grace. When I entered that uninviting field, the church had but a nominal existence. There were three ruling elders, with one deacon, and a few communicants, hard to find, scattered and disheartened. I looked after them, and found that several, whose names were enrolled, had died or moved away. I preached to the few that could be collected, twice on the Sabbath, lectured on Wednesday evenings, and opened a rotary prayer-meeting on Friday evenings; and thus we moved on very slowly, but harmoniously. I introduced the keeping of sessional records, which was a new measure there; as they had not been used to anything more than a register of members, admissions to the Lord's table, baptisms, marriages, and deaths. It was a day of small things, yet we grew by little and little, with ebbings and flowings; for the population was sparse and fluctuating. Presbyterianism was at a ruinous discount, and materials for a church of that name very scarce. The few church-going people in and about the town were Lutheran,

German Reformed, Methodist, Episcopalians, Men-
nonists, &c. Great numbers were of no creed, and
passed the Sabbath in visiting and amusement; some
continued their secular pursuits. A few men of wealth
and leisure gave all their influence in favour of practical infidelity, and against the Bible.

Still we held on quietly, and, at one time, we really
had a refreshing from the Lord, and received as its
fruits some twelve or fourteen persons to the communion of the church on a sacramental occasion. We
built a comfortable lecture-room, and had a flourishing
Sunday-school. At my suggestion, a subscription was
opened to procure a congregational library, and we
kept it in the lecture-room. It was small at first, but
very select, containing some of the choice works published by our Board of Publication. Such a library,
under proper regulations, should be in every church.
"Give attention to reading," is addressed to all people, as well as ministers. Reading, hearing, preaching, and prayer, are mutual helpers of each other, and
if rightly used, will be found to be greatly conducive
to our growth in grace, and the knowledge of God our
Saviour.

During my stay among them, the people increased
in number and strength, manifested a good degree of
zeal in the cause of missions, temperance, and the
colonization enterprise on the western coast of Africa.
They contributed, as they felt able, for the support of
the gospel at home and abroad. There was a debt of
long standing pressing upon us. In my farewell discourse, I urged the necessity of paying off this incum-

brance; and my successor, Mr. Bradford, did them good service by his strenuous and successful efforts to get them out of debt, and off the Missionary Board.

They are now (1853) a strong, self-sustaining church, and have an excellent pastor, the Rev. Henry J. Van Dyke, in whom they are all well united; and at Chestnut Hill, the upper part of the town, there has been a church organized with good prospects, under the ministry of the Rev. Roger Owen. They have erected a chaste and commodious house, which is nearly ready to occupy; and I see now, that my humble labours were not in vain in the Lord among this people; they were thus kept together till the day of their prosperity came, by favour of Providence. By the rapid increase of people in and about Philadelphia, Germantown has become a large and beautiful village, and we have now, instead of one feeble church, two of considerable strength with fine prospects. "Who hath despised the day of small things?"

Since my return to Philadelphia I have been fully occupied in serving vacant churches, and acting as a missionary in some of the charitable institutions of the city, particularly the "Widows' Asylum," and one of the "Magdalen Asylums," where I have seen with pleasure the benign influence of the gospel on the afflicted and the lowly. Though I have neither had, nor wish to have, a special pastoral charge, since leaving Germantown, yet I have continued in the work of the ministry, not only in compliance with my ordination vows, but from preference, and from a deep and settled conviction of its Divine appointment and benign

6*

bearing on the temporal and eternal interests of mankind. Besides preaching almost as much as in former
years, I have written, and delivered twice, a course of
lectures on the "Evidences of Christianity," prepared and published a volume of "Lectures on Biblical History" to the time of Joshua, and a "Practical
Exposition of the Epistle to the Ephesians;" besides
occasional discourses and fugitive pieces. Yet, alas!
how little have I done, and how imperfectly, for my
dear Lord and Saviour, who has died for me, and
given me the sweet hope of forgiveness and eternal
life!

Here Dr. Neill's account of himself ends, in a manner so abrupt as to indicate that it was not finished.
Not many days before his death he expressed regret that he had not resumed his narrative, and
brought it nearer to the close of his life. But the
seven years that followed this last record of his own
pen, were characterized by experiences and deeds
which would be more faithfully written by others than
by himself. There was a gradual increase of Christian zeal and earnestness in doing good. His prayers,
addresses, and sermons, during this period, equalled
those of the best days of his ministry, in strength of
thought, in propriety, correctness of language, arrangement and argument, while they greatly excelled
them in earnestness, pungency, directness, and unc-
tion. The writer listened to no preacher whom he

had the privilege to hear, with more uniform interest and edification than to Dr. Neill. His strong sympathy and hearty coöperation in what, with so much fitness, is called the "Great Awakening" of our times, were apparent to all. Those who heard his prayers and his affectionate and earnest exhortations, will not forget them while they live. That his delicate frame should have had such power of endurance, could labour so long, and accomplish so much, is evidence of the special care of that Providence on which he habitually relied. He was well aware of his feeble hold on life, and not only conversed familiarly with his friends about his death, but was habitually so prepared, as to live divested of all fear. The calm, dispassionate, and collected manner in which he delivered his last messages to friends, and gave directions concerning his funeral, reminded one of the parting instructions of a father about to leave his family for a week, or for only a night. In Dr. Neill's death we saw nothing of the "king of terrors." When not engaged in conversation with others, his mind was filled with heavenly meditations, while the precious doctrines and promises of the gospel were repeated with an almost supernatural copiousness and fluency. They came to him with an adaptedness and pertinency that indicated a special ministry of the Comforter in suggesting them. His physical sufferings, which at times were very severe, extorted no expressions of impatience or complaint. His habitual language, whenever we were at his bedside, was that of submission, thankfulness, and praise. For several hours that preceded the last, he was apparently unconscious of what was passing around him; and when the time of his exit came, at three o'clock on the morning of the 8th of August, 1860, it was made so gently, that the exact moment was not perceived.

The interment of Dr. Neill was postponed till the 13th, when it was conducted in accordance with the instructions that had been given by himself. It was deemed a just tribute of respect to one who had been held in so high esteem, that a discourse should be preached commemorative of his labours and life.

DISCOURSE

LIFE AND CHARACTER OF REV. DR. NEILL,

By JOSEPH H. JONES, D. D.

———————

FOR ME TO LIVE IS CHRIST, AND TO DIE IS GAIN.
Philippians i. 21.

WHEN Cicero had reached the age of sixty-one, he wrote in five books his "Tusculan Disputations." They are a discussion of five different questions in heathen philosophy, relating to the happiness of human life. The first of these books treats of death—in which all the skill of his eloquent and graceful pen is put in requisition to divest the last enemy of his terrors, and make his readers think that "to die is gain." He condemns suicide, and any agency of a man in procuring his own death, and teaches a better morality on this and several other subjects than many who have borne the Christian name. But all his arguments fail to convince. He says that "Cato exulted in the opportunity of dying when his time came;" but he mentions no good reason why. "That the life of a philosopher is but a continuous meditation on death." But when he attempts to tell us what the philosopher hoped for after death, we wonder that he should have thought of it so much, or have cared to think of it at all. No; the teachings of this illustrious Roman do not suggest a single hint to allay the slavish fears of the dying. He could not speak "with authority;" he knew not what to say. He wanted light on this occult subject. Cato's freedom from fear, therefore, was not intelligent; it was studied or pretended, and not real. It belonged only to those who, like the author of our text, were taught in a better and more enlightened school, to assure us, not only that "death is gain," but for whom it is gain, and why or how it is gain;—to show some support or rational basis on which a truth of such unspeakable importance can rest. All this we find in the new philosophy of our apostle, which connects the end of life with its antecedent works and faith; which couples the man's gain at death with Christ, to whom he has been united in life.

Those who are accustomed to read the Scriptures critically and in different versions, are aware, that there is a slight discrepancy among them in relation to the passage before us. Calvin says, that its precise meaning has been mistaken by both translators and expounders. He would render it, "Christ is my gain whether in life or in death." Some other versions translate it in the same way. But while these learned men differ, to some extent, in changing Paul's language into their own, they agree essentially in their ideas of his meaning—that the gainful death he speaks of, was the legitimate result of his peculiar life. For him "to die was gain," because "to live was Christ."

All that the apostle designs to teach, therefore, may be set forth with sufficient fulness for the purpose of this discourse, by a brief exposition,

I. Of the sort of life here referred to; and

II. Of the gain by such a death as follows it.

Every hearer has doubtless noticed the unusual phraseology in which this wonderful existence is expressed. "For me to live is Christ;" which, as describing Paul's alliance to his Master, and teaching a great truth of Christian experience, is perfectly intelligible. But taken into any different connection, for the purpose of setting forth the relation of other disciples to their head, it is an unwarrantable solecism. Antigonus, one of the kings of Macedonia, was an enthusiastic admirer of Zeno, the founder of the Stoic philosophy; but who that desired to express this high regard would say, that for him to live was Zeno? Nor would it have struck the ear less strangely for one to have said, that for Xenophon to live was Socrates, because the former was such an earnest believer and advocate of this great teacher's doctrines. But nobody thinks it anomalous, either in thought or diction, when the Apostle says, that "for me to live is Christ." His meaning is discovered and is readily understood as descriptive of a certain experience which is known to be a reality, though incapable of being adequately set forth in any form of words.

Every disciple of Christ is a witness to its truth. It is the most significant and comprehensive mode possible, of describing his thoughts of Christ, his dependence on Christ, his obligations to him, and his hopes from him as the Alpha and Omega of his salvation.

Among the many thoughts which this language comprehends, the apostle would recognize Christ as being,

1. *The Source of his life.*

As the body imparts life to the limbs—as streams live upon the fountains from which they issue—as the vine is the source of life to the branches—so were all of Paul's life-springs in Christ. This deriving of life from Christ, or living on him, is taught in the symbols of the sacramental table, alluded to in John vi. 53, where it is said, "Except ye eat the flesh of the Son of man, and drink his blood, ye have no life in you." Another idea embraced in this language of Paul is,

2. *That to advance Christ's kingdom was the main purpose and object of his life.*

It was the continued motive, irresistible and enduring, which led him onward, from the beginning of his Christian life to its end. "What things were gain" to him—all the wealth and worldly honour that awaited him as a popular leader among the Pharisees, he "counted loss for Christ." To preach His gospel, he did not shrink from the exhausting labours— stripes above measure, beatings with rods, stonings, shipwrecks, perils of waters, perils of robbers, perils of his own countrymen, perils by the heathen; in the city, in the wilderness, in the sea, and among false brethren, of which he writes so graphically in his second Epistle to the Corinthians, xi. 23—27. None of these things moved him; neither did he count his life dear unto himself, so that he might finish his course with joy, and the ministry which he had received of the Lord Jesus, to testify the gospel of the grace of God. Acts xx. 24, 25. Another meaning conveyed by this language of Paul is,

3. *That the highest happiness of his life was derived from communion with Christ;* and hence his trials, severe and appalling as they would have been to most men, did not frighten him nor impair his enjoyment. His happiness was drawn from such a source, that no changes in his circumstances could in any sensible degree affect it. He could sing, and praise God, with as much joyfulness in the dungeon at Philippi, as in the house of Lydia.

> Christ was the spring of all his joys,
> The life of his delights,
> The glory of his brightest days,
> And comfort of his nights.

When he stood in disgrace before Agrippa, the gazing-stock of a heathen multitude, he was not unhappy; nor would he have then exchanged places with his royal judge, even if he could. And to mention but a single thought more—Paul's language implies an abiding impression

4. *That his own honour was identified with the cause of Christ.* He felt the liveliest sympathy on every indignity done to his beloved Master, or to any of his true disciples. Who that reads his epistles, can fail to see that, with the apostle John, he had "no greater joy than to hear that his children walked

7

in truth," (3 John 4;) and no greater sorrow, than when they relapsed into sin, and covered themselves and the Christian cause with dishonour. Their integrity, consistency, and perseverance in their appropriate duties, were his life. "Now we live," he says to his endeared brethren at Thessalonica, "if ye stand fast in the Lord." As an affectionate father shares in all that touches the honour of his children, so did our illustrious apostle, and so does every other friend of Christ feel himself to be personally interested in all that concerns his fellow-disciples, or their glorious Head.

Such, very imperfectly expounded, is the meaning of Paul in this peculiar language descriptive of his life. Nor need any, who can say in such an acceptation, "for me to live is Christ," falter in adopting the triumphant clause that follows, "to die is gain."

II. But to what special advantage does the Apostle refer as the issue of such a life? "To die," as the hearer well knows, is to undergo a change which is proverbial for its terror. Among all the fearful things from which our nature shrinks, this holds the preëminence, and is fitly styled by Bildad the Shuhite, their "king." It is this which makes the existence of thousands so bitter, that they regret their ever having entered the world, such is their tormenting dread of going out of it. Death is the alloy which makes the finest gold dim. It is the "dead fly" in the sweetest "ointment of the apothecary." It is the portentous hand that writes "tekel" on all our worldly gains. Nor have the terrors of this enemy been overrated in relation to those who are unprepared to meet him. Death to them is the end of privileges and means of grace. He that is unchanged and is morally "filthy" at death, must be "filthy still" to all eternity. If lost then, he is lost for ever. And O the thought, how ineffably dreadful! of being shut out from heaven, and of having our never-ending existence in all the sins and sufferings, and the godless companionship of hell! We have said that the way to escape the terrors of an accusing conscience and banish the fear of death, has eluded all the searchings of human philosophy. The secret was not found in the almost three hundred systems of the ancients mentioned by Varro. But it was first brought to light in the heaven-disclosed science of this inspired volume. This is a new system of truth, hitherto unknown, containing the chief duty, as well as the "chief end of man," in which death is an essential element. A new song of joy and triumph is put into the mouth of trembling humanity. Her tears are wiped away; her days of mourning are ended, and the "king of terrors" becomes an angel of mercy. If death be the loss of some things to such a man as Paul, it is the gain of others, that are infinitely greater and better.

1. *It is a happy release from all the natural evils of life;* from all the trouble that "man is born to," as the sparks fly upward; from sickness, oppression, care, anxiety, melancholy, heart-ache; from all that can give pain to the body or disquiet to the soul. Such a death "is gain," because,

2. *It is the end of all the spiritual evils of life,*

of all conflicts with "the world, the flesh, and the devil." It is the hour of the soul's triumph over every adversary, and the "fight of faith" is now ended for ever. There are no more struggles with an evil heart of unbelief; with its apathy, wandering affections, its envy, jealousy, pride, malice, and uncharitableness. The Divine image, which was lost at the apostasy, is now restored, and the child of God at death becomes perfect as his Father in Heaven is perfect. But death is gain in a higher and more important sense than that.

3. *It is to depart and be with Christ.* But what this language comprehends in all its import—what it is to be with Him and like Him; to be a sharer in his happiness and glory, who can tell but they who know what it means by their personal experience? Eye hath not seen nor ear heard it, and when the apostle returned from the "third heaven," where he had enjoyed it for a season, he wanted the powers of speech to express it. The things he saw, and heard, and felt, were "unutterable." But we are dwelling too long in our exposition, which was designed to be only a preface to what you have been invited to hear this evening, of one in whose Paul-like life and death the apostle's words were so well exemplified.

And in preparing this tribute to our departed friend, it is gratefully acknowledged that we have been greatly aided by his own suggestion of our text. More than a year before his death, when in the enjoyment of his ordinary health, the request was

made that, should such a service as we now render
fall to the lot of the speaker, these words of Paul
should be the text.   To any preacher who had known
Dr. Neill intimately, the passage would have occurred
umprompted, as affording the most appropriate theme
for such an occasion, that he could select.   We need
not remark, that the wish was expressed with perfect
modesty, and without the least savour of complacency
. in his Christian attainments, by which he would seem
to liken himself to Paul.   No man was ever more
backward to make either his personal religion or his
official labours the topic of conversation, much less of
boasting; but when referred to in our private intercourse, I know not how often he has dwelt in the most
disparaging terms on his numberless delinquencies,
neglected opportunities of usefulness, and sins of
omission.   And yet, who that ever enjoyed the benefit
of his ministry, heard his sermons, and witnessed his
daily conduct, ever doubted that Christ was his life, in
every acceptation of that strong language, as interpreted in this discourse; that Christ was habitually
recognized as the source of his life?   To advance
Christ's kingdom was the main object of his life.
The highest enjoyment of his life was derived from
communion with Christ.   His honour was identified
with the cause of Christ.   Indeed, our text is so
exact a description of Dr. Neill's life, that when I
have expounded its meaning, I seem to myself to
have accomplished all that this service requires.   It
is the biography of our lamented friend in epitome.
What need be added, what can be added, to make our
7*

narrative complete, when we have said that for him "to live was Christ?" It comprehends every moral excellency and every good work that our minds can conceive or our tongues express. It embraces every detail that we wish to hear or know of his private, domestic, social, and official life. It is enough to say, that in each and every department, in every relation and station of life, for him "to live was Christ." His precepts were the rule of his life, and His holy example was the pattern of his life. To exemplify these remarks by the number of facts which might be cited from his Autobiography, would only be the anticipation of what you may soon have the privilege of reading. All, therefore, that the hearer would expect or desire on this occasion, is only an expression of opinion, or a delineation of such traits of character as the writer of his own memoirs would of course omit; such, for example, as those which relate to himself as a father, a husband, and a member of society. But the integrity, tenderness, and fidelity with which he performed the duties of these several relations is too well known to most whom I address, to make such an account more than a rehearsal of what is as familiar to themselves as it is to the speaker. They all know him to have been of a most tender spirit, charitable to the infirmities and weaknesses of others, ever ready to forgive their faults and injuries to himself, and utterly incapable of resentment.

Dr. Neill was liberal in his contributions to the poor who needed clothing or bread, and had a lively sympathy with indigent students in pursuit of education, as has been significantly proclaimed since his death, by the bequest of two hundred dollars, (all that he could well afford,) to the College at Princeton, for the aid of beneficiaries. This he regarded as the paying of a debt of honour, contracted when a student there. He also gave one hundred and fifty dollars as an expression of his sympathy with disabled ministers in need, and the suffering widows and orphans of deceased ministers.

Such gifts, in view of the donor's limited means, are bountiful. They are the "two mites" mentioned in Luke xxi. 21, that in Christ's esteem are more than the costly offerings of the rich, and evince a stronger love for him. He had written "holiness to the Lord" on all his possessions, which he kept in hand only so long as he needed them to furnish him his daily bread; and then he cast not a small proportion of them all into the treasury of the Lord. The most of his theological books were left to the Ashmun Institute, as an expression of his interest for the welfare of the Africans among us. Other bequests bear similar testimony to Dr. Neill's generosity of heart.

He was also affectionate and urbane; uniformly dignified and courteous, never descending to what was frivolous, and unbecoming the manners of a Christian minister and a true gentleman. He suffered, at various periods of his life, the sort of physical indisposition to which scholars and persons generally of sedentary habits are peculiarly subject, by which the spirits are often depressed, and the temper tried; yet his graces were made to shine the brighter by these attritions between the flesh and the spirit—conflicts which are inseparable from the experience of every person of susceptible nerves and imperfect health.

Dr. Neill was an industrious and successful student, with intellect and acquisitions which procured him an elevated place among scholars. His triumph over the obstacles which in youth impeded his way to an education; his appointment to the post of teacher in the College of New Jersey at Princeton, immediately after receiving his bachelor's degree; his early and continued acceptance and success as a preacher to congregations as intelligent and discriminating as any in our land; his election to the high place of President of the College at Carlisle; the respect shown in the literary honours that were conferred on him, unsolicited by friends; his influence in the numerous literary, philanthropic, and religious institutions of our land, which he helped to originate and sustain; the manifest interest and favour with which he was always heard in our ecclesiastical assemblies, when he arose to speak—are all so many testimonials to the superiority of his mental powers, his weight of character, and the high respect in which he was held as a man of letters and a minister of the gospel.

The same view of Dr. Neill's talents, various reading, and scholarly culture, is sustained by his published works. His Lectures on Biblical History, and Practical Exposition of the Epistle to the Ephesians, evince a critical and enlightened study of the Scriptures, a chaste and classical pen, a thorough understanding of the doctrines of our faith, and a commendable zeal to proclaim and defend them. Tho character of Dr. Neill's mind, his taste, and the extent of his reading, were exhibited in his library, which contained some of the best works, theological and miscellaneous, in our language. Nor could any one enjoy his confidence, hear his opinions, read with care his writings, and not receive a deep impression of his excellent judgment, sound sense, extensive knowledge, and many gifts, which might have justly raised him to the higher places of honour held by persons of less modesty and pretence, without a moiety of his merit and qualifications.

Dr. Neill, it is well known, was constitutionally cautious and conservative; yet he was kept from the extremes of party, not by timidity, but by principle. He was not a man of indecision; not vacillating, nor a trimmer, as all will bear witness, who recollect the bold and independent tone of his public addresses; but he was, from conviction, a man of prudence, in a sense of that ambiguous term, which is honourable and healthful. He could not withdraw his confidence from a brother, "for whom Christ died," because he could only say "Sibboleth;" but he gave the hand of fraternal fellowship to all who loved the same Saviour, and whose hopes of salvation rested on the same foundation with his own.

Nor did any difference of opinion between himself and others on matters of ecclesiastical policy, impair the respect or confidence of either. "You know my feelings on the subject of Christian union," he said, in one of our last interviews, "how low I hold sectarian names and forms about which Christians differ, compared with those glorious truths in which they agree. I wish to have these sentiments published at my funeral." Then followed his instructions, to select from different denominations those clerical brethren who should be invited to take part in that solemnity. Thus proclaiming, in the arrangements for the last official service which they would ever be able to render, the catholicism of his heart. "Though dead" he would yet "speak," and make this *post mortem* declaration of a love for Christ's disciples, which was paramount to all the modes by which their discipleship was declared. But to give an adequate view of the life of a minister who was spared so long, who filled so many useful and important posts, doing, in his humble, unostentatious way, so much good, belongs to his biographer. It cannot be compressed within the limits of a sermon. But the fact is not to be overlooked, as an encouraging example to ministers in advanced age, that Dr. Neill's last years were among the most useful of his life, and, as he said to the speaker, the happiest. At no former period were his "labours more abundant" according to his strength, his habits more devotional; never was he more "fervent in spirit," instructive in conversation and preaching, or more eloquent. No part of his labours since his return to the city, has been more useful than his ministrations among the inmates of some of our institutions of philanthropy. The infirmities, sorrows, and sins that he witnessed in his visits of mercy, touched his heart, and elicited its liveliest sympathies. His conversations, and familiar instructions, at the Asylum for Widows, were peculiarly edifying, judicious, and comforting. No mourners beyond the circle of his kindred are so sincere, and feel so much bereaved by Dr. Neill's death, as they. His impromptu address in the Synod of Philadelphia, at their last meeting in this city, and that before the American Board of Commissioners for Foreign Missions, in October last, will never be forgotten by any one who heard them. His many discourses uttered without manuscript in our hearing, his conversational discourses in the lecture room, and at the communion table, could not be surpassed in tenderness, simplicity of manner, and richness in evangelical truth. Indeed, these delightful meetings with our departed friend and teacher have been so recent, that we have not begun to realize that we shall see and hear him no more; that we shall never again listen to those prayers of unsurpassed excellence, so humble, so penitent and earnest, so well expressed, conveying in the most appropriate language the thoughts of every devotional heart in the assembly; that we have seen for the last time, that tall and venerable form, bending over the low desk to the sacred volume, on account of his imperfect vision. That we shall never more take his hand, and receive his affectionate greetings, brings back a solemn reality which has seemed more like a vision.

Such an illusion is promoted by our recurrence to

the surprising calmness and self-possession with which
he withdrew. His freedom from all that fear of
death, by which he had been at times disquieted during
his life; his perfect readiness for the sundering of all
earthly ties which had been so tender and so strong;
his directions, so deliberately given, concerning the
time, place, and mode of his interment; the persons
to officiate; his funeral sermon; the psalm to be sung;
the preparation for the press of the modest and too
brief memoir of his life; the unruffled composure with
which he bade his beloved friends and kindred farewell; were all exemplifications of our text, and proofs
of its sustaining power. Nothing but an assurance
that "to die was gain" could have given such support
and composure to his soul, when flesh and heart were
failing. Such a death, fellow-survivors, is of untold
importance to us, as another demonstration both of
the reality of religion, and of its efficacy in that last
hour, when mere physical courage quails, the strongest
heart faints for fear, and philosophy becomes a fool.
Think of the horror with which some of the stoutest
boasters of their courage have shrunk from the grave,
when contrasted with such a tranquil, hopeful, joyful
exit as his. Think how the scoffer of Ferney left the
world, compared with the triumphant departure of
Paul.

But while our meditations on the happy end of our
ascended friend are full of comfort in view of his
"gain," we cannot be unmindful of our "loss." I am
well aware of the levity with which the unthinking
world are accustomed to speak of death, especially in

the ease of those who have lived to a great age. Detached as it is in their mind from its moral results, it is regarded as only one of those physical changes in nature, which come of course, and we must all look for —a mere common place event, not to be noticed too seriously, and one which it is bootless and foolish to lament. Alexander Pope, the poet and wit, thus discourses concerning his own departure, which occurred at the age of fifty-six. "When I think what an inconsiderable little atom every single man is, with respect to the whole creation, methinks it is a shame to be concerned about the removal of such a trivial animal as I am. The morning after my exit, the sun will rise as bright as ever, the flowers will smell as sweet, the plants spring as green. The world will proceed in its old course, people will laugh as heartily and marry as fast as they used to do." All this is very true, but while the world is moving on in its usual carelessness and unconcern, what has become of the departed soul? Has it gone to a state of sorrow or of joy? Is our friend to be for ever happy or miserable? Has he gone to heaven—or where is he? The old disciple, of whose death the world speaks so slightingly, may have come to his grave as a shock of corn in his season, and it is well with him. But who is to take his fallen mantle, offer his prayers, give his faithful exhortations, exhibit his godly example? The treasures of heavenly wisdom which are invested in every enlightened Christian of four-score, are beyond any appreciable value. To his family, his congregation, and to the public at large, the loss is not to be repaired. God grant, my fellow-mourners, that the burden of our loss may be lightened in some degree by our recollections of his teachings, of his exemplary living, and especially in the answer of his prayers. To myself, the loss of this valuable helper in my ministry is great. It fills me with emotions which no tongue can utter, when I think that I am left the only survivor of the four pastors who have filled your pulpit; that Dr. Neill has joined the company of Kennedy and Winchester; and how soon the sacred place shall cease to know the speaker, is a grave secret which Omniscience reserves to himself.

May the great Watchman and Shepherd of Israel, a symbol of whose presence hovered between the wings of the cherubim, be ever present with his servant, and with the people to whom he ministers. Touch their lips, and inspire their hearts, O God, whenever they approach thy mercy-seat in prayer. Endue us all more plentifully with thy grace, that with our ascended friend and brother, we may at last depart in peace, with his hope in our hearts, and his words on our lips, "for me to live is Christ, and to die is gain."

SERMONS

BY THE

Rev. WILLIAM NEILL, D. D.

SELF-DENIAL A CHRISTIAN DUTY.

Then said Jesus unto his disciples, If any man will come after me, let him deny himself.—MATTHEW xvi. 24.

By many this is accounted a hard saying. Hence the vain attempt to confine its application to the apostles and primitive disciples of our Lord: or if this cannot be made out satisfactorily, then its meaning must be frittered down to suit the corrupt propensities of the human heart. But the terms of discipleship are not changed; and it is idle, dangerous, and wicked, to employ an ingenious criticism in opposing or explaining away the obvious meaning and express testimony of God's word. The law bears upon all—it is promulged in comprehensive terms—"If any man will come after me, let him deny himself." There is no alternative, brethren; as we would be the followers and friends of Christ, we must submit to his laws, and surrender ourselves to the influence of his grace.

Self-denial, it is freely admitted, is not in itself pleasant, nor does it possess any intrinsic merit or efficacy. But the Saviour requires it; and were we

8*

unable to discover the reasonableness or necessity of the requirement, his authority has undisputable claims upon our obedience. But the goodness of God forbids us to suppose that he would wantonly or needlessly grieve the children of men. He who has given understanding to man, can promulgate no laws which are not founded on reason and equity. This inference flows irresistibly from the Divine perfection. It is no doubt correct in the case before us. Our blessed Lord commands us, as we would follow him, and share in his salvation, to deny ourselves. Let us see whether we cannot discover enough to satisfy us that the command is holy, just, and good. Be it carefully observed, then,

I. That the Lord Jesus Christ came into the world to *save sinners*. Had he come to place himself at the head of a race of innocent beings, then, and in that case, protection and defence would have been sufficient. Discipline, restraint, and self-control, for aught that we know, might not have been necessary. But as the case is, protection alone will not answer the end proposed. The Saviour finds us in a state of sin and misery. He finds us far gone—gone beyond the reach of an angel's arm, and sinking under a deadly disease. To save us, therefore, he must prescribe the proper remedies, and unless we follow his prescriptions a cure is not to be expected. It is a maxim in the healing art, universally admitted, that "inveterate diseases require powerful, and sometimes very painful applications."

Now when the depravity of our nature is taken

into the account, who does not see the necessity of self-denial? We are not upright—our passions and appetites have, by the sad apostasy, obtained the ascendency. They are not, naturally, disposed to follow the dictates of reason. They are turbulent, clamorous, and headstrong, and, if not restrained, they will precipitate us into ruin. It is the province of self-denial, through help obtained of God, to reduce them to order and subordination, and it is impossible to make any advances in holiness without exercising self-discipline. It is, in short, a principal means of attaining to all those tempers and dispositions which compose the character of a good man. To illustrate this remark, let us descend to particulars. By nature we are prone to love and serve the creature more than the Creator. This is wrong. How is the evil to be corrected? By refusing to follow this propensity of our nature—by setting our affections on things above, not on things which are on the earth. Here is need of self-denial. We are naturally proud. But pride is not becoming a dependent sinful creature; and we are just so far humble as we refuse to indulge pride. We are naturally inclined to avenge an injury—the language of the unrenewed heart is, "revenge is sweet." But the gospel says, "avenge not yourselves," and our Lord has set us an example of forgiveness, that we should follow his steps. Here is work for self-denial.

We are naturally selfish, avaricous, covetous. But our Divine religion requires us to devise liberal things;

to regard them that are in bonds, as being ourselves also in the body; to stand ready for every good word and work, and to give alms of such things as we have. Here again is work for self-denial. We are prone to waste our time in idleness, or vain and trifling pursuits. But the gospel calls upon us to redeem time; to give all diligence to make our calling and election sure; to be sober, and watch unto prayer. And if we would secure the true riches, we must refuse to gratify the desires of the flesh; we must dissent from the usages of the world, and follow Christ. Thus we see the necessity of self-denial results from the corruption of our nature. It is indispensable; it lies at the foundation of the Christian character; it is, if I may so speak, the process by which we are to be transformed in the spirit of our minds, and restored to the Divine likeness; and, without exercising it, we shall in vain expect to arrive at the stature of a perfect man in Christ Jesus.

II. Another argument in favour of self-denial may be deduced from the design of Christianity. What is this design, my hearers, as it relates to us? What is it, but to free us from the dominion of sin; to purify our hearts, and bring us into a state of communion and fellowship with God; to produce and cherish those dispositions and tempers which shall fit us for the felicity of heaven? What, then, are those qualities which go to prepare us for the happiness of heaven? You will find a specimen of them in the fifth chapter of the Gospel by Matthew: humility, meekness, repentance, purity, heavenly-mindedness, peace, patience, and resignation to the Divine will. On each of these traits of character the Saviour pronounces a benediction; and we cannot dispute their excellence, without rejecting the gospel, and opposing our own judgment to the decisions of infinite wisdom. Now every one of these dispositions has its opposite in our corrupt hearts. And in so far as we yield to these opposites, we refuse to fall in with the design of Christianity, which is to elevate our affections and sanctify our souls.

III. The necessity of self-denial will appear still more clearly, if we consider the influence which the body and its animal appetites have upon the soul and its moral qualities. It is observed by a judicious writer,* "that the fall of man seems to have consisted very much in the subjection of the soul to the power and dominion of the body; as the characteristic mark of his restoration through Christ is the reduction of the body under the power and dominion of the soul. For thus the Scriptures describe the whole process as a contest between the flesh and the spirit, ending, after many struggles and vicissitudes, in the victory of the latter." This observation is supported by a saying of the ancients: "The corruptible body presseth down the soul, and the earthly tabernacle weigheth down the mind."

This being the case, how careful should we be, my hearers, not to indulge our animal appetites to the degradation of our intellectual and moral powers.

* Bishop Horne.

The body is by Divine appointment the soul's servant; and it is justly entitled to all needful nourishment, in meat and drink. But if it be pampered to excess, it will refuse obedience; and when it once obtains the mastery, it is, of all masters, the most sottish and inexorable. Indeed, it will be found invariably true that the excessive gratification of our sensual appetites blunts and benumbs the intellectual faculties. Let a man, for instance, indulge freely in eating and drinking, in the intermission of public worship on the Sabbath, and he will be less disposed to go to the house of God in the afternoon than ho was in the forenoon; and if he docs go, he will be more inclined to sleep, than to pray and hear the gospel.

We see, then, that the Christian doctrine of self-denial is founded on the constitution of our nature. We are composed of two parts, soul and body. These, though possessed of distinct qualities, and capable of a separato existence, arc closely united, and exert on one another a mutual influence. And he who prefers his rational to his animal nature, must take care of his soul; and in doing this he will find it absolutely necessary, in many instances, to deny and mortify the body with its affections and lusts. Thus St. Paul reasons, "Therefore, brethren, we arc debtors, not to the flesh, to live after the flesh; for if ye live after the flesh ye shall die; but if ye, through the Spirit, do mortify the deeds of the body, ye shall live." Rom. viii. 12, 13.

IV. The last argument that we shall adduco in

support of the doctrine of self-denial, we derive from the fact, that it is the price set upon everything that forms the object of man's pursuit. It is not peculiar to the Christian life. Let a man select what object he pleases, if he will prosecute it with zeal and effect, he must exercise self-denial. And really, however paradoxical the remark may seem, there are not wanting witnesses who can attest, that the self-denial of sinners is often more painful than that which is required of the Christian. See the miser, whose aim it is to add continually to his piles of minted dust. He denies himself, not only the pleasure of helping the needy, and making the widow's heart sing for joy, but the conveniences, and even necessaries of life. He lives in constant fear of being robbed, and, in many instances, dies hugging his chest, in fearful apprehension of coming to want.

The gamester denies himself sleep, which, to the honest labouring man, is sweet, and resigns the plaudits of a good conscience, which, to the upright in heart, are better than rubies. He finds it often necessary to refuse to his hunger and thirst their wonted supplies, to maintain a steady hand and a clear head, for the purpose of cheating with adroitness, and so as to escape detection. The courtier of popular favour applies himself with suppleness and cringing to the prejudices, whims, and vices of his fellow-mortals. O what toils, what anxieties, what mortifications, and disappointments he is doomed to endure! All that is manly, all that is independent, all that is dignified, all that is

honourable in the human character, must be sacri-
ficed—to what? a name, fleeting as the air, a
bubble, a vanity, a thing of nought!

The votary of fashion and amusement is often
borne down to weariness and yawning with the
giddy whirl of changing modes of dress and manners.
The theatre, the ball room, and the splendid party,
are not unfrequently followed with· a disgust and
languor of spirits, which extort from the bosom of
folly the bitterest execrations against the inexorable
laws of custom. O how much to be pitied, as well
as blamed, are they who resign the ease, and half
the simple sanctified pleasures of home, and go in
chase of happiness in public and brilliant entertainments, where neither nature nor nature's God ever
intended it should be found!

But not to mention other characters, who, in the
service of their respective masters, are obliged to
make great and painful sacrifices—tell me, hearers,
is it reasonable, is it fair, to account the Lord Jesus
Christ a hard Master, because he requires us, on
becoming his followers, to deny ourselves? Can we
avoid self-denial, serve what master we may? Is not
the doctrine founded on the depravity of our hearts,
the design of the gospel, the constitution of our
nature? and does it not correspond with what we see
constantly practised by all descriptions of persons, in
pursuing their several favourite objects? And, when
we take into account "the prize of our high calling of
God in Christ Jesus," and compare this with those
things for which so many spend their strength, and

deprive themselves of rest, who would hesitate to comply with the Divine requirement, "If any man will come after me, let him deny himself"? The duty, rightly understood, is not, as some affect to represent it, repulsive to the dictates of good sense and right reason. It is not a cant phrase, without rational meaning. It is a term of sober and significant import, expressive of a temper without which no man can be a Christian. "It does not consist in denying what a man is, or what he has; in refusing favours conferred on us in the course of providence; in rejecting the use of God's creatures; in being careless of life, health, or family; in macerating the body, or abusing it in any respect; but in renouncing those pleasures, profits, connections, and practices, which are prejudicial to the true interests of the soul, and offensive to God."

As all the faculties of our nature are deranged and vitiated by the fall, so they all furnish occasion for the exercise of self-denial. Thus the understanding is to be so far denied as not to lean upon it, independent of Divine instruction: "Trust in the Lord with all thy heart," says Solomon, "and lean not unto thine own understanding." Prov. iii. 5. The will is to be denied, so far as it opposes the will of God: "Wherefore, be ye not unwise," says Paul, "but understanding what the will of the Lord is." Eph. v. 17. The affections are to be denied, when they claim inordinate indulgence: "Mortify your members which are upon the earth," says the same apostle; "fornication, uncleanness, inordinate affection, evil

9

concupiscence, and covetousness, which is idolatry; for which things' sake the wrath of God cometh on the children of disobedience." Col. iii. 5, 6. The honours of the world and the praise of men are to be rejected, when they come in competition with our duty to God: "By faith, Moses, when he was come to years, refused to be called the son of Pharaoh's daughter; choosing rather to suffer affliction with the people of God, than to enjoy the pleasures of sin for a season: esteeming the reproach of Christ greater riches than the treasures of Egypt." Heb. xi. 25, 26. Our own righteousness is to be denied, so as not to depend upon it. Like St. Paul, we are to account all things but loss in comparison with Christ, and desire to be found in him, and to be saved through his righteousness and merits. In a word, everything that is sinful in itself, or that militates against our growth in grace, is to be denied: "For without holiness no man shall see the Lord." Heb. xii. 14.

Having now seen the grounds and nature of the duty, let us attend to the inducements to practise it. These are many and various. We shall confine our attention at present to the authority, the example, and the promises of Christ. We have the authority of Christ in our text. He here proposes self-denial as an indispensable term of discipleship. And as he is always of one mind, we may not expect that any of the laws of his kingdom will ever be changed. They are the result of the combined counsels of wisdom, justice, and mercy. He knows what is in man. He knows the deplorable state to which sin has reduced us. He knows what means are most fit to be used for our salvation from sin. The infinite benignity of his heart forbids us to suppose that he would impose a needless burden or arbitrary restraint on his disciples; and verily his authority is not to be contemned with impunity. It is the will of God, that all men honour the Son, even as they honour the Father. His will is made known to us, not as a matter of speculative curiosity, but as a law of duty, having for its sanction the worm that never dies, the fire that is not quenched, and the wrath of the Lamb. If we do not the things which he commands us, we prove ourselves his enemies. If we refuse to follow his prescriptions, when he comes to us in his gospel, as the Physician and Saviour of our souls, we pour contempt on his Godhead, reject his mercy, and resolve to die in our sins. And for this triple crime of having outraged his authority, despised his grace, and ruined ourselves, he will reckon with us at a future day: "For we must all appear before the judgment-seat of Christ."

Secondly, consider his example as a motive to self-denial. Of his example, in this respect, you have an inimitable picture drawn by the pencil of inspiration, in the Epistle to the Philippians ii. 5—8: "Let this mind be in you, which was also in Christ Jesus; who, being in the form of God, thought it not robbery to be equal with God; but made himself of no reputation, and took upon him the form of a servant, and was made in the likeness of men. And being found in fashion as a man, he humbled himself, and became obedient unto death, even the death of the cross."

No self-denial that we can be required to exercise, will bear a comparison with this. The blessed Master disrobed himself of his glory, and assumed the fashion of a man, and the form of a servant, voluntarily, and for the sake of sinners. Whereas, with us, the duty involves our interest; our case requires it; it is designed for our good: "He that humbleth himself, shall be exalted." The mouth of the Lord hath spoken it.

O my hearers, when we contemplate the Divine Redeemer, in his native majesty; when we behold him, the express image of the Father, encompassed with angels, illumining all heaven with the beams of his glory; and then view him it that state of matchless humiliation to which he submitted for our sake, can we, for a moment, refuse any sacrifices of self-indulgence to such a Master? Ah, Christian, whatever may be your temptations; whatever obloquy, scorn, and contempt you have to meet, in adhering to your duty; whatever injuries, neglects, or insults from your fellow-men you have to forgive; whatever hindrances and persecutions you have to meet with in the service of your Lord, they are but as the small dust of the balance when compared with the contradiction of sinners, the sorrows and sufferings which he endured, and to which you owe all your hopes of pardon, perseverance, and eternal life. "Consider this, lest you be weary and faint in your minds." Do not refuse to follow him, because he requires you to deny yourselves. No obstacles stopped him, when engaged in working out your redemption. If your trials be great, your temptations violent, and your corruptions strong, you have the promise of "grace sufficient." And here you have a third motive to the duty of self-denial.

It is not a work which you are required to do in your own strength. He who enjoins the duty, promises all needful aid in performing it. Here is the ground on which you may confidently hope for ultimate success. "When I am weak, then am I strong," is Divine philosophy. This is St. Paul's philosophy. Hence the bold declaration, "I can do all things through Christ, who strengtheneth me." Hence, too, those seeming paradoxes which he utters in relation to himself and fellow-sufferers for the word of God and the testimony of Jesus: "As unknown, and yet well known; as dying, and behold we live; as chastened, and not killed; as sorrowful, yet always rejoicing; as poor, yet making many rich; as having nothing, and yet possessing all things." 2 Cor. vi. 9, 10.

O then, Christian, with such helps, promises, and encouragements, how can you fail of success, unless you neglect to avail yourself of the resources which are placed in your offer? But remember, without these Divine succours, you will make but a feeble and ineffectual resistance to the enemies of your salvation. "Without me ye can do nothing," contains more useful instruction than you can find in many volumes of casuistry. In the work of self-denial, as in every other duty, "our sufficiency is of God."

Let us now recapitulate what has been said. Self-denial is an indispensable term of Christian disciple-

9*

ship: "If any man will come after me," &c. It consists in the renunciation of self-confidence; in the
utter abandonment of all those passions, pursuits, and
pleasures which impede the sanctification of our hearts,
or interfere with our duty to God, our Saviour. The
necessity of it arises out of the degeneracy of our
nature; it is not an arbitrary or needless law. The
glorious design of the gospel scheme of salvation to
restore us to communion with God requires it; and it
is a price set on all moral and religious attainments.
The duty of exercising it is enforced by the authority,
the example, and promised grace of the Lord Jesus
Christ.

HEAVENLY MANSIONS.

(A COMMUNION SERMON.)

------◆◆◆------

"Let not your heart be troubled: ye believe in God, believe also
in me. In my Father's house are many mansions: if it were
not so, I would have told you. I go to prepare a place for you.
And if I go and prepare a place for you, I will come again, and
receive you unto myself; that where I am, there ye may be
also."—JOHN xiv. 1—3.

THESE words were addressed to the apostles by our
blessed Lord very soon after he had instituted the
holy ordinance which we are now to celebrate, in
commemoration of his death. To those who had
been favoured with his personal friendship and
counsels, the address must have been in a high
degree interesting and consolatory. But we shall
consider it as intended for the benefit of his followers in every period of his Church. In this point
of view the subject, it is hoped, will be useful to
many, and not unsuitable to the business before us.

A series of observations, unfolding the sense of
the passage, with some practical reflections adapted
to the present occasion, is all that I propose in this
discourse.

I. "Ye believe in God: believe also in me." The

apostles believed in God as the Creator and Preserver of all things. They believed in the testimony of the prophets respecting the promised Messiah. But now when he, who they expected should redeem Israel, was about to be cut off by a violent and ignominious death, their faith in him was in danger of being diminished. In propagating his gospel, and maintaining his cause, they had a world of opposition to encounter. To be deprived of his company and animating example—to be obliged to meet the prejudices of Jews, the idolatry of pagans, and the pride of philosophy, without the aid of his personal influence, was a sore trial. This the Saviour foresaw, and endeavoured to provide against it. With all the tenderness of a father and a friend, he exhorts them not to give up their confidence in him. It was expedient, indeed, that he should go and leave them for a time. He must be delivered into the hands of sinners—he must die—his blood must be shed for the remission of sins. But this was necessary to the attainment of the great end for which he had become incarnate. It had been predicted by the prophets, and therefore his death, as the fulfilment of prophecy, instead of weakening, should confirm their faith in him, as the Lord their righteousness, and the propitiation for their sins. "Let not your heart be troubled:" as if he had said, let not the gloomy prospect of my death oppress your spirits. I have counted the cost of the great work in which I am engaged. I must give my life a ransom for many; but I shall not be holden of death; after three days I will rise, as I have said, and meet you in Galilee. You shall find that I am the faithful and true witness. I have power to lay down my life, and I have power to take it up again. Be not faithless, therefore, but believing. Think not that I am going to deceive you. Heaven and earth shall pass away, but my word shall not fail.

Christians, apply this observation to yourselves. If you are indeed Christ's followers, as you profess to be, he says to you, "Let not your hearts be troubled; ye believe in God; believe also in me." You doubtless have your fightings without, and fears within. Whence arise these distressing apprehensions? Are they not attributable to the weakness of your faith in Christ? Your Saviour has told you that his yoke is easy, and his burden light. He has invited you to come unto him that you may find rest to your souls. You have come; but you have not found that uniform satisfaction and comfort which you expected. When you examine and try to ascertain whether you bear the marks of true discipleship, you are often oppressed, and ready to sink under the fearful apprehension, that you have neither part nor lot in the great salvation. And instead of saying with the apostle, "I know whom I have believed," you complain, with the poet:

'Tis a point I long to know,
Oft it causes anxious thought:
Do I love the Lord, or no?
Am I his, or am I not?

If I love, why am I thus?
  Why this dull and lifeless frame?
Hardly, sure, can they be worse,
  Who have never heard his name.

Lord, decide the doubtful case;
  Thou who art thy people's Sun!
Shine upon thy work of grace,
  If it be indeed begun!

Whence these mournful complaints? Is it not because you do not believe in Christ, as you believe in God? Faith in God, without regard to the Mediator of the new covenant, cannot give comfort to a fallen creature, under a sense of his sin. If you would have joy in believing, and rise above the terrors of eternal death, you must commit your souls into the hands of your Redeemer, with entire and unqualified confidence. Hear his word, then, and lay hold of the hope which it sets before you: "I am the way, the truth, and the life: no man cometh to the Father, but by me. Without me, ye can do nothing. Ye believe in God; believe also in me." Do you feel your insufficiency for the duties required of you as a professor of the gospel? Are you sensible of your unworthiness to approach the table of the Lord? You are unworthy; and it is well you feel it. But Christ is worthy. In him the Father is well pleased. Venture forward, therefore, in his name. Plead his righteousness, and trust in his merits. He ever liveth to make intercession for us. He has passed through this vale of tears; he has borne our griefs and carried our sorrows; the everlasting doors have been lifted up; and the heavens have received him from the sight of mortals; but he is still touched with a feeling of our infirmities—his delight is with the sons of men, and to every humble follower his language is, "My grace is sufficient for thee: ye believe in God, believe also in me."

II. Observe the familiar and satisfactory style in which the Saviour speaks of the heavenly state. He calls it his Father's house. "In my Father's house," says he, "are many mansions; if it were not so, I would have told you." The apostles, from their Jewish habits and education, had heretofore indulged a hope that the Messiah would set up a temporal kingdom. In this temporal kingdom, they expected preferment and distinction. This was the grand error of the nation. Hence the cross of Christ became to the Jews a stumbling-block. When the time came in which the Redeemer must lay down his life and pour out his blood for the salvation of his people, this visionary idea of wordly distinction was to be given up. And, as the minds of the disciples might not, as yet, be well established in the doctrine of the immortality of the soul, their Lord endeavours, on this interesting occasion, to direct their attention to that state of perfect bliss which remains for the people of God in the world to come. He points them to heaven—the house—the delightful, glorious residence of *his* Father, and their Father. There, says he, are many mansions. Behold a house not made with hands, eternal in the heavens! In that happy house there is ample room—the apartments are numerous, and of various dimensions—suited to the various capacities and pious attainments of my followers. There is a heaven, a place of rest, of safety and triumph, where you shall exchange the cross for a crown, the sigh of mourning for the song of triumph. Your hope of future bliss shall not be disappointed. "If it were not so, I would have told you." As if he had said, Have I not proved myself a faithful teacher? And can you suppose that I would deceive you on so important a point as that which involves your eternal life? I came from the bosom of the Father. I have a delightful remembrance of the glories of the upper world. In my gospel I have brought life and immortality to light; and as soon as I shall have finished the work assigned me in the covenant of mercy and grace, I will return to heaven in your name, and in the name of all who shall believe in me to the end of time. I will enter into the holy of holies with my blood and righteousness. These shall avail for the admission of my humble followers. As the High Priest of your profession, I will bear upon my breast the names of the faithful. In due time, the redeemed of all nations shall come to the heavenly Mount Zion, with joy and triumph, and sorrow and sighing shall flee away. "I go to prepare a place for you."

Here, then, communicants, let me suppose you to be Christians indeed, and call upon you to cherish the hope of a blessed immortality. You are Christ's and Christ is God's. At present you travel through a wilderness, where you share in the sorrows and hardships incident to the human family. But what signify the trials and fatigues of a journey to those who are drawing near home, with the certain expectation of everything that is soothing and comfortable! Heaven is your home; God is your Father; Christ, who deigns to call you brethren, is preparing a place for you in that holy, happy house, where you are to obtain the end of your faith, even life everlasting. With you, it is not a matter of doubtful disputation, whether you shall live after the present life. You receive it as an indubitable truth, on the testimony of Jesus, who is emphatically styled the faithful and true witness. "Because I live, ye shall live also." Seize this truth then, believer, and let it cheer you in the house of your pilgrimage. Everything on earth is transient and unsatisfying. Here the fairest flower fades; the finest prospects are soon beclouded; the soundest health must yield to the infirmities of age; the strongest intellect fail; the richest inheritance be relinquished; the tenderest ties of nature be dissolved; and all the pleasures of the world terminate in disappointment and the grave. But on the objects of your faith and hope, eternity impresses reality and incomparable worth. The Saviour, whose death you are now to commemorate, lives for ever; and he lives for you: "Your life is hid with Christ in God." With a hope full of immortality, and a heart overflowing with gratitude, you may sing, as you pass along the journey of life,

"Now to the shining realms above,
I stretch my hands, and glance my eyes;
O for the pinions of a dove
To bear me to the upper skies!

10

> There from the bosom of my God,
>   Oceans of endless pleasure roll;
> There would I fix my last abode,
>   And drain the sorrows of my soul."

III. Observe, thirdly, the Saviour's determination to complete the happiness of his disciples: "And if I go and prepare a place for you, I will come again, and receive you unto myself; that where I am, there ye may be also." Think not, Christians, that your Lord will leave the work of your redemption unfinished. He does nothing in vain. His grace is incorruptible seed; whom he loves, he loves unto the end. He will conduct you safely through all the dangers of the way, and put you in possession of the promised inheritance. There are two cases in which he comes again, and receives his people unto himself.

First, he comes to them individually at death. Here it is that he draws near, and affords support and comfort in time of need. O it is a consolatory thought, my hearers; for we must die. "Dust thou art, and unto dust thou shalt return." And who can think of dying without wishing to die in the Lord? Poor, feeble mortal, canst thou think of meeting the king of terrors in thy own strength! Be assured thy courage will fail thee; and thou wilt then feel thy need of Him who is the resurrection and the life! The weakest believer may say with David: "Though I walk through the valley of the shadow of death, I will fear no evil; for thou art with me; thy rod and staff, they comfort me." Yes, Christian, if you cleave to him, following him from a principle of love, in the way of his commands and ordinances, he will come graciously near you in a dying hour; he will take you in from a world of storms to the haven of eternal rest, where you shall see his face and sing his praise who has loved you and washed you from your sins in his own blood.

But there is another case in which the Saviour will come again and receive his followers unto himself. He will come in power and great glory, at the end of the world; when his gospel shall have been preached unto all nations; when the ends of the earth shall have received his salvation; when he shall have seen of the travail of his soul and be satisfied; when the designs of his mercy shall have been accomplished among our fallen race;· when the Jews shall have been gathered into the gospel fold, with the fulness of the Gentiles; then, "to them that look for him, will he appear a second time, without sin unto salvation." When he came to his people individually at death, he received their souls only unto himself, but now he will receive their bodies also. When this corruptible shall be so modified as to be incorruptible, a re-union is to take place between the body and its immortal tenant. The bodies of the pious are the temples of the Holy Ghost, and not one of them shall be lost. So St. Paul teaches us in his Epistle to the Philippians, "Our conversation is in heaven, from whence we also look for the Saviour, the Lord Jesus Christ; who shall change our vile body, that it may be fashioned like unto his glorious body; according to the working whereby he is able even to subdue all things unto himself." O blessed and happy day, when our Divine Redeemer shall come to collect the thousands of his people into his Father's house! There shall be the best society, the most exalted employment, with fulness of joy, and pleasures ever more! There the spirits of just men made perfect, shall join with angels in pouring forth the highest praises to Him that sitteth upon the throne, and to the Lamb for ever. There will be Abraham, Isaac, and Jacob, the prophets, the apostles, and martyrs, with the redeemed of all nations, engaged in the same delightful work. My hearers, will you be there? Would it afford you pleasure to be where Jesus displays his glories, and cheers the souls of his people with the holy pleasures of heaven? Do you love him, believe in him, and keep his commandments? Remember, the mansions of bliss are prepared for those who are made "meet for the inheritance of the saints in light." The vessels of mercy are "afore prepared unto glory." Heaven has no charms for the ungodly; it can give no happiness to those who love sin. Indeed, my hearers, so essential is holiness, that St. Paul teaches us that without it no man shall see the Lord.

Communicants, you expect, when done with this world, to go where Jesus is. You indulge a hope that he is now engaged preparing a place for you in his Father's house. You trust he has bought you with his blood, and quickened you by his Spirit. You expect to realize the promise, "Where I am there shall my servant be also." How shall you express your gratitude to Him who has given you these cheering hopes and glorious prospects? Is it a hard condition, that you should be required "to deny yourselves, and take up your cross, and follow Christ? Can the service of such a Master be a weariness? No, no, says the true disciple; "his love constraineth us"! It is this that makes "his yoke easy and his burden light." Come, then, to his table, under the constraining influence of his love. Come, express your sense of obligation, by a cheerful compliance with his dying request, "This do in remembrance of me."

"The love of Christ constraineth us; because we thus judge, that if one died for all, then were all dead; and that he died for all, that they who live, should live, not unto themselves, but to him who died for them, and rose again." This should be the judgment of every professed disciple of Christ. "Herein is my Father glorified," says he, "that ye bear much fruit." Yes, Christians, it is your proper business, and ought to be your constant aim, to glorify God with your bodies and spirits, which are his. Let not the corrupting influence of a wicked world obliterate from your minds the law of redeeming love. While busied with the affairs of this life, forget not whose you are, and whither you are going. Every day, every moment is bringing your redemption nearer and nearer. You are, at present, in a vale of tears; but, yet a little while, and your Saviour will come and receive you graciously into those places which he is

10*

now preparing for you. Be it, then, as your meat and drink to do the will of your Father who is in heaven. Examine yourselves whether ye be in the faith; give all diligence to make your calling and election sure.

But, my hearers, are you all interested in the love and friendship of the Lord Jesus? Can you all look up to God, and indulge, on good grounds, the cheering hope that Christ is interceding for you at the right hand of the Father, that he owns you as disciples, and that he will say to you, at the last day, "Come, ye blessed of my Father, inherit the kingdom prepared for you from the foundation of the world?" Alas! I fear some of you cannot lay claim to these high privileges, on scriptural authority! And should this be the case with any who now hear me, let them know, assuredly, that it is a fearful thing to live without God in the world. Dear friends, we bring no railing accusation against you; but we entreat you, by the mercies and by the terrors of the Lord, to repent, to lay hold of the hope set before you in the gospel. As ambassadors for Christ, we pray you be reconciled to God.' If you are not united to Jesus by a true faith, you are living in a state of condemnation. Hear the Redeemer's own words on this point: "He that believeth not, is condemned already." God has given you space for repentance, and has set before you an open door. A great salvation is offered to you freely, without money and without price. But your day of grace is passing while I address you.

Your Sabbaths, your sanctuary privileges, and your sacramental seasons will soon be over; and should death arrest you in a Christless state, then will be brought to pass upon you that fearful saying, "He that is filthy, let him be filthy still." "Behold, now is the accepted time; behold, now is the day of salvation!"

CHRISTIAN'S CREED AND TRIUMPH.

————◆◆◆————

Who is he that overcometh the world, but he that believeth that Jesus is the Son of God?—1 JOHN v. 5.

THESE words place before us, at one view, the Christian's creed and triumph. He believeth that Jesus is the Son of God—this is his creed. He overcometh the world—this is his triumph.

Let us examine this creed, and try to ascertain the import of the victory which it secures. The language of our text evidently supposes that there are evils to be met with in the world; and that faith in Jesus the Son of God, is the only means by which these evils can be surmounted. This is an idea that pervades the New Testament. The world lieth in wickedness. Its spirit, its manners, and its maxims, are hostile to godliness; and whosoever permits himself to be carried along by the current of its fashion, must not only sustain loss, but, in the end, be utterly ruined. Hence Paul the apostle charges us, "Be not conformed to this world; but be ye transformed by the renewing of your minds, that you may prove what is that good, and acceptable, and perfect will of God."

To the good man, this world presents a scene of trial. It abounds in dangers and troubles, against which faith in the Redeemer affords the only sufficient defence: "In the world," says the Divine Saviour, "ye shall have tribulation; but, be of good cheer, I have overcome the world." To true believers, this passage is full of the richest consolation, while to the ungodly it is unintelligible and uninteresting; for it is the believer, and the believer only, that can participate in the benefits of Christ's victory over the world. Let us inquire, then,

I. What is implied in believing that Jesus is the Son of God? It is a concise and comprehensive expression of evangelical faith. This, my hearers, is a subject of vast importance in the Christian scheme of redemption. It implies two things, viz., credit and trust. *Faith*, in the general acceptation of the term, has relation to testimony. *Gospel faith* has immediate and special relation to the testimony of God respecting his Son. This testimony of God we have in the Bible. Here we are assured that Christ Jesus is the only Saviour of our fallen race; that he is able and ready to save to the uttermost all that come to God by him; that he has removed every obstacle which opposed our salvation; that he has wrought out a righteousness every way answerable to the demands of the Divine law; that he has shed his blood for the remission of sin, and made provision for its ultimate and entire extirpation from the soul that confides in him. The first and most obvious exercise of faith is to believe this testimony. That is, to believe that Jesus Christ is just such a glorious personage—such an able, willing, and compassionate Saviour, as the sacred oracles pronounce him to be. But faith includes another very important idea, viz., *trust.* A mere assent to what the Scripture teaches respecting Jesus Christ, is nothing more than an act of the understanding; or a kind of historical faith, which may have little or no sanctifying influence on the heart and life: "With the heart man believeth unto righteousness." Rom. x. 10. And in order to a hearty reception of the truth, as it is in Jesus, the sinner must feel his sinfulness, and need of a Saviour. So long as he remains unimpressed with a sense of his guilt, he cannot perceive the necessity of embracing Christ.

Hence it is that the tidings of salvation are treated with indifference by so large a portion of mankind. Many persons consider the gospel as a very decent system of religion, who cannot bear to be urged to repentance, and an entire surrender of themselves to Christ. What is the reason? Because their consciences have never been impressed with a conviction of sin. This insensibility to the evil of sin, and the awful danger to which it exposes the transgressor, has always been a hindrance to the success of the gospel. The Redeemer has taught us in his word, that no one will accept of salvation, who does not feel himself a helpless and guilty creature. "The Son of man," says he, "is come to save that which was lost—they that are whole need not a physician; but they that are sick." "I came not to call the righteous, but sinners to repentance." But when sin is felt to be exceeding sinful, the soul cleaves to Christ, and confides in him as its all in all.

The plan of redemption, through the mediation of Jesus, the Son of God, appears not only true and wise, but gracious and necessary. Observe here, the distinction between saving faith and a barren, joyless profession. The merely nominal Christian may entertain a high degree of respect for the Saviour; he may yield a cold assent to the truths of the gospel; he may even be a strenuous advocate for orthodox sentiments; but his religion consists in orthodoxy; it never touches his heart, or sanctifies his affections. Whereas every article of the true believer's creed has a practical and sanctifying influence on his temper and conduct. He not only believes, but obeys the truth. And, in keeping his Lord's commandments, he finds great reward. Christ is precious; his yoke is easy, and his burden light. The true principle of evangelical obedience is to be found in those remarkable words of Paul: "The love of Christ constraineth us, because we thus judge that if one died for all, then were all dead: and that he died for all, that they which live should not henceforth live unto themselves, but unto him who died for them and rose again." 2 Cor. v. 14, 15.

This trust in the Redeemer, and devotion to his service, necessarily presupposes the admission of his Divine character. For what man of common sense would entrust his soul, with all its immortal interests, to a mere creature? I could not feel secure in building my hopes of pardon and eternal life, even on an angel. The brightest seraph in heaven can do no more than his duty. He cannot make atonement for the smallest transgression of the Divine law. But when I find Jesus, the Son of God, set forth in the sacred Scriptures as the Lord our righteousness and the propitiation for our sins, believing the infallible word of inspiration, I feel no hesitation in reposing entire confidence in him. I know that Jehovah Jesus is able to save; that his atonement is of infinite efficacy; that his grace is sufficient, and his promise sure and infallible to all who hope in his mercy. Do not think it strange, my friends, that God requires you to believe in the Lord Jesus Christ, on pain of everlasting misery. The whole gospel of our salvation proceeds on the melancholy fact that man is a guilty, ruined creature. And that faith, on which the sacred Scriptures lay so much stress, is something more than an assent to the truths of God's word. It implies a personal appropriation of Jesus, and the benefits of his redemption. It involves a dependence on his righteousness for justification, and an application to the sacrifice of his blood for pardon, together with an unreserved surrender of ourselves to Christ, as our King, our Lord, our Master, our Defender, and the Captain of our salvation. Jesus is the Son of God in a sense which is inapplicable to any other being in the universe. He is the only begotten, the brightness of the Father's glory, and the express image of his person. He is God manifest in the flesh, and over all, blessed for ever. His name is precious, as ointment poured forth. His death gave life to the world, his blood was shed for the remission of sins, and his righteousness is unto and upon all them that believe. "Blessed are all they who put their trust in him!"

My hearers, do you believe that Jesus is the Son of God? Do you believe him to be the only Mediator between God and man? Do you believe that he is Immanuel, uniting in his sacred person the seed of Abraham, and the essence of the adorable Godhead? Do you believe what the prophet says of him? "He was wounded for our transgressions; he was bruised for our iniquities; the chastisement of our peace was upon him, and with his stripes we are healed. All we like sheep have gone astray; we have turned every one to his own way, and the Lord hath laid on him the iniquity of us all." In a word, do you believe that he is able and willing to save you, and have you committed your souls to him, in a covenant never to be forgotten? Is your faith an operative principle? Is it attended by peace with God, and productive of good works? Put these questions to your consciences. "Examine yourselves, whether ye be in the faith."

Having taken a cursory view of the Christian's creed, let us

II. Attend to his triumph. "Who is he that overcometh the world, but he that believeth that Jesus is the Son of God?" It is not without good reason that the apostle gives this challenge. The true believer does obtain a triumph with which no other conquest will bear a comparison. It is a complete victory over the world, and all the evils with

11

which it abounds. "Thanks be to God, who always causeth us to triumph in Christ."

The Christian has many troubles and dangers to meet with in this world, but his blessed Lord causes him to triumph over them all. He is not exempt from the common calamities of life; but he has one peculiar advantage, God is with him in his afflictions, and makes all things work together for his ultimate good. We know that affliction is good and necessary for us, so long as we are in the body. This is one of the means which God employs to prepare a people for his praise. And that his people may neither despise his chastening, nor faint when rebuked of him, he has given them promises of succour suited to all cases that may occur, however distressing. Hence they are directed to account it a blessing when they fall into divers trials; for by these trials God intends to prove that their faith is more precious than gold which perisheth. "Call upon me in the day of trouble, saith the Lord, I will deliver thee, and thou shalt glorify me." "My grace is sufficient for thee." "I will never leave thee, nor forsake thee." When these and the like promises are fully credited, and their consolations realized by the believer, he can interpret Paul's language, when he says, "Sorrowful, yet always rejoicing;" and sing with the prophet Jonah, "I will sacrifice unto thee with the voice of thanksgiving—salvation is of the Lord." In all ages God has proved himself to his people a very present help in time of need. Whatever affliction he sends upon them, his blessing accompanies it. So we hear them testifying, "We know that all things work together for good to them that love God." They knew it from his promise, and they felt it by experience. Hence we find them triumphant in the severest persecutions for righteousness' sake. "If God be for us, who can be against us? He that spared not his own Son, but delivered him up for us all, how shall he not with him, also, freely give us all things? Who shall lay anything to the charge of God's elect? It is God that justifieth, who is he that condemneth? It is Christ that died, yea, rather that is risen again, who is even at the right hand of God, who also maketh intercession for us."

The disciple of Christ is a believer in the particular providence of God. "Are not two sparrows sold for a farthing; and one of them doth not fall to the ground without your heavenly Father?" "The hairs of your head are all numbered." This doctrine is happily calculated to give relief to the pious mind under the heaviest trials. "Whom the Lord loveth he chasteneth, and scourgeth every son whom he receiveth." What, may the Christian say, what if I am called to suffer the loss of all things? What if I suffer in my person, in my family, or estate? What if I am to part with kindred and friends? It is my heavenly Father's will. He knows my frame. He sees what is best for me. If he is pleased to visit with the rod, I am sure that infinite goodness dictates and directs every stroke that his hand inflicts. He has admitted me to the adoption of children, and why should I be offended on receiving the treatment of a child? If he corrects me, it is for his glory and my improvement. "Shall I receive good at the hand of God, and shall I not receive evil also?" "No chastening, for the present, seemeth to be joyous, but grievous; nevertheless, afterwards, it yieldeth the peaceable fruit of righteousness unto them which are exercised thereby." Heb. xii. 11. And, "I reckon that the sufferings of this present time are not worthy to be compared with the glory that shall be revealed in us." Rom. viii. 18.

Such is the believer's triumph over the common afflictions of this life; equally decisive is his victory over the temptations and allurements of the world. Against these insidious enemies of his salvation he sets a watch, and makes his continual prayer to God, "Lead me not into temptation, but deliver me from evil!" The blessed Saviour, who was tempted in all points, like as we are, knows how to deliver them that are tempted: and to those who trust in him, he always administers relief in times of danger. He has taught his disciples that the Prince of the power of the air is a defeated adversary, that if they resist him, he will flee from them. He has taught them, also, that the promises of the world are fallacious, and its enjoyments transient and unsatisfactory. He has taught them that one thing is needful; that true religion is the pearl of great price, and that all else is chaff, driven and scattered by the wind. He has given to the minds of his followers a new and heavenly direction; he has created in them a thirst for glory, honour, and immortality, which causes them to look with comparative contempt on all inferior things, and with utter abhorrence on those sensual indulgences which war against the soul.   Earthly minds may and will live after the flesh, and pursue earthly things; but the heaven-born soul cannot live upon husks; it aspires after the celestial manna, and pants for the waters of the sanctuary.

Try yourselves, professing Christians, by this criterion.   If you prefer Jerusalem to your chief earthly joy—if you account a day in God's courts better than a thousand in the tents of wickedness and folly, there is ground to hope that you are born of the Spirit, and that the good work which has been begun within you will be carried on till the day of Jesus Christ.   But, if the glare of wealth, if titles and distinctions among men, if the frivolous amusements, and fashionable dissipations of the world engross more of your attention, and afford you more pleasure than the ordinances of God, and the sober duties of your religious profession, you have awful cause to fear that your faith is not the faith of God's elect.   That faith which does not regenerate the moral taste of its possessor, and supply him with new objects of pursuit, and open to him new and sanctifying sources of enjoyment, is radically defective; it is the shadow, without the substance—the name, without the thing—a creed, connected with *no* triumph.

The Christian's grand triumph is that which he obtains over the fears of dying.   "By one man sin

11*

entered into the world, and death by sin; and so, death passed upon all men, for that all have sinned." "It is appointed unto men once to die." It is an event incident to us all. Death is inevitable; and to the worldling it is an object of unutterable terror. Here, then, we have abundant reason to bless God, who causeth us to triumph in Christ, the second Adam, the Lord from heaven! Forasmuch as they whom he came to redeem "were partakers of flesh and blood, he also took part of the same, that, through death, he might destroy him who had the power of death, i. e., the devil; and might deliver them who, through fear of death, were, all their life-time, subject to bondage." Yes, ten thousand blessings on his precious name! He became bone of our bone, and flesh of our flesh, that he might subdue the king of terrors, and teach his followers to say, with Paul, "For me to live is Christ, and to die is gain!" He died for our sins, and rose again as the first-fruits from the dead. In his glorious resurrection we have the most complete demonstration 'that he plucked away the sting of death. He raises us from the grave of sin, and quickens us to newness of life. He has taught us that, if these bodies were dissolved, "we have a building of God—a house not made with hands, eternal in the heavens." The sting of death is sin—but sin once removed from the conscience, the song of triumph breaks from the lips of the dying believer, "O grave, where is thy victory? O death, where is thy sting? Thanks be to God, who giveth us the victory, through our Lord Jesus Christ."

Hearers, would you wish to share in the Christian's joyful prospects at the close of this mortal life? Have faith in Jesus, the Son of God. Surrender yourselves to his service. Seek by fervent prayer, and by a diligent attention to all gospel means, to be washed, and sanctified, and justified, in the name of the Lord, and by the Spirit of our God. We could produce you a thousand witnesses that infidelity, either professed, or practised upon, invariably brings men to a miserable end. If you live after the flesh, and are governed by the spirit and maxims of the world, you cannot expect to die either safely or comfortably. To die!—blessed is the exclusive privilege of him who dies in the Lord. It is in Christ, and in Christ only, that any of our fallen race can triumph in a dying hour. "Seek the Lord, therefore, while he may be found; call upon him while he is near." Risk not the immortal interests of your souls on the dubious result of a death-bed repentance. Amidst the cares and vanities of this world, forget not that you are travelling to the house appointed for all the living. While you have Sabbaths and sanctuary privileges, improve them for eternity. These opportunities of securing the true riches will soon be past, and you will have to account for them all at the judgment-seat of Christ. Examine well the ground of your hopes for the world to come. If you profess to be the disciples of Jesus, try to feel, at all times, the obligations of redeeming love. If ye be risen with Christ, seek those things which are above. If you

are redeemed sinners, you are debtors to grace, but
not to the flesh, that ye should live after the flesh.
"Put off the old man with his deeds, and put on the
new man, which, after God, is created in righteousness and true holiness." And, O if any of you are
living without God, and without hope in the world,
be persuaded to lay hold on the hope set before
you in the gospel. You know, sinner, that the world
will, by and by, abandon you. Why should you
continue to serve it? Believe in the Son of God;
devote yourself to his service, and he will never leave
nor forsake you. While I once more repeat in your
hearing the messages of his mercy, may the Spirit of
all grace incline your heart to receive the truth, in
the love thereof. "Him that cometh unto me I will
in no wise cast out." "Behold, I stand at the door
and knock; if any man hear my voice, and open the
door, I will come in to him, and sup with him, and
he with me." "All things are now ready." "And
the Spirit and the bride say, Come; and let him
that heareth say, Come; and let him that is athirst
come; and whosoever will, let him take the water
of life freely." Amen.

ENOCH'S WALK WITH GOD.

———————

And Enoch walked with God, and he was not; for God took him.
GENESIS v. 24.

IN all ages of the world the righteous have been few in comparison with the multitude of evil-doers. There have always, however, been some that feared the Lord, and thought upon his name. Even in the antediluvian world, we find, here and there, a pious character. Such was Enoch, the son of Jared, and the seventh from Adam of whom we have any account in Scripture. The sacred historian says but little respecting him; that little, however, is much to his credit. It furnishes us with an example worthy of imitation, and teaches us that the service of God is not a vain thing.

The first thing that claims our notice is Enoch's manner of life. "He walked with God." These four words give us a short, but comprehensive and expressive description of a pious deportment. True piety impresses the heart with a deep and solemn sense of the majesty, goodness, and omnipresence of God. It opens a delightful intercourse between the believing

soul and the infinite Father of spirits. It creates a
love of holiness, and a hatred of sin; a hungering
and thirsting after righteousness, a panting for God—
the living God—which nothing short of heaven and
eternal glory can satisfy: and God indulges his
children, even in this dark world, with the light of
his countenance, and the comforts of his grace.
Hence they love to cultivate a sense of his presence,
and all those acts of worship which promote a devotional spirit, are regarded by them, not only as
duties, but as privileges. In the works of his hand,
and the acts of his providence, they contemplate the
perfections of Jehovah. In the closet, around the
domestic altar, and in the courts of his house, it is
the prevailing desire of their hearts to feel the
gracious influence of his Spirit, enlightening their
minds, subduing their sins, and preparing them for
the inheritance of the saints in light. By serious
meditation, by prayer, by reading and hearing his
word, by conversing with his people, by celebrating
the ordinances of his grace, they aim habitually to
live "as seeing Him who is invisible." Thus they
walk with God; they carry the thoughts of him into
all the concerns of life. In everything, by supplication and thanksgiving, they make known their
wants and express their gratitude to him. They cast
their cares upon him; they commit their souls to him,
as to a faithful Creator. He receives them into
his family, and gives them the Spirit of adoption,
whereby they cry, "Abba Father."

But, seeing mankind are by nature the enemies of

God, sold under sin, and liable to the curse of the Divine law, how are any of them recovered from the snare of the devil, and restored to this happy state of intercourse and favour with their Maker? By grace, extended to the guilty through the mediation of Jesus Christ. By this means Enoch was redeemed from the power of sin, and enabled to please God. The apostle Paul tells us that it was through faith that this eminent man of God attained all his excellence, and all his high privileges. He received with confidence and joy the Divine testimony; he entertained a firm persuasion of what God had then revealed respecting the fall and recovery of man. He had the faith of God's elect, and being justified by faith, he had peace with God; he lived a cotemporary with Adam three hundred years. With him he, no doubt, often conversed, and joined in religious worship. From him, as well as from various other sources, he had an opportunity of learning the character, the law, the government, and perfections of God. That gracious promise, "The seed of the woman shall bruise the serpent's head," could not have been unknown to him. The Lamb slain from the foundation of the world formed the basis of his hope. Like Abraham, he saw the Messiah's day, and rejoiced. He felt and bewailed his sinfulness; he revered his Maker and sought his blessing, in the use of such means of religious improvement as had been prescribed by Divine authority. The great outlines of redemption, by the sacrifice of the cross, to be offered in due time, were revealed to his believing mind; he saw enough of the glory of

Christ to secure his faith, to inspire him with hope, and to engage his best affections. We are authorized to speak thus of Enoch's hope in Christ, not only by what is said of his faith in the eleventh chapter of Hebrews, but also by a passage in the Epistle of Jude, at the fourteenth verse: "And Enoch, also, the seventh from Adam, prophesied of these, *i. e.*, (of certain bad characters of whom the apostle is speaking,) saying, Behold, the Lord cometh with ten thousand of his saints, to execute judgment upon all, and to convince all that are ungodly among them, of all their ungodly deeds which they have ungodly committed; and of all their hard speeches, which ungodly sinners have spoken against him."

Here is a prophecy, purporting to have been uttered by Enoch; and as it is not to be found in the Old Testament, curiosity naturally asks, where the apostle found it. The probability is, that St. Jude took it from a roll of traditions held in high veneration by the Jews. And, though the quotation does not prove the authenticity of the whole volume from which it is taken, yet, to us, who receive the New Testament, as given by inspiration of God, it clearly proves the fact that Enoch was a prophet, and that he foretold the second coming of our Lord to judgment. Hence we may fairly conclude that he was not ignorant of the Divine purpose, that the Son of God should appear in the flesh to take away sin by the sacrifice of his own blood; to finish transgression, and complete a righteousness which should be unto and upon all them that believe. In the faith of this precious truth Enoch walked with God, enjoyed a peace with heaven, and a hope of glory which all the wisdom and treasures of the world could not give, and of which all the scoffers of the age in which he lived could not deprive him. If any of you, my hearers, are living in sin, strangers to pure fellowship with God, allow me to urge you to seek these blessings with all diligence, in that blood which cleanseth from all sin. Implore forgiving mercy and recovering grace through the sacrifice of the cross. "Be reconciled to God; for he hath made him to be sin for us, who knew no sin; that we might be made the righteousness of God in him." You may dream of peace, and happiness, and heaven, on the ground of your own comparative or fancied goodness, but know assuredly that the whole world is become guilty, and that without the shedding of blood there is no remission. "Woe to him that striveth with his Maker!" There is no walking with God; no fellowship with the Father of your spirits; no pardon; no peace; no heaven for you, till Christ is formed in you the hope of glory. "The carnal mind is enmity against God." "The ploughing of the wicked is sin, and God is angry with them every day." "How can two walk together, except they be agreed?" Frail, dependent creature—poor miserable sinner, cast away the weapons of your rebellion. Touch the sceptre of peace; lay hold of the hope set before you; hear the accents of mercy; receive with faith and love the tidings of grace, and the offers of infinite condescension. "Behold," saith the Saviour, "I stand at the door and knock; if any man hear my voice, and open

12

the door, I will come in to him, and sup with him, and he with me!"

Those of you who have been brought into the blessed state of fellow-citizens with the saints, and of the household of God, need not be told that you obtained this inestimable privilege through the merits of Christ. You know by happy experience that he is made of God unto you wisdom, and righteousness, and sanctification, and redemption. You, who were once afar off, have been brought nigh by the blood of sprinkling; you have been made accepted in the beloved; and you can join the apostle Paul in that impassioned burst of gratitude to redeeming love, "God forbid that I should glory, save in the cross of our Lord Jesus Christ, by which the world is crucified unto me, and I unto the world." Restored to the favour of God, through faith in his dear Son, it is now your business, your duty, and your privilege, to walk with, to keep near the throne of his grace, and rejoice beneath the covert of his parental wing. To assist and encourage you in so doing, let me call your attention for a few moments to Enoch's example. It is recorded and held out to us, as an inducement to go and do likewise. He walked with God; which implies several particulars; as,

First, a deep sense of dependence on his Maker, not only as a creature, but as a subject of Divine grace. Under the teaching of the Holy Spirit, he had learned his own frailty. He knew that all his springs were in God; and felt no hesitation in acknowledging that it was fit and proper for God's intelligent creatures to lean upon him for support, and look to him as the Author of all good, and the only inexhaustible source of happiness. Hence the law of God, and not his own will, or the maxims of the world, would become of choice the rule of his conduct. No doubt a large majority of those around him minded earthly things, neglectful of the Lord that made them; making a mock of sin, and holding in derision the few pious whose conduct reproved, and whose light exposed the deeds of darkness that characterized that age of degeneracy and sin. But Enoch was not one of those who deemed it safe to follow a multitude to do evil. He had more respect for the law of his God than for the practice of his neighbours. He was willing to sacrifice the smiles of the world to the approbation of his Maker. He felt, also, that he was sanctified but in part; that he must look to God for the completion of the work which Divine grace had begun in his soul. This sense of dependence would naturally beget a holy jealousy of himself, and produce a tender concern to avoid temptation, to flee the company of the wicked, and to give himself to watching and prayer.

Do you, my Christian brethren, endeavour in this way to grow in grace, and in the knowledge of our Lord Jesus Christ? You have solemnly engaged to renounce sin, and serve God in newness of life. What effect have the loose manners and licentious maxims of the world, upon your religious vows and pious resolutions made in your closets, or at the table of your blessed Lord? Do you not sometimes find yourselves yielding to the opinion, that common practice cannot be greatly wrong, or seriously dangerous? Amidst the hurry and pressure of earthly pursuits, do you not often forget what manner of spirit you ought to cultivate? When conscience checks you, and admonishes you not to forget the Rock that begat you, or the Saviour that bought you, does not Satan, or your own backsliding hearts, suggest an apology: "We would act otherwise; but company seduces; we cannot help yielding to the importunity of friends; we must do a little as other people do, or else we must needs go out of the world." Ah, Christians, and is this the way in which you expect to perfect holiness in the fear of God? Is this the way to fall in with the gracious designs of your Saviour, who redeemed you with his blood, that you might be unto God a peculiar people, zealous of good works? Do you not know who has said, "If any man will come after me, let him deny himself, and take up his cross and follow me? Have you forgotten the exhortation, "Be not conformed to this world; but be ye transformed by the renewing of your minds, that ye may prove what is that good, and acceptable, and perfect will of God?" "Quench not the Spirit." "If any man love the world, the love of the Father is not in him." Though you may forget your vows, God will not forget them. Call to mind, then, your obligations to redeeming love. Cherish a sense of your dependence. By the grace of God you are what you are. As ye have received Christ Jesus the Lord, so walk ye in him, with the same self-diffidence, the same faith, the same abhorrence of sin, and the same zeal for his glory.

Another means which Enoch, no doubt, used to maintain a close and comfortable walk with God, was to consider himself continually in the Divine presence; to endure, like Moses, as seeing Him who is invisible. An ancient philosopher advised his scholars, as a means of confirming their virtuous habits, to fancy themselves, at all times, in the presence of some person of high respectability and eminent piety. The wisdom of this rule is readily perceived. Few persons are so fool-hardy as not to feel restrained and awed by the presence of goodness. Substitute the only wise God in the place of the philosopher's good man, and the efficacy of the rule must be vastly increased. God searches the hearts and tries the reins of the children of men. He beholds and abhors sin, in thought and purpose, no less than in word and deed; and we are for ever in his presence. Darkness and light are both alike to him. He is privy to all our ways and designs; all things are naked and open to the view of Him with whom we have to do. "Thou God seest me." Let us carry this thought with us, brethren, wherever we go, or whatever we do. If we forget God, vanity or sin will occupy our minds, and temptation will easily overcome us. If we would walk with God, we must regard his presence as a pavilion round about us.

12*

We may be deprived of outward privileges by a variety of causes, but nothing, except sin, can interrupt our intercourse with the Father of our spirits. The Lord is a sun and shield to his people; and will give both grace and glory to them that walk uprightly.

Again, Enoch, in maintaining a walk with God, doubtless abounded in prayer and praise. He loved God; his affections were placed on things above. He had many wants to be supplied, and enjoyed many blessings, for which to give thanks. This sense of his wants and obligations would draw him frequently to the throne of grace. And, my hearers, have not we equal need and equal encouragement to draw near to God, that we may obtain mercy, and find grace to help? Is the Lord's arm shortened, that it cannot save, or his ear heavy, that it cannot hear? No! "God is the same, yesterday, to-day, and for ever." The same grace that enabled Enoch to lead a holy life, will be imparted to you, if you feel your need of it, and ask it in the name of Christ. Fellowship with God was not a privilege peculiar to Scripture characters. It is the privilege of every true penitent and sincere believer in Christ, to draw near the Father of mercies, with full assurance of hope. "Pray without ceasing." "Ask, and ye shall receive." "If ye, being evil, know how to give good gifts unto your children; how much more shall your Father who is in heaven give the Holy Spirit unto them that ask him!"

But what was the result of Enoch's walk with God?

We are told, in a few words, in a style of force and sublimity peculiar to the sacred volume, "He was not, for God took him;" or, in the language of Paul, "by faith Enoch was translated, that he should not see death; and was not found, because God had translated him: for, before his translation, he had this testimony, that he pleased God." Heb. xi. 5. He was suddenly removed from this world of sin and sorrow, without sickness, or any of the pains of dissolution. As it shall be with the living in the day of judgment, his body was changed and immortalized, and conveyed by the angels into that blissful state, where is fulness of joy and pleasures for evermore.

What a signal token of Divine favour! What encouragement it affords to faithful and patient continuance in well-doing! You do not expect, indeed, my Christian brethren, to be translated to heaven in the manner of Enoch, or Elijah: you will have to endure the decay of nature, and pass through the agonies of death. But if, like Enoch, you walk with God, unto all well-pleasing, he will take you to himself, and entrance shall be ministered unto you abundantly into the everlasting kingdom of our Lord and Saviour Jesus Christ. While your bodies rest in their graves till the resurrection, under the guardian care of angels, your spirits shall return unto God who gave them. "Be ye followers of them, who, through faith and patience, are now inheriting the promises." Aspire after glory, honour, and immortality. Be animated by the shouts of victory that flow from the lips of those who, through grace, have attained to the heights of glory, where they reign with Christ, as kings and priests unto God the Father. My dear hearers, one and all, a price is put into your hands, with which you may secure the good part that shall never be taken from you. O then, let not the transient cares and engagements of this dying world deprive you of the true riches! Your souls are of more value than all the gold of Ophir and the gems of India. Secure their salvation by laying hold of the hope set before you in the gospel. Believe in the Lord Jesus Christ, and you shall be saved. Rouse up from your native lethargy! It is high time to awake out of sleep. The day of grace is passing while I address you; the scenes of eternity will soon burst upon us with un-rivalled splendor and ineffable interest. The Bridegroom is coming, and, immediately on his arrival, they that shall be found ready, will go in with him to the marriage supper, and the door will be shut! Amen!

THE WANDERER RECLAIMED.

For ye were as sheep going astray; but are now returned unto the Shepherd and Bishop of your souls.—1 PETER ii. 25.

WE have in this passage of sacred Scripture the natural state of mankind, justly and strikingly contrasted with that into which they are brought by the grace of God. By nature we are "as sheep going astray;" our wandering begins early. "We go astray," says the Psalmist, "as soon as we are born;" and we continue to press onward, in the ways of sin and death, till redeeming mercy visits our hearts, and turns our feet from the paths of the destroyer. Then, O happy change! we are convinced of our folly, our danger, and our guilt; and are sweetly and effectually constrained, by the influence of all-conquering grace, to bow to the authority, and resign ourselves to the protection and guidance of "the Shepherd and Bishop of our souls."

There are two particulars in this text that claim special notice, viz.

I. The unhappy state of an unconverted sinner.

II. His restoration to the favour and protection of God the Saviour.

I. The unconverted sinner is described in our text as a lost and wandering creature: "Ye were as sheep going astray." The point of comparison between the sheep and the sinner is a propensity, common to both, to forsake the right way, and to pursue heedlessly the paths of misery and ruin. And who that reads the Bible, and is in any measure attentive to what passes around and within him, can hesitate for a moment to acknowledge that man, in his unsanctified state, is exceedingly neglectful of the law of his duty, and prone to forsake his own mercies? Nor is this perverse inclination peculiar to any one age or description of mankind. "All we, like sheep," says the prophet, "have gone astray; we have turned, every one to his own way." Isa. liii. 6. Yes, my hearers, this propensity to wander in the mazes of sin and folly, is one of the strongest and deepest features in the character of our fallen race! By nature we are all "as sheep going astray." Let us acknowledge the humbling truth. The more deeply we are affected by it, in reference to ourselves, the more likely we shall be to appreciate and admire the grace which provides for our restoration to the verdant pastures and peaceful ways of the good Shepherd.

Let us not hastily conclude that we are in the right way, because we do not associate with certain classes of wanderers, whose particular course may have been determined by peculiar circumstances. So various and multiform is error, that "every one may pursue his own course," and yet be "as sheep going astray." The way of transgressors is broad, comprising within its limits innumerable pathways suited to all manner of depraved taste; and however the ways of sin differ in other respects, they all agree in leading men away from God, the source of blessedness, and in conducting infatuated wanderers to the dreary regions of despair and perdition. "There is a way that seemeth right unto a man; but the end thereof are the ways of death." Prov. xiv. 12. "Destruction and misery are in their paths: and the way of peace have they not known." Rom. iii. 16, 17. "There is none that seeketh after God; they are all gone out of the way." Rom. iii. 11, 12.

These testimonies of sacred Scripture are abundantly confirmed by facts with which we are all but too well acquainted. Observe the tempers and practices of mankind, from infancy up to old age, and what a melancholy spectacle of waywardness and wandering do they exhibit! With what difficulty are children trained to habits of industry, kindness, and honesty! What disrelish, what aversion, do youth generally manifest in regard to devotional exercises and religious duties! How are their imaginations charmed, and their hearts drawn away from God and holiness, by the pleasures and pageantry of the world! In riper years, when maturity of judgment might be expected to correct the vagaries of passion, what ambitious contests do we often witness for distinction, which must all vanish at death, and leave the victor and the vanquished, the prince and the poor man, on a perfect level! And among the aged, to whom the pursuits of ambition are impossible, how many do we see sinking into the grave without God, and utterly destitute of the Christian's cheering hope of a blessed immortality!

But, perhaps, we may be ready to congratulate ourselves that we do not belong to any of these classes of wanderers. We are not haughty and self-willed. We are not seeking great things for ourselves. We are endeavouring to be content with the allotments of Providence, and are careful to cherish a humane disposition, and to establish and deserve the character of honest men and good citizens. So far, it is well. But then, my hearers, God looks at the heart. How is it with us, in regard to heart-wanderings? We are taught in Scripture, that "the heart is deceitful above all things, and desperately wicked." If this be wrong, all is not right. "Keep thy heart with all diligence, for out of it are the issues of life." Prov. iv. 23. Is God uppermost in our thoughts? Do we love to meditate on his precepts, and find our chief delight, our richest consolations in his promises? Is his glory a prominent object in all our plans and enterprises? Alas, for our fallen nature! How often, when outwardly engaged in the most solemn acts of religious duty, do we find the heart going after its idols! Many a foolish excursion has it taken this morning, even since we have been here, in God's house. I appeal to your consciences, hearers; is it not so? I appeal to Scripture: "They come and sit before me as my people, (saith the Lord,) but their heart is after their covetousness." Ezek. xxxiii. 31. "An evil heart of unbelief in departing from the living

God," is the source and spring of all our wanderings. This is the deep-rooted malady of our nature; and until it is cured, we are all "as sheep going astray." Thanks be to God, for the provisions of redeeming grace! Many a wandering heart has been reclaimed, and filled with peace and joy unspeakable; and the expostulatory voice is still heard from the sacred word, "Turn ye, turn ye; for why will ye die?" Let us, then, attend a little to the sinner's restoration to the favour and protection of God, the Saviour.

II. This is the second particular in the text, which claims our special notice—"but are now returned to the Shepherd and Bishop of your souls." Who is the Shepherd and Bishop of souls? And how is the return of the guilty wanderers brought about? For, my hearers, our wanderings are not only pitiable, but blameworthy. In forsaking the good ways of the Lord, we have dishonoured and insulted him; we have preferred the creature to the Creator, and have paid to idols that homage which is due only to Him, who is over all blessed for ever. And the Holy One of Israel is jealous for his honour, and will not give his glory to another. If He, from whom we have revolted, ever receive us back to favour, we may rest assured it will be in a way that shall not impair the claims of justice, or the majesty of his holy law. Hence the necessity of a Mediator, a Daysman, one who is qualified to effect a reconciliation in a way that shall discountenance sin, and, at the same time, maintain the rights of Divine government. Such a one is the Lord Jesus Christ; and he is the Shepherd and

13

Bishop of souls. He says, "I am the good Shepherd;" "I am the door; by me, if any man enter in, he shall be saved;" "I am the way, the truth, and the life; no man cometh unto the Father but by me." Here, brethren, is the chosen, and consecrated, and only medium of our return to the favour and protection of our Heavenly Father. Jesus, the Son of God, is eminently qualified to perform the office of Mediator; for, while he is bone of our bone, and flesh of our flesh, he is also the brightness of the Father's glory, and the express image of his person; and, in him, it hath pleased the Father that all fulness should dwell. Accordingly, he not only commiserates the sinner, and does and suffers whatever is needful to reclaim and save him; he, also, entertains and manifests a just regard for the holiness and authority of the Creator. Such a Redeemer is Christ the Lord—the Shepherd and Bishop of our souls. To him let us repair, confident that he is "able to save to the uttermost all that come to God through him." And, that we may be induced to put our trust in him, let us consider his mediatorial work in a few of its most important particulars.

1. He has shed his blood for the remission of sins. This is alluded to in the verse preceding our text; "By whose stripes ye were healed." In the fifty-third chapter of Isaiah, it is said, "The Lord hath laid on him the iniquity of us all:" and again, "For the transgression of my people was he stricken." The apostle Peter urges Christians to a holy life, by assuring them that they were redeemed by "the

precious blood of Christ, as of a lamb, without blemish and without spot." 1 Peter i. 19. This blood of atonement being shed, forgiveness of sins is offered to the chief of sinners. Yes, hearers, through the efficacy of this one offering, the guilt of our wanderings may be pardoned; and let it never be forgotten, that without the shedding of this blood, which cleanseth from all sin, there could have been no remission. But blessed be God for his unspeakable gift, "in whom we have redemption, through his blood, the forgiveness of sins, according to the riches of his grace." The Shepherd and Bishop of souls, then, has opened a fountain in which we may wash and be cleansed from the sin of our past wanderings.

2. He has magnified the law of God, and, in obeying it perfectly, has wrought a righteousness, which, by imputation, is unto and upon all that believe, for justification: so that God can be just, and yet be the justifier of him that believeth in Jesus. This righteousness is perfect and available because of the infinite dignity of the Redeemer; and it is imputable to the believer, or capable of being reckoned his, in law and justice, because it has been wrought out by Christ, expressly for his people, while obeying and suffering, the just for the unjust, as their voluntary substitute, that he might bring them to God. Hence, in every sinner that is freed from condemnation, and restored to the Divine favour, "grace reigns, through righteousness, unto eternal life, by Jesus Christ, our Lord." Rom. v. 21. Thus the redemption price is paid, and everlasting righteousness procured,

by the interposing grace of the Redeemer, without the agency, and even without the knowledge of the bewildered, wandering sinner; and such is the stupefying influence of sin, that the poor infatuated creature is quite insensible to the danger of his condition. If, therefore, the work of the Shepherd and Bishop of souls were to cease here, it would be ineffectual. No change would be produced in the character or conduct of those who are going astray as lost sheep. But the work does not cease here. The only wise God does nothing in vain, nothing by halves; none of his undertakings prove abortive. "Whom he did foreknow, he also did predestinate to be conformed to the image of his Son." Rom. viii. 29. We observe,

3. That the Good Shepherd looks after, searches out, and brings back that which is lost. He publishes the glad tidings—liberty to the captives, and the opening of the prison to them that are bound. He visits the wanderers by his Spirit, arrests their attention, apprizes them of their error, convicts them of sin, turns their feet into the way of life, and applies to their souls the redemption which he has wrought. Now this part of the great work of our deliverance is accomplished by a Divine agency, no less than those parts which have been just noticed. But in the application of gospel blessings, sinners are made sensible of their misery, and need of a Saviour. Their wills are not forced; but they are made willing in a day of gracious power; and, through sanctification of the Spirit and belief of the truth, they are gradually made meet for the inheritance of the saints in

light. They work out their own salvation with fear and trembling; because God works in them, both to will and to do that which is well-pleasing in his sight.

That this view is just, will appear by attending to that branch of the text on which this article is founded—"but are now returned," &c. Observe, it is not *ye have returned*, as it would be if the return were effected by the wanderer's own unaided efforts. "Ye are returned" is the passive form of an active verb; and its import is equivalent to *ye are converted*, or *restored*, or *caused to return*. But our statement does not depend on the construction of a single text. Hear the language of prophecy by the mouth of Ezekiel, xxxiv. 11, &c.: "Behold, saith the Lord, I, even I, will both search my sheep and seek them out. I will deliver them out of all places where they have been scattered in the cloudy and dark day: I will seek that which was lost, and bring again that which was driven away." Hear the voice of the redeeming Shepherd himself: "The Son of Man is come to seek and to save that which was lost." Luke xiv. 10. And again, he says, "Other sheep I have, which are not of this fold, (*i. e.*, not Jews by birth,) them, also, I must bring, and they shall hear my voice; and there shall be one fold and one Shepherd." John x. 16. The same doctrine is taught in the parable of the lost sheep, Luke xv. 4, 5. The shepherd goes after the wanderer till he finds it; and when he has found it, he does not merely show it the way, and command it to return, and then leave it exposed to

13*

the voracious beasts of the forest; but he lays it on his shoulders, and bears it homeward rejoicing. This representation is just and striking. Man, left to himself, unawakened, unrenewed, and unaided by the life-giving Spirit of God, will never return from the error of his way, or lay hold on the hope set before him in the gospel. Mere moral suasion can have no saving effect on souls that are dead in trespasses and sins. A new heart and a right spirit are indispensable to salvation; and these are the fruit of the washing of regeneration, and the renewing of the Holy Ghost. "By grace are ye saved, through faith, and that not of yourselves; it is the gift of God." Such, my hearers, is our dependence on free grace. Let us not indulge the notion that we can turn from our sins at any time when we may judge it convenient. This is one of Satan's most popular maxims. "Can the Ethiopian change his skin, or the leopard his spots?" "Not by might nor by power; but by my Spirit, saith the Lord." Let your prayer to God be, "Turn thou me, and I shall be turned; draw me, and I will follow after thee; wash me, and I shall be clean." But we observe,

4. The Shepherd and Bishop of souls performs for his flock all that which is implied in these significant and expressive titles. He guides, and feeds, and oversees, and defends them. He leads them into green pastures, and by still waters. His eyes are continually upon them for good, and his ears are open to their cries. To the weak he gives strength, and to

the heavy-laden rest and peace. The wanderer is restored, the sick healed, and the lambs are carried in his arms. They all hear his voice and follow him, and he gives them eternal life; and none can pluck them out of his hand. Happy flock! May we all know by experience the blessedness of those who "are returned to the Shepherd and Bishop of their souls!"

Two or three reflections from what has been said, will close the discourse.

1. Let sinners consider, that so long as they persist in treating with neglect the gospel and its gracious provisions, they wander farther and farther from the fountain of life, and do really slight their own best and most precious interests. Dear fellow-immortals, the capacities and desires of your souls can never be filled and satisfied with the unsubstantial pleasures of the world. The grand end of your being is to glorify God, and enjoy him for ever; and if through negligence and sin you fail of this most desirable attainment, disappointment and ruin will be your inevitable portion. Think of your frailty and dependence on Him who made you. You have forsaken the fountain of living waters, and in a little while your broken cisterns will utterly fail you. If you are not returned unto the Shepherd and Bishop of souls, you will continue to go astray, as lost sheep, till your feet stumble on the dark mountains, and your fall will be tremendous, in proportion to the calls and mercies that you have slighted and despised.

2. Let those who have been reclaimed from their wanderings cherish a grateful sense of their obligations to the good Shepherd, who not only died for them, but sought them out, and brought them within the safe inclosure of his consecrated fold.   O Christians, never forget the horrible pit and the miry clay whence your feet have been taken!

HOW TO OBTAIN ETERNAL LIFE.

From that time many of his disciples went back and walked no more with him. Then said Jesus unto the twelve, Will ye also go away? Then Simon Peter answered him, Lord, to whom shall we go? thou hast the words of eternal life.—John vi. 66—68.

IN all ages of the church there have been some to whom the doctrines of the gospel have proved a stumbling-block. Our Lord, in the chapter from which our text is taken, had been teaching the principles of his religion in figurative language. He knew that many of his professed followers entertained very superficial views of him and his kingdom, and that they associated with his true disciples from unworthy motives. In order, therefore, to correct their mistakes, and prevent a consequent disappointment of their expectations, he gave them to understand, that, though constantly about his person, and permitted to behold his miracles, they could not come to him and give their souls up to him, without a Divine influence upon their hearts: "No man can come to me, except the Father which hath sent me draw him," verse 44. And that they might be convinced that faith in him was something more than a cold assent to the precepts of his gospel, he represented the benefits of his atonement under the idea of bread; and taught them that they must eat his flesh and drink his blood, before they could obtain the remission of their sins, or a title to eternal life. Taking his words literally, they murmured and said, "This is a hard saying, who can hear it?" These false-hearted disciples were inexcusable in taking offence at our Lord's doctrine, because he explained his meaning, and taught them that his language was not to be taken in its literal sense, as appears from a fair interpretation of verses 61, 62, 63: "When Jesus knew, in himself, that his disciples murmured at what they had just heard, he said unto them, Doth this offend you?" That is, do you consider my doctrine incredible and stumble at it? "What, then, if ye shall see the Son of Man ascending up into heaven where he was before?" Would you then understand what was meant by the bread of life coming down from thence, as the food of the world? Or would you then believe that I came from heaven, notwithstanding the objection you have made as to the meanness of my parentage? Thus Christ plainly intimated his intended ascension, and in the meantime, as a key to the whole of his discourse on this occasion, he added, "It is the Spirit that quickeneth; the flesh profiteth nothing; the words that I speak unto you, they are spirit, and they are life:" which an eminent commentator* explains thus: "As in the human frame, it is the indwelling soul that quickens every part of it—

---

* Dr. Doddridge.

and the flesh, how exactly soever organized and adorned, if separate from the soul, profits nothing, but is an inactive and insensible mass; so, also, the words which I speak unto you are spirit; that is, they are to be taken in a spiritual sense, and then you will find they are life to your soul; whereas, to take them in a literal sense would be equally unprofitable and monstrous." But this explanation, it seems, was not satisfactory. These disciples, like many in our own times, wanted a religion of forms and outward appearances; they would believe nothing that was mysterious, or that transcended the limits of reason; and, particularly, they revolted at the idea of dependence on Divine grace. "From that time, therefore, they turned back, determined no longer to follow a master who taught such unintelligible doctrines, and who gave no countenance to their self-righteous and secular views."

What the number of these apostles was, we are not informed; they were many, however; and our Lord deemed it proper to improve the occasion, by putting the question pointedly to the twelve apostles, "Will ye also go away?" This question did not proceed from any apprehensions that he might be totally forsaken. The Saviour knew what was in man. He knew perfectly well who was to betray him, who would deny him, who would forsake him, and who would adhere to him amidst all perils. It was designed for the good of his apostles, to make them examine the grounds of their attachment to him. He wished them not to begin to build without count-

ing the cost; he would neither force them nor
entice them to follow him. They must make up
their minds on the evidence before them, and look
forward to consequences. He wished them, if they
did continue in his service, to do so from a conviction
of duty. He would not deceive them either as to
the nature of his religion, or the consequences of a
firm adherence to his cause. If they determined to
serve him, they must calculate on hardships and
cruel mockings, which nothing but a love of truth,
and a consciousness of duty could patiently endure.
Observe the candour and honesty of the Saviour.
Impostors always accommodate themselves to the prejudices and flatter the passions of those whom they
wish to proselyte. But the Son of God resorts to
no such unworthy means for the promotion of his
cause. He states explicitly the terms of discipleship.
He keeps nothing back, offers no palliatives, holds
out no lure to selfishness, or sensual desires. He
points out the sacrifices, the sufferings, the labours,
and self-denials attendant on his service; and in
view of these discouragements, says to the twelve,
Will you follow me? See, yonder are many persons
going away, offended at the terms of discipleship;
will you go with them, or are you resolved deliberately to continue in my service? "Will ye also
go away?" The true believer abhors the thoughts
of apostasy. Accordingly, Peter answers, in the name
of the other eleven, charitably thinking them of one
mind with himself, "Lord, to whom shall we go?
thou hast the words of eternal life." This is an

important sentiment. To illustrate and impress it more deeply upon your minds, is my design in this discourse. I say *to impress it more deeply upon your minds;* for I take it for granted that you all believe with Peter, that Jesus Christ teaches the true way of obtaining eternal life. Whether this belief has all that influence upon your hearts and your conduct that it should have, is best known to yourselves and your Maker.

Jesus Christ in his gospel has set before us the doctrines to be believed, and the precepts to be obeyed, in order to the attainment of eternal life. This proposition is evidently comprised in our text. Let us set our minds to the serious consideration of it.

I. The essential and fundamental doctrines to be believed are few, but vastly important. They are entitled to our chief attention, and they are taught so fully and plainly in the New Testament that he who runs may read. They are such as these—the entire depravity of our nature; our absolute need of a Divine influence to renew and sanctify our hearts; the mediatorial character and work of Jesus Christ, his Divinity, incarnation, atonement, resurrection, ascension, and intercession for his people; and the necessity of confiding in his merits as the sole ground of our justification and acceptance with God; a general judgment and a future state, in which the wicked shall go away into everlasting punishment, and the righteous be confirmed in eternal glory. These are some of the leading doctrines of the Christain faith; they are intended to be received as prin-

14

ciples of action; and it is by a faithful adherence to these principles, that the disciples of Christ may hope to be enabled, through grace, to adorn the doctrine of God their Saviour in all things, and to enjoy communion with the Father of their spirits. These doctrines, I am well aware, are lightly esteemed even by some who bear the Christian name. But they are taught and inculcated in the sacred writings, in terms as decisive and explicit as language can express them. They are, in fact, so intimately interwoven in the tenor and entire substance of Christianity, that they cannot be rejected without sapping the foundation of our immortal hopes.

Now suffer me to urge you to a firm belief of, and steady attachment to the doctrines of Christ. They comprise the essence of that revelation of mercy, which it has pleased God to bestow upon a guilty world—an authentic and satisfactory solution of the momentous question, "What shall I do to be saved?" The redemption of sinners by the blood of Christ is the distinguishing feature of the gospel. Let us receive the Divine message with cordiality and gratitude. Either to despise or neglect the way of salvation through Christ, is a certain indication of an ungrateful and degenerate mind. Men talk foolishly of the sufficiency of natural religion. The utmost aim of natural religion is to teach the natural perfections of God. But the most luminous display of the Divine power, wisdom, and righteousness, cannot infuse hope into the guilty heart, or soothe the troubled conscience. Our sad apostasy has produced an embarrassment and perplexity in our prospects, which nothing but an express assurance of forgiveness can remove. We find ourselves a race of miserable offenders. And how our Creator and rightful Lord might see fit to dispose of us, is a question on which the light of nature could give us no certain information. "For who hath known the mind of the Lord; or, being his counsellor, hath taught him?" But the words of the Divine Saviour solve the difficulty; the silence of ages is broken; the darkness of reason gives way to the light of the Sun of Righteousness; and we behold the astonishing spectacle, "God in Christ, reconciling the world unto himself!"

If you wish, then, to have a good hope, seek it in Christ: learn of him, trust in him, commit your souls to him, and you have all the perfections of the adorable Godhead engaged for your eternal safety. "In him you have the knowledge of salvation by the remission of sins, through the tender mercy of our God, whereby the dayspring from on high hath visited us, to give light to them that sit in darkness and the shadow of death, to guide our feet in the way of peace." Let us not then flatter ourselves, that we may disregard the words of Christ with impunity. If we turn away from Him who addresses us from heaven, we do it at our peril. He came from the bosom of the Father, and claims, amid ten thousand witnesses, to be "the way, the truth, and the life." He has the words of eternal life—neither is there salvation in any other. Turn away from him, and where will you go, with any hope of forgiveness and acceptance with God? To philosophy? It may amuse you with fine theories and waking dreams; but it cannot atone for your sin, or enlighten before you the valley of the shadow of death. To the law? It is inflexible, and makes no allowance for the smallest sin; its language is, "Cursed is every one that continueth not in all things that are written in the book of the law, to do them." To Moses? He will send you back again to Christ; for he wrote of him as that prophet which the Lord God should raise up, that all men might hear and obey him. Will you not then receive the truth from the lips of Him who came a light into the world, that whosoever believeth in him should not abide in darkness? He is a teacher come from God. His credentials are clear; his words are spirit and life; his promise is extensive and sure: "Him that cometh unto me, I will in nowise cast out. If any man thirst, let him come unto me and drink. I am the bread of life: he that cometh to me shall never hunger; and he that believeth on me shall never thirst."

II. Christ, having the words of eternal life, prescribes the path that leads to glory. He is our Lawgiver; he promulgates and interprets his laws, and requires obedience as the test of our attachment to his person: "Ye are my friends," says he, "if ye do whatsoever I command you."

It is not my intention to go into particular specification of the precepts of the gospel. They are much better known than practised. The single point to which I now invite your attention, is the inconsistency of living according to the course of this world, while we profess to acknowledge the authority of Christ. The conduct which he requires of his disciples is different from that of the world in general; and that the Christian name can be of no avail, except when joined with Christian practice, is an obvious and indisputable truth. When I admit that Jesus Christ is a Divine teacher, clothed with Divine authority, and qualified to lead me to heaven and eternal glory, I implicitly engage to regulate my conduct and temper by the rules which he prescribes. And if it be not my constant aim to live up to this engagement, I fall under the cutting reproof, "Why call ye me Lord, Lord, and keep not my sayings?"

Duplicity in religious concerns cannot be practised with success; for "all things are naked and open to Him with whom we have to do." Now, any person who reads the gospel of Christ with the least attention, must observe that we are there required to exercise repentance towards God, and faith in the Redeemer; to renounce all sin; to avoid conformity to the world; to abstain from fleshly lusts, which war against the soul; to be sober, and watch unto prayer; to set our affections on things above, and not on things on the earth; to have our conversation in heaven; to take up our cross, and follow Christ; to break off all connections and pursuits which impede our growth in grace; to lay aside every weight, and run the race that is set before us, looking unto Jesus. These and the like precepts, though not to be so rigorously inter-

14*

preted as to interfere with the social and active duties
of life, certainly require us to seek the glory of God
and the sanctification of our souls, in a course of conscientious obedience to Christ, and devotion to the
interests of his kingdom.

The religion of Christ is an active religion. It has
fair claims to our best affections; and it furnishes
employment for the longest life. Its blessed Author
went about doing good. He had no time to spend in
a state of indecision and hesitancy between duty and
folly, virtue and vice. And they that are joined to
the Lord are of one spirit. They resemble him in
temper and conduct. It is the law of his kingdom:
"If any man have not the Spirit of Christ, he is none
of his." I do not address myself to professed unbe-
lievers, whose hopes and wishes are bounded by the
narrow limits of this short life. The practice of such
persons may be consistent with their principles; but
it is an awful consistency, in rejecting that life and
immortality which are brought to light in the gospel.
My aim is to correct a mistake too prevalent among
those who admit the truth of Christianity. The mistake to which I allude is this—that a kind of neutral-
ity in religion is wiser and safer than an open and
decided attachment to the cause of Christ. It is
alleged that a man may have faith quietly, and to
himself. Were this notion to prevail, it would inevitably strip the Christian church of its visible form.
Had it obtained among the apostles and primitive
Christians, there would have been no ministry of
reconciliation; no churches, no baptism, no com-

munion of the body and blood of Christ. We would have had no assembling of ourselves together for public worship, which St. Paul charges us not to forget, though it is the manner of some to forget or neglect. The truth is, this notion of having faith to one's-self is, for the most part, intended as an apology to conscience for being ashamed of the gospel of Christ. He who has the words of eternal life, says: "Ye are the light of the world: neither do men light a candle, and put it under a bushel, but on a candle-stick; and it giveth light unto all that are in the house. Let your light so shine before men, that they may see your good works, and glorify your Father which is in heaven."

Another mistake, nearly allied to the one just no-ticed, is, that a life not marked with any open vice, cannot be a sinful life, and cannot fail to meet the approbation of God. If the gospel required nothing more than negative goodness, and had no respect to the state of the heart, this opinion would be, at least, plausible. But, on the principles of Christian morals, to do nothing, is often to do a positive evil, and to incur a positive punishment. The slothful servant, in the parable, is pronounced wicked, and treated as such. In the case of the barren fig-tree, also, our Lord teaches, by a significant action, the same doc-trine: "Cut it down." Why? Not because it bears bad fruit; but because it bears none. The famous Athenian lawgiver declared, that "to stand neuter in dangerous commotions of the State, was a crime against the State." The same principle is recognized in the kingdom of Christ. "He that is not with me is against me; and he that gathereth not with me, scattereth abroad."

"Will ye also go away?" Many, from one pretence and another, have turned their backs upon Christ, determined to have nothing to do with him and his religion. I now put the question to you, my hearers, in his name. And should any of you feel inclined to answer, Yes, I would submit to you a few previous questions, to which I entreat you to pay serious attention. Are you sure that death is an eternal sleep; that this mortal shall not put on immortality; and that you will never be roused by the voice of the archangel, and the trump of God, to stand before the judgment-seat of Christ? Or, if you believe in a future state, are you fully satisfied that you need no expiation of your sins? Are you willing to appear in the presence of your Maker and plead your own cause, before inflexible justice and immaculate purity? Are you sure, after candid investigation, that the Bible is a tissue of falsehood and cunningly devised fables? Are you sure that Jesus Christ . . . But I dare not proceed farther. If you are prepared to answer these questions in the affirmative, then, indeed, to be consistent, you must go away. We will follow you with the eye of compassion, and sound after you this tender expostulation of Heaven's mercy: "Turn ye, turn ye; for why will ye die!" But I hope in God, with Peter in the text you will all answer, "To whom shall we go? Thou hast the words of eternal life." You believe that Jesus is the only

Saviour. You see no gleam of hope from any other quarter. Receive, then, a short advice, intended to assist you in making a right application and improvement of our subject.

If you find yourselves to be sinners, helpless and guilty, without righteousness or strength of your own; if you wish a happiness suited to the capacities of immortal souls; if you perceive that Christ is such a Saviour as you need, and that the truth of his gospel is founded on such sort of evidence as no man on earth was ever yet deceived by trusting to, in any other case, then repose entire confidence in him. Receive his doctrines in love. Question not the efficacy, the all-sufficiency of his atonement. Cast your polluted souls beneath the droppings of his blood, and they shall be cleansed from all sin. Lay hold, by faith, on his righteousness, and it shall be unto and upon you for justification. "He that hath the Son of God, hath life. There is now, therefore, no condemnation to them that are in Christ Jesus, who walk not after the flesh, but after the Spirit." So, also, in regard to practice. If you feel that longing after immortality which, supported by reason and confirmed by revelation, more than intimates that you are children of eternity; if, on comparing things temporal with things eternal, you are convinced the pains and pleasures of this life are not fit to be compared with the rewards and punishments of the life to come, then follow Christ, let who will go away from him. Prove to your own satisfaction that your faith is a living, victorious, Divine principle. Seek no compromise between the precepts of the gospel and the maxims of the world. Be not staggered at the question, "Have any of the rulers believed on him?" Not many wise men after the flesh, not many noble or mighty are called; enough are called, however, to secure the suffrages of intellects of the first order. If you belong to a little flock, it is that little flock to which it is the "Father's good pleasure to give the kingdom."

TEMPERANCE:

ITS NECESSITY AND OBLIGATION.

———————

Every man that striveth for the mastery is temperate in all things. Now they do it to obtain a corruptible crown; but we an incorruptible.—1 Cor. ix. 25.

THERE is, in this passage of sacred Scripture, a manifest allusion to the celebrated Isthmian games, which were celebrated in the neighbourhood of Corinth. The athletes, *i. e.*, those who took part in the exercises of the stadium, were required to observe the strictest regimen in their meals and drinks. This was deemed essential to the vigour and agility of their bodies; and to this they cheerfully submitted, in the hope of obtaining those honorary premiums which were awarded to the successful competitor. From this custom St. Paul draws an argument in favour of that self-government and discipline of the passions enjoined upon Christians, and which is so important to the attainment of the prize of their high calling.

"Every man that striveth for the mastery is temperate in all things." From the constitution of our nature, temperance is indispensably necessary to success in any enterprise. So judged the managers of these Grecian games; so judged the great apostle of the Gentiles; and we are sure that his judgment was right, for it was formed under the influence of the Spirit of truth. To give force to his argument he goes on to remark, "Now they do it," *i. e.*, these combatants are temperate in all things "to obtain a corruptible crown," a wreath composed of fading and perishable leaves; "but we an incorruptible," a crown of righteousness and glory, that fadeth not away. The apostle's argument is this: If they who seek the applause of their fellow mortals, and who strive to gain an insignificant, fading crown, submit to be temperate in all things; if they observe the strictest abstemiousness, renouncing every sensual indulgence which tends to debilitate their bodily powers; if they voluntarily endure hardships, and are content with whatever kind of discipline may be deemed proper to qualify them for "running so that they may obtain;" if they do all this, knowing, at the same time, "that they who run in a race run all, but one receiveth the prize;" shall not Christians, to whom God opens the rich treasures of his grace, and to whom he proffers glory, honour, and immortality, be temperate in all things? Will not they give up all corrupting gratifications, and mortify those lusts of the flesh which war against the soul, to secure an incorruptible crown, a sure and permanent inherit- ance, commensurate with the existence, and suited to the growing capacities of an immortal spirit? Nothing is more reasonable, and it is as needful as it is reasonable. It is the law of the Lord's house, a law which from which none of his disciples need look for a dispensation. "If any man," says he, "will come after me, let him deny himself, and take up his cross, and follow me."

The duty inculcated in our text, my hearers, is temperance—"temperance in all things." By which, in its extended sense, I understand the right government of our passions and appetites. That temperance, or which is the same thing, self-government and self-denial, is a Christian duty, none will dispute, who understand the nature and design of Christianity. It is deplorable that any who admit the obligation of the duty, should live regardless of its dictates. But it is so. Christ is often wounded in the house of his professed disciples; while his gospel is unjustly charged with their failings and their crimes. To be temperate in all things is not, indeed, an easy duty. In our fallen nature it meets with a repellent principle, which, if a man be not influenced by that faith which brings all the powers of the soul into subjugation to the laws of Jesus Christ, will not only dispute its authority but utterly reject its claims. Hence it comes to pass, that men have the hardihood at once to deny their obligation to be temperate, and turn away with scorn from the religion which prescribes the duty. They allege that, as our passions and animal desires form a part of our nature, there can be no harm in gratifying them. Our native propensities were intended to be indulged; to indulge them, therefore, is but to obey the law of our nature. This is plausible, but it is not sound

15

reasoning. Let us try if we cannot detect its sophistry.

To this end we propose, in the first place, to prove that the necessity of temperance results from the depravity of our nature. Secondly, that the exercise of this virtue is favourable to happiness. Thirdly, urge the motive presented in the latter clause of our text, "now they do it to obtain a corruptible crown, but we an incorruptible."

I. The necessity of temperance results from the depravity of our nature. A certain modern philosopher, with much more of the pride than of the light of philosophy, has ventured to make the following assertion: "To imagine that the gratifying any of the senses, or the indulging any delicacy in meats, drinks, or apparel, is of itself a vice, can never enter into a head that is not disordered by the frenzies of a fanatical enthusiasm." This doctrine may go down readily enough with those who are not in the habit of distinguishing between sound and sense, between bold assumption and solid argument. But it will not satisfy a man of sobriety and discernment. It is undeniable that the gospel of our salvation prohibits intemperance under the most fearful penalty. The laws of our Lord's kingdom are pointed and positive on the subject, and are not to be disregarded with impunity. "Avenge not yourselves; vengeance is mine; I will repay, saith the Lord." "Therefore, brethren, we are debtors, not to the flesh, to live after the flesh; for if ye live after the flesh ye shall die; but if ye, through the Spirit, do mortify the deeds of the body ye shall live." Now it is not supposable that our blessed Saviour would lay his followers under any needless restraint. Indeed, he tells us himself, that "his yoke is easy and his burden light." That is, as easy and as light as our miserable circumstances and his merciful design of purifying us unto himself will admit of. Why then does he require us to restrain, to deny, and govern our natural propensities? Because we are depraved creatures. Because, ever since the fall of Adam, our passions and sensual appetites have exerted an undue influence over our reason and conscience, and aim at nothing short of the entire dominion of the soul.

Let the fact, then, of man's depravity be admitted. He is not upright; his mind is disordered. Sin has produced anarchy and confusion in the soul. The passions and affections do not move in quiet subordination to the higher principles of reason and conscience. We have evil desires and wayward propensities, which will either govern us, or we must govern them. The truth, my hearers, lies within a narrow compass, and may be expressed in a few words. The heart of man is depraved. This depravity consists very much in the predominance of the inferior over the superior powers of the mind. Reformation commences by the restoration of reason to the throne, and conscience to her due influence, the direction of the passions to their proper objects, and the subjection of the whole man to the law and authority of God. In effecting this radical change in our minds, man's moral agency is not superseded. The sinner is still free and accountable; commanded to work out his own salvation with fear and trembling, while God works in him both to will and to do. Hence our obligation to be temperate in all things, to control our passions, to restrain our appetites, and abstain from fleshly lusts. Self-discipline must be maintained; and, however painful and difficult it may be, it is not to be given up. It is salutary, it is necessary. The Saviour requires it, not in the wantonness of power, but in the exercise of his redeeming mercy. To the philosophical remark, therefore, that there can be no harm in gratifying our senses and appetites, because in so doing we obey the law of our nature, we are prepared to reply, and the reply is short. Were we upright, as God made man at first, then virtue would consist in following our natural inclinations, because these inclinations would tend only to good; but, as we are fallen and depraved creatures, and as our inclinations are consequently often wrong, and our passions always exorbitant in their claims to indulgence, to follow our inclinations, and yield to our passions, is the certain road to complete degradation and everlasting ruin. Thus much for the necessity of temperance. It arises out of the corruption of the human heart. The remedy which the Saviour, like a good physician, applies to our souls is not more severe than the disease under which we labour requires.

II. We proposed, secondly, to show that the exercise of this virtue is favourable to happiness. And this, we think, will not be a difficult task. Look at the miseries which its opposite, intemperance, produces. "From whence," saith the apostle, "come wars and fightings among you? Come they not hence, even of your lusts, which war in your members?" Whence, my hearers, come murders, robberies, oppression, and fraud? Whence come breaches of friendship, violations of the marriage covenant, and the seduction of the innocent? Whence comes the loss of health, reputation, and fortune, to individuals? Whence come the penury, the disorder, the feuds and broils, the wretchedness, the infamy, of many families, once the abode of peace, the pride of their neighbours, and the hope of the church? These are the effects, these the trophies of head-strong passion and unbridled appetite. In fact, my hearers, happiness is not to be enjoyed under the misrule of intemperate passions.

Consider the subject in what point of light you please, this conclusion will force itself upon you with irresistible evidence. Look at the man of an angry and waspish temper. What is he? Can he be happy whose bosom is a stranger to peace and the soothing charities of social intercourse? Can he be happy whose language and conduct are calculated to make all around him miserable—the tyrant of his family, and the scorn and scourge of his neighbourhood? Take the envious man; his soul is the seat of discontent and malevolence; his brother's success is his misfortune. A stranger to good-will and the sweet sympathies of human kindness, he lives wretched, and dies unloved and unlamented. The same may be said

15*

of revenge, ambition, jealousy, and the other strong passions. When indulged, they not only destroy the peace of the mind that cherishes them, but spread confusion and misery wide as the sphere of their influence.

The indulgence of our sensual appetites is equally hostile to happiness. Take an instance. Behold the man who is yielding to an inordinate fondness for intoxicating liquors, and you see one who, in so far as he gives in to this pernicious habit, resigns his health, his peace, his intellect, his reputation, his usefulness, and, though he may not suspect it, his hope of heaven. It is painful to touch upon so humiliating a subject in a Christian assembly, because it seems to imply the existence of a vice among us, not only unworthy the Christian name, but degrading and reproachful to the character of a man. But we dare not forbear. The Spirit of truth has declared unequivocally, that no drunkard shall inherit the kingdom of God. You see it is a sin which, if persisted in, will exclude a man from heaven.

Perhaps there may be some among us who are falling heedlessly and imperceptibly into this vice. Should there be such, let them take seasonable warning. Let them pause and repent, and correct a habit which, if not speedily corrected, will fasten upon them as immovably as the Ethiopian's skin, or the leopard's spots. Let those young men who seem to think it allowable to indulge freely in the inebriating draught on some rare and special occasions, be admonished, that in tampering with drunkenness they are sporting with danger. That is an admirable precept, "Beware, lest any of you be hardened through the deceitfulness of sin." Sensual pleasure is one of sin's most insinuating and deceptive forms. In this character the syren plays her part with fatal success. By her fascinating arts she decoys and ensnares the unsuspecting victim, while she conceals the hideous scorpions, the quenchless fires, and deathless worm, that follow in her train.

The time would fail us to do justice to the subject. And, indeed, it is a subject on which argument would be useless. Drunkenness is a vice of notorious and preëminent turpitude. It preys alike upon body and soul. It debases our nature; obscures the brightest powers of intellect; robs a man of his best enjoyments, and compels him at last to give up his hopes of heaven. In short, the mischiefs of intemperance are incalculable, and may be eternal. To guard against these mischiefs, let us resolve, with St. Paul, to keep under our body, and bring it into subjection. There is no alternative; if we do not govern our passions and appetites, they will govern and ruin us. The task is a difficult one; but let us call in the aid which Divine grace has provided for us.

Christianity has a right to require a stricter command over the lusts of the flesh, and a higher sanctity of manners, than any other religion, because it affords to its votaries ample assistance and glorious rewards. "We can do all things through Christ, who strengtheneth us." With this sure word of promise, who would despair of success? Can any one who believes the gospel, account it useless to mortify the deeds of the body, and restrain his sensual appetites, when they who strive for the mastery in the most trivial contests, and for the silliest rewards, submit to be temperate in all things? "Now they do it to obtain a corruptible crown, but we an incorruptible."

III. The prize, my hearers, for which you are called upon to strive, is worth contending for. It is the prize of the high calling of God in Christ Jesus. It is the richest that Heaven can bestow. It implies whatever is desirable, with whatever is suitable to complete the felicity of an immortal soul. And the question will soon be decided whether we shall obtain it or not. Our characters are forming for eternity. The irrevocable sentence will soon go forth, "He that is filthy, let him be filthy still." Time rolls on like a resistless torrent; the pleasures of sense will soon be over. "The things which are seen are temporal, but the things which are not seen are eternal." "Labour not for the meat that perisheth, but for that which endureth unto everlasting life." Corruptible crowns wither on the brow, and blast the hopes of their votaries. The voice of Divine mercy calls upon us to choose the good part, that shall never be taken from us—an incorruptible crown, a fulness of joy, an eternal heaven. Let none say, despairingly, Our passions have gained the mastery; our habits of intemperance have become fixed and unconquerable. Make the attempt humbly, but resolutely, and you will find

Omnipotent grace sufficient for you. Your guilt may be great, and your danger is certainly imminent; but the blood of Christ cleanseth from all sin, and the grace of God is sufficient to enable you to relinquish all bad habits, and resist all temptations. And, O consider, I beseech you, the folly, the madness, of expecting the heavenly prize, while you continue in sin! Sin is a native of hell; and whomsoever it governs, it carries, in the end, to its own place. If ever you are saved, you must part with all sin. So long as you retain a relish for sinful indulgences, heaven, where all is pure and holy, were you admitted there, must be to you a place of bondage and intolerable restraint.

As you would be happy, useful, and respected in this world; as you would wish to die in the exercise of a good hope; as you would mingle in the songs of the redeemed; as you would see God and your Saviour, and be blessed in his presence for ever, "be temperate in all things." My young friends, I have brought this subject before you, not because I have any reason to think that intemperance prevails among you in any remarkable degree; but because I know that persons, at your age, and in your circumstances, need to be seasonably and solemnly warned of its baneful influence. It has ruined thousands, in relation to both worlds. That it may not ruin any of you; that none of you may yield yourselves to its degrading and accursed dominion, is my earnest desire and prayer to God. Your safety will much depend on your steering clear of its first approaches. For your assistance against this insidious enemy of all righteousness, usefulness, and peace, let me submit to you, in conclusion, two short pieces of advice.

1. Give your attention regularly to some useful occupation. Idleness is the mother of a numerous and hateful progeny of vices. It invariably nourishes our worst and most dangerous passions, and almost always induces intemperance of one sort or other. If you yield yourselves to her soft embraces, she will either lull you to sleep in the spring and seed-time of of life, or drench you with the maddening draughts of intoxication, as a miserable refuge for your ennui, or the gnawings of an empty, besotted, unoccupied mind. Those of you, therefore, who will soon have completed your domestic training, will do well to bend your minds to those studies and pursuits which have an immediate bearing upon the business which you may select. Remember that this life is short; and in its relation to that which is to come, it is too precious to admit of our spending much of it in amusement, or even in miscellaneous pursuits which have in view no definite object.

2. If you wish to be temperate in all things, and in all circumstances, and from right motives, ask of God, with all importunity, and in the name of Christ, that he will give you a holy heart, a tender sense of duty, and a deep, fixed, and unconquerable abhorrence of sin, in its varied and deceitful forms. The restraints of honour, of self-respect, of self-interest,

may for awhile keep you from gross outbreakings of sin; but, believe me, nothing but the grace of God, through the redemption that is in Christ, can renovate your fallen nature, effectually rescue you from the wiles of Satan, the wickedness of your own hearts, and the snares of the world, and make you meet for the inheritance of the saints in light. May God bless you, and save you, to the praise of his glorious grace!

A CONVENIENT SEASON.

And as he reasoned of righteousness, temperance, and judgment to come, Felix trembled, and answered, Go thy way for this time; when I have a convenient season, I will call for thee.—Acts xxiv. 25.

WE have in these words something to admire, and something to deplore. The conduct of the apostle is admirable, that of Felix is deplorable. The former is worthy to be imitated by the ministers of religion, the latter should be carefully avoided by all men. St. Paul now stood charged with the high crimes of sedition, profanation of the temple, and sundry violations of the law of Moses. The high-priest, and the Sanhedrim, the supreme ecclesiastical council of the Jewish nation, were his prosecutors. Tertullus, an insidious barrister, who seems to have been equally regardless of humanity and truth, was employed to manage their cause. Paul stood alone at the bar of the Procurator, with whom it rested to condemn or acquit him. What a temptation this to keep back the solemn and awakening truths of the gospel! In such circumstances any but a good man would have used flattery and artful management. But the cause

in which the apostle was engaged needed none of the
helps which sin could afford. He preferred a good
conscience to the favour of man; and faithfulness to
his adorable Master was too high a price to pay for
life itself. When permitted to speak in his own
defence, he declared his innocence, and challenged
his accusers to substantiate their allegations. He
affirmed that his religious opinions were perfectly
consistent with the writings of Moses and the prophets; that his late journey to Jerusalem had been
for the purposes of charity and devotion; that his
entrance into the temple was attended with no tumul-
tuous proceedings; nor had he entertained any sedi-
tious designs against the civil authority or peace of
the State; protested his constant care to have been
to have a conscience void of offence towards God and
man; and boldly asserted that his enemies could not
prove the things whereof they accused him. In all
the firmness of conscious truth and rectitude, he
appeals to his persecutors, "Let these same here say,
if they have found any evil doing in me; except it
be for this one voice that I uttered, standing among
them, Touching the resurrection of the dead, I am
called in question by you this day." After hearing his defence, Felix, under pretence of hearing
farther evidence in the case, ordered the prisoner to
be held in safe keeping, with permission, in the mean
time, to receive the visits of his friends.

After certain days, the sacred historian informs
us, "Felix sent for Paul, and heard him concerning
the faith in Christ." The Roman governor, and

16

the adulterous Drusilla, who was a Jewess, having heard many rumours about Christianity, were, it seems, desirous, from motives of curiosity, to hear what could be said in its favour by this extraordinary man. Paul, always ready to publish and defend the gospel, complied with their wishes. But his discourse proved to be of a very different kind, no doubt, from what was expected. The historian may not have recorded all that he said on the occasion. From what is related, we find that Paul was a practical and pointed preacher. To gratify an idle, speculative curiosity, seems to have been regarded by him as an unworthy aim. He kept in view the character and conduct of his audience. Regardless of the trappings of oratory, which often disguise the truth, and prevent its effect by blunting its edge, his grand object in all his discourses was to convict of sin and persuade to holiness.

Accordingly, instead of entertaining his noble auditory with an elaborate defence of the Christian faith, he addresses them on subjects calculated to alarm their fears, awaken in them a sense of guilt, and produce a reformation in their sentiments and manners. The character of Felix was notoriously bad. Two historians, Tacitus and Josephus, agree in representing him as a man of cruelty and wickedness. Licentiousness and avarice constituted the odious and conflicting features of his private character. His government was a continued scene of injustice and oppression. Of the wicked companion of this wicked man nothing need be said. She was the lawful wife of Azizus, king of Emesa, whom she abandoned. Her sin has long been proverbial; so that, by common consent, Drusilla is but another name for whatever is most depraved and hateful in the conduct of her sex. Such were the principal persons before whom the apostle was now called to speak. And it will be readily admitted that the topics on which he chose to expatiate, were not at all calculated to flatter or conciliate the favour of his hearers. He reasoned of righteousness, before the man whose public character was tarnished with cruelty and oppression; of temperance and judgment to come, before those who were living in a state of unblushing incontinence, unmindful of death, and a day of fearful retribution. Admirable example of Christian heroism and ministerial fidelity! In the fervour of his zeal for the honour of his Lord and the salvation of souls, he forgets that he is a prisoner, and loses sight of the effect which the plainness and pungency of his reproofs might have upon upon his personal safety. Here is the noble spirit that should influence all who preach the gospel of Christ.

Personalities are never to be used in the pulpit. They invariably offend the pious, and confirm the prejudices of the wicked against the cause of truth and goodness. But he who does not study the character of his hearers; who does not adapt his style to their capacities, and level his discourses against the sins to which they are addicted, greatly mistakes the nature of his business, and falls far short of the grand design of the sacred ministry. There is a wide

difference between respect for an audience, and a
temporizing regard to the persons of men. The
former is never to be neglected. The latter is wholly
inadmissible. Such appear to have been the views
of St. Paul on this subject. Accordingly, we find
him everywhere, even in circumstances of external
danger, with the utmost plainness, urging all men,.
both high and low, to abandon their sins, and "flee
from the wrath to come." This method is to be preferred, not only because it was the method of Christ
and his apostles, but also because it is the most successful. It is not always, however, attended with
success. For, my brethren, unless the word of life
be carried to the heart by a Divine influence, the
eloquence and fervour of an angel would be of no
avail to the saving of a soul. Of this fact we have
a striking exemplification before us. What effect
the reasoning of Paul had upon Drusilla we are not
informed. On Felix it had a powerful effect. In
him, though a great sinner, conscience still retained
a degree of sensibility, which had he cherished, and
had he yielded to the impressions of sacred truth, his
trembling might have issued in a saving change of
heart and of life. But he loved his sins, and could not
consent to part with them at present. The partial
glimpse which the apostle's reasoning had given him
of his guilt and danger, filled him with fearfulness,
and he hastened to bring the interview to a close.
The faithful monitor for whom he had sent, that he
might hear him concerning the faith in Christ, was
interrupted and dismissed with a "Go thy way for

this time; when I have a convenient season I will call for thee."

Infatuated man! why not hear the messenger of God through, and decide for yourself upon the question respecting the faith in Christ without farther delay? No doubt his numerous and weighty engagements of a secular nature, were pleaded as a sufficient apology for the postponement of concerns which reason and conscience told him demanded his most serious attention. But the momentous affairs of salvation and eternity were, for a while at least, to give place to the trifles of time; perhaps the gratification of a sensual appetite, or the attainment of some imaginary good, incompatible with the Christian temper. What an affecting picture of the folly and depravity of man! "When I have a convenient season, I will call for thee."

And did Felix ever find this convenient season, on which he hazarded his soul, and the imperishable glories of heaven? That he did, there is not a particle of evidence to be found in the history of his after conduct. We find him, indeed, conferring with Paul after this, but it was in hopes of obtaining money, for which he would have released him. We hear no more of his trembling, or wishing to hear anything farther respecting the faith in Christ. Disappointed in his avaricious views, he resolved, in all the wantonness of power, to hold in imprisonment for two years, a man against whom had not been proved the semblance of a crime; and, at last, upon being recalled from the government for his own crimes, he left Paul bound,

16*

from the base motive of courting the favour and gratifying the malice of the Jews. What complicated
iniquity—what deliberate wickedness! How affecting
to observe, that the deep impressions of truth made on
the heart of a sinner sometimes tend, through his
own neglect, to aggravate his guilt and prepare him
for the fearful doom of being beaten with many
stripes!

My hearers, I have presented to you the conduct of
Felix, not for your imitation, but for your avoidance.
You see he promised well. The force of gospel truth
reached his conscience, and he trembled at the danger
of his state. But refusing to give due attention to
the subject at the proper time, his good impressions
gradually wore off, and he became hardened through
the deceitfulness of sin. His case is recorded for
our admonition. We have a solemn lesson to learn
from it. It teaches us that procrastination in religious concerns is a destroyer of souls. This is a species of self-deception which thousands are practising
on themselves, in the face of Scripture, conscience,
and reason. It is a kind of madness common to persons of all ranks, and at every period of life. The
young cannot become religious on account of this,
that, and the other frivolous accomplishment, or
fashionable amusement, which engages their pursuit,
or occupies their mind. The middle aged, full of
business, eagerly grasping at the world's treasures and
distinctions, cannot embrace the faith in Christ, because they have no time to spare for reading, meditation, prayer, and the duties of piety. The old and

infirm cannot, because in them the habits of sin have grown inveterate. By each class, in turn, the messages of grace and the awakening impression of God's word are dismissed with the maxim of Felix, "Go thy way for this time; when I have a convenient season, I will call for thee." How shall we account for so general a compliance with the spirit of a maxim so manifestly false and delusive? Undoubtedly its source is to be found in the extreme depravity of the human heart. By nature we do not love to retain God in our thoughts; for the exalted pleasures of devotion we have no relish. The things of the Spirit are foolishness to us; nor can we discover their glory and excellence, because they are spiritually discerned. Hence the common preference given to the pleasures of sin. And in the indulgence of this depraved bias, our fears are quieted by the fallacious opinion that, when the pleasures of the world abandon us, we can easily obtain religion enough to save us from hell, and furnish us with a title to heaven. But really this opinion ought to be given up, at least by those who believe the Scriptures speak truth. To become religious, in the gospel sense, is to become a new creature; to undergo an entire change of heart, and enter on a new course of life. The lively oracles of God tell us that we are "dead in trespasses and sins," and ascribe our regeneration expressly and exclusively to God, who worketh in us, both to will and to do of his good pleasure.

It is said by some that a man may become religious whenever he pleases. There cannot be found a more absurd and deceptive sophism; for the will is the seat of human depravity; and if not operated upon by a Divine influence, it must eternally retain its perverseness and opposition to God. This fact furnishes no solid objection to the use of means. The same passage of sacred writ that assures us it is God that worketh in us, commands us to work out our own salvation, with fear and trembling. The gospel is to be preached, the word is to be read, and prayer is to be made without ceasing. The good seed is to be sown, Paul is to plant and Apollos to water; but it is God's prerogative to give the increase. There is a certain course of conduct in which the Divine blessing is to be expected, and he who does not pursue this course may look for a curse. The man who neglects the means of grace, under pretext of not being able to change his heart, not only challenges the displeasure of his Maker, but offers an insult to his own understanding, and outrages common sense. From our complete dependence on God for a right temper of mind, the plain and legitimate inference is, that we should seek it of him in the way he has prescribed.

Suffer me, then, in the conclusion of this discourse, to submit to you a few remarks on the unreasonableness, ingratitude, and danger of waiting for a more convenient season than the present, to embrace the Saviour and enter cordially into his service. I doubt not that to many of you these remarks will not apply, because you have made up your minds and chosen the good part. But, if there be any whose consciences tell them they are not, in religion, what they ought to be; any who have hitherto put off their convictions with a promise to call for them at some future period, their serious attention is affectionately solicited to the following considerations.

First, this procrastinating spirit—this waiting for a more convenient season to become religious, is unreasonable. What does the word of God teach you—that word which you cannot reject without casting away with it the hope of immortality? It teaches you that, by nature, you are under the condemnatory sentence of God's law; that, except you repent, you shall perish; that, without holiness, no man shall the Lord; that, except you are born again, you cannot enter into the kingdom of God; that you go astray from the womb; that, till you believe and obey the gospel, you have neither part nor lot in the great salvation. These things you admit, and yet when God, by his word, his providence, or Spirit, calls you to reflection and thoughtfulness, you say, " Go thy way for this time; when I have a convenient season, I will call for thee." Is not this unwise in the extreme? You do not act thus in other concerns of far less moment. When taken sick, you lose no time, spare no pains, to have the disease checked at its commencement. Should a skilful physician offer you his services, at such a crisis, would you put him off, as you do that Divine Saviour who proffers to heal all your diseases, and restore to your soul perfect moral health and vigour? Suppose an estate left you by the bequest of a friend, and you are informed, that unless measures are taken to get possession of it immediately, you will be in danger of losing it, would you say to the friendly adviser, "Go thy way, it will be time enough at a more convenient season"? The answer is obvious. And is the pearl of great price so trifling an object in your estimation, that you are willing to risk it on an imaginary convenient season which you may not live to see? Do you not know that the present is the only time you have any right to count upon? The future belongs to God, and he tells you expressly, that "now is the accepted time, and day of salvation." Is happiness your aim? And do you not know that for the attainment of this object of universal pursuit, the advantages are on the side of piety, with regard to both worlds? "Godliness is profitable unto all things, having promise of the life that now is, and of that which is to come." Wisdom's ways are pleasant, and her end glory and honour. But the way of transgressors is hard, and their end infamy and ruin. Are you afraid, then, of being safe and happy too soon? Can you, without incurring the imputation of folly, continue longer feeding on husks, and rejecting the food of angels, that bread of life which cometh down from heaven?

Secondly, there is extreme ingratitude in postponing the claims of religion. That son who riots on the bounty, disobeys the commands, and presumes on the clemency of a kind and indulgent parent, is justly considered disingenuous and wicked. He who can trifle with parental solicitude and kindness, must be in the last stage of depravity. Are you, then, under no obligations to the Father of mercies? Your sin has rendered you obnoxious to his wrath, and he might ong ago have cast you off as cumberers of his ground; but, instead of this, he has rescued you from a thousand dangers, and provided for you a thousand unmerited and unsolicited comforts. Through all the windings of a prodigal life, he has commissioned messenger after messenger to pursue you, and give you assurance of his tender regard, and readiness to receive you back again to the honours and privileges of his house. Often as you have rejected his authority, and refused to submit to his wise and gentle control, still he is reluctant to abandon you; and while you are making haste to get beyond the reach of his voice, he sends after you this heart-melting expostulation of mercy: "How shall I give thee up, Ephraim? How shall I deliver thee, O Judah?" "Turn ye, turn ye, for why will ye die?"

And can you treat the kindly counsels of such a Parent with coldness and neglect? Have you not grieved his Spirit and exercised his patience long enough? You intend returning to your duty, and hope for a restoration to his favour, when your convenient season arrives; but after so long a course of disobedience, how will you approach him? What excuse will you offer for contempt of authority and abuse of mercy? Will you tell him, that because of the freeness of his grace and compassion, you ventured deliberately to try his forbearance; that from his overflowing goodness, you took encouragement to continue longer in sin than you would have done, had he been a hard master, and strict to mark iniquity? O, what disingenuousness, what presumption, what blackness of ingratitude is this! How can you trifle with the mercy on which you are dependent for life and salvation?

Consider, in the last place, the danger of putting off the things which belong to your everlasting peace. As the path of the just shineth more and more to the perfect day, so evil men wax worse and worse. It is a fearful truth, taught in Scripture, and confirmed by experience. The habit of sinning may become unconquerable. What says the word of God? "Can the Ethiopian change his skin, or the leopard his spots? Then may ye also do good, that are accustomed to do evil." What says your own experience? Do not some of you now listen, with indifference, to Divine truths, which once produced in you the tenderest emotions, and the fullest purposes of amendment? And is there no danger of the gospel proving to you a savour of death unto death? Will the Redeemer always knock at the door of your hearts? Has not God forewarned you, that his Spirit shall not always strive with man? "Ephraim is joined to his idols; let him alone." This tremendous sentence passed, the case of the impenitent sinner is hopeless, and nothing remains but a fearful looking for of judgment and fiery indignation.

Now, admit the possibility that God may leave you to fill up the measure of your iniquity; that he may withdraw from you the awakening and regenerating influence of his Holy Spirit; that he may leave you to your refuges of lies; and how can you neglect religion in this day of your merciful visitation? Hear the compassionate Saviour's lamentation over that devoted city, once the glory of the whole earth, but whose destruction admonishes us to beware lest a promise of entering into rest being left us, any of us should seem to come short of it: "O Jerusalem, Jerusalem! thou that killest the prophets, and stonest them that are sent unto thee; how often would I have gathered thy children together, even as a hen gathereth her chickens under her wings; and ye would not! Behold, your house is left unto you desolate!" The things which belong to your peace are hid from your eyes!

Dear brethren, think not that these are the representations of a disordered imagination. They are the words of truth and soberness; let them sink down into your hearts. Be admonished to give all diligence to make your calling and election sure. "He that hath ears to hear, let him hear what the Spirit saith unto the churches." "Behold, now is the accepted time! Behold, now is the day of salvation!" "Whatsoever thy hand findeth to do, do it with thy might; for there is no knowledge, nor device, nor wisdom, in the grave, whither thou goest."

THE HAPPY MAN.

Blessed is the man that walketh not in the counsel of the ungodly, nor standeth in the way of sinners, nor sitteth in the seat of the scornful.—PSALM i. 1.

THIS Psalm seems to have been designed as a preface to the whole book. Like the sermon on the mount, it begins with a benediction. It establishes a marked distinction between the righteous and the wicked, and sets before us, in striking contrast, the felicity of the one, and the misery and ultimate ruin of the other. The character of the happy man is described, first, negatively. "Blessed," or, as the word signifies, *happy*, "is the man that walketh not in the counsel of the ungodly, nor standeth in the way of sinners, nor sitteth in the seat of the scornful." Here is what may be called the climax of wickedness; beginning in a want of suitable sentiments towards God, and terminating in open contempt for his authority and grace.

By the *ungodly*, in this gradation, we understand those persons who, in the Scripture sense of the phrase, live without God in the world; persons who, though they may be honest and humane in their intercourse with their fellow-men, are, nevertheless,

destitute of evangelical faith and piety. They acknowledge the existence of a God, and a future state of
rewards and punishments. They abhor vice, applaud
virtue, are strenuous advocates, and, in some instances, examples of good morals, so far as the social
duties are concerned. But still they are ungodly.
They favour the cause of morality, not so much from
a regard to the authority and glory of the Creator,
as from a conviction of its salutary influence in promoting the peace of society, and the general happiness of human life. The distinguishing principles of
revealed religion are neither understood nor relished
by them. The Bible account of man's apostasy,
guilt, and dependence on free grace, for his recovery
from the pollution and dominion of sin; the necessity
of regeneration by the Holy Spirit, of faith in the
Lord Jesus Christ, of pardon through the sacrifice of
his blood, and justification by the merit of his righteousness, are doctrines with which they have no
experimental acquaintance, and for which they entertain no serious or reverential regard. Accustomed to
"think more highly of themselves than they ought to
think," they cannot readily give in to the prophet's
declaration, "The heart is deceitful above all things,
and desperately wicked"—nor to the apostle's, "The
carnal mind is enmity against God; for it is not subject to the law of God, neither, indeed, can be."
Self-complacent and wise in their own conceits, they
are strangers to that humility and self-abasement
which the gospel inculcates. Having never been
transformed by the renewing of their mind, they

know nothing of that joy in the Holy Ghost, of that communion with the Father, and with his Son, Jesus Christ, which the sacred Scriptures represent as at once the evidence, the glory, and the privilege of vital godliness. Their views of Divine Providence are vague and inefficient. Regarding it as general, not condescending to individual concerns, they find but little inducement to pray, or acknowledge God in the common events and duties of life. Thus, they live without God: he has no place in their affections. They feed upon his bounty from day to day; but render him no thankful acknowledgments. Their plans, their wishes, and their hopes are all worldly, selfish, and contracted. In short, they are the ungodly, who, "through the pride of their hearts, will not seek after God."

It is easy to see that the counsel or advice which such persons might give on religious subjects would not accord with the dictates of Scripture. However plausible, philosophic, and seemingly rational, its direct tendency would be to flatter the native vanity of our hearts, and keep us from the Saviour, under the delusive idea that we stand in no need of his salvation. "Blessed is the man that walketh not in the counsel of the ungodly." He who would keep himself unspotted from the world, and obtain an interest in the Christian plan of redemption; he who would wish to experience the renovating grace of the gospel, and secure a part in the inheritance of the saints in light, had need to beware of the "wise, the scribe, and the disputer of this world." "The wisdom of the world is foolishness with God." "Godliness is profitable unto all things; having promise of the life that now is, and of that which is to come." "The Lord hath set apart him that is godly for himself"—"but the way of the ungodly shall perish"!

"Nor standeth in the way of sinners." Here is the second step in the downward road of sin. By *sinners*, in this connection, we understand the openly vicious, in contradistinction to the mere moralist, who, though destitute of saving grace, is often a useful member of society. The *way* of sinners means their practice, and to stand in their way, is to join them in their fleshly indulgences and evil deeds. Happy the man that shuns their company, and loiters not in the place of their concourse! Vice, however commonly practised, has few advocates. Its influence is so palpably destructive of the peace, happiness, and dignity of mankind, as well in their individual capacity, as in their social state, that no person of common sense will venture deliberately to vindicate the way of sinners. But alas! what numbers there are who connive at it, and occasionally, at least, partake of its forbidden fruits and fancied pleasures! This is matter of deepest regret to the friends of piety and good morals. Solitary wickedness must, necessarily, be limited in its pernicious effects. Public sentiment, decidedly and strongly expressed, would soon drive it back to its lurking-places, where, deprived of nutriment, it must pine away and die. But if we stand in the way of sinners—if we associate with them now and then, though with no intention of continuing in

17*

their society, we thereby give them countenance; we practically say to them, "Your way is good, and safe enough; we should have no objections to going all lengths with you, did our circumstances permit." Is not this to bid the wicked God-speed? Do we not thus become partakers of their sins, and accessory to their ruin?

There is an abominable sentiment, which passes by far too current even with men who are not remarkably deficient in their moral deportment. It is this: "Some bad practices, or sinful indulgences, may be encouraged, or, at least, connived at, with a view to *prevent greater evils.*" Here are certain sins, prohibited indeed by laws both human and Divine, but they must be spared, lest when removed something worse may occupy their place. This is one of the devil's most ingenious maxims. It is a maxim that operates immeasurable mischief. It contains an apology for whatever vice happens, for the time being, to be fashionable and prevalent. It contributes largely to perpetuate and screen several sins of a scarlet colour and crimson hue; sins punishable by the laws of the land, and which, therefore, if permitted to pass unpunished, become the sins of the land, and provoke the just judgments of Heaven. Christian morality knows nothing about sparing one class of sins for the sake of keeping out others. It knows no necessary moral evils which it does not propose to remedy. St. Paul's charge is, "Have no fellowship with the unfruitful works of darkness, but rather reprove them."

But he who stands in the way of sinners not only encourages them in their evil deeds, but places himself voluntarily under a course of training for the seat of the scornful. That "evil communications corrupt good manners," is an article of inspired truth, confirmed by the experience of ages. Society produces a similarity of manners, with much the same certainty and uniformity, that consanguinity does a family likeness in the size, complexion, and features of the body. It is on this principle that Solomon declares, "A companion of fools shall be destroyed." Voluntary association supposes a congeniality of disposition; and all men have naturally a sinful propensity, which only wants occasion and a little excitement to call it forth into action. Should it be asked here, whether we may not become Christians by imitating the pious, and frequenting their company, we answer, no: because in this case their exists no congeniality of disposition. "That which is born of the flesh is flesh, and that which is born of the Spirit is Spirit." There is, indeed, a form of godliness, which may be assumed or acquired by imitation; but the power, the transforming, the sanctifying, the elevating power of true religion, is of supernatural origin. The new man in Christ is not self-created. "By grace are ye saved, through faith; and that not of yourselves: it is the gift of God." Good men, however, possessing in common a gracious principle, though in unequal degrees, may derive great benefit from associating. "Iron sharpeneth iron; so a man sharpeneth the countenance of his friend." Prov. xxvii. 17.

Brethren of the same family, dwelling together in unity, may be greatly helpful to each other. They may exhort, comfort, encourage, and provoke one another to love and good works. The social principle is the same in the wicked; but it operates in a different direction. The use which they make of it, is to banish the fear of God, and stifle the voice of conscience. Their aim is to keep each other in countenance, while fulfilling the lusts of the flesh. "Come," say they, "let us eat, and drink, and be merry; let us deck ourselves with rose-buds, ere they be withered; let us indulge every passion, and give care and thoughtfulness to the wind."

To the human heart, already predisposed to every moral malady, such language is generally irresistible. And many, very many have been lured on, by promises of liberty and pleasure, to their utter and everlasting undoing. In fact, my hearers, the only safe maxim in regard to criminal association is, "Touch not, taste not, handle not." "The way of sinners" is down hill. If you associate with the profane, you will soon adopt their dialect; if you hang around the gambling table, you will soon be a gambler; if you visit the dram shop, you cherish an appetite that will issue in drunkenness; one violation of the Sabbath paves the way for another, and another still more flagrant; if you frequent the theatre, and acquire a relish for its entertainments, you will soon disrelish the exercises of God's house; for they are contrary the one to the other. Let all, then, but especially the young and inexperienced adventurer into life, listen with reverence to the monitory dictates of heavenly wisdom: "My son, if sinners entice thee, consent thou not; walk not thou in the way with them; refrain thy foot from their path; for their feet run to evil, and make haste to shed blood. Shun the house of the strange woman; it is the antechamber of hell; it inclineth unto death; none that go unto her return again; neither take they hold of the paths of life." Prov. i. and ii. "Blessed is the man who standeth not in the way of sinners."

"Nor sitteth in the seat of the scornful." The *scornful* are those monsters in the moral world who set their face against the heavens, and treat with contempt and levity the awful realities of religion and eternity; and to sit in their seat, is to join them in their low and blasphemous ribaldry. This is the last, the lowest, and the most hopeless stage of human infamy and folly. Few, one would fondly hope, adventure, in this enlightened age, to scoff at the well-authenticated and long-tried truths of the Christian faith. The being and providence of God are so clearly apparent, in the visible creation, and in the great events of the present age, that none but a fool would be guilty of saying in his heart, "There is no God." And the truth of Christianity is attested by such a cloud of witnesses, and strikes the candid mind with so much force of evidence, that professed unbelief seems to have no rational ground to stand on. We are forewarned, however, that there should be "scoffers in the last days, walking after their own lusts." 2 Pet. iii. 3.

It is pleasing to observe that infidelity has no individual subsistence given it in the system of prophecy. "It is not a beast; but a mere putrid excrescence, which, though it may diffuse death through every vein of the body over which it grows, yet shall die along with it." Its enormities effect its own overthrow. Indeed, it is impossible that a system which wages war with the good sense, the order, the refinement, the charity and civilization of the world, should long escape the execration and contempt of all honest and discerning men. "It is, in no shape, formed for perpetuity," says a learned and pious writer, (Hall;) "sudden in its rise and impetuous in its progress, it resembles a mountain torrent, which is loud, filthy, and desolating; but being fed by no perennial spring, is soon drained off, and disappears. We flatter ourselves, its day is near a close; and that it will never again assume the attitude of an assailant. That religious and generous influence which now pervades every section of the habitable globe, which is sending the heralds of the cross to and fro; which is giving the lively oracles of revealed truth to all nations in their own tongues, reminds us of the angel in the Apocalypse, 'flying through the midst of heaven, having the everlasting gospel to preach to them that dwell on the earth, and to every nation, and kindred, and tongue, and people; saying with a loud voice, Fear God, and give glory to him; for the hour of his judgment is come; worship him that made heaven and earth, and the sea, and the fountains of waters.'"

To embrace the principles of infidelity, and become scoffers of Divine things, is to sacrifice our peace of mind and hope of immortality to the dreams of a distempered brain; it is to throw away the refined pleasures of devotion and the ineffable comforts of faith in a risen Saviour, for the sordid gratification of appetites and passions, at once debasing to all that is noble, and destructive to whatever is cheering in the character and prospects of man. The man who rejects and scoffs at the gospel of Jesus Christ, forsakes his own mercies, and seals his own ruin. He scorns that scheme of redeeming grace, which the Scriptures reveal, without pretending to have discovered any other way of pardon and acceptance with God. He aims, with a sort of wanton inhumanity, to extinguish the light of the Sun of Righteousness graciously vouchsafed to guide us to heaven. He spurns and strikes from his lips the only cup of consolation put into the hand of fallen man, to soothe the broken spirit amid that flood of sorrow and wretchedness with which sin has deluged our guilty world. He discredits the testimony of the only wise God, corroborated by a thousand undeniable facts; he tramples on the blood of atonement; challenges the wrath of heaven; turns away from Him who has the words of eternal life, and resolves to die in his sins, cherishing the delusive, damning hope, that death is an eternal sleep. Verily, "This is the condemnation, that light hath come into the world, but men love darkness rather than light, because their deeds are evil."

As you would escape this fearful condemnation,

embrace the truth, as it is in Jesus. "He is the way, the truth, and the life." Neither is there salvation in any other. His gospel sets before you the only good hope. Lay hold of it. His cross is the tree of life; his blood cleanseth from all sin; and his righteousness is unto and upon all them that believe. O taste and see that the Lord is gracious. Blessed are all they that put their trust in him!

We may infer from this subject, the importance of a speedy and unreserved devotion of our hearts to the Lord. Evil men wax worse and worse. The moral malady of our nature becomes more and more inveterate and alarming, till its power is broken by the regenerating grace of the gospel. He who walks in the counsel of the ungodly, walks in the direct and downward road to the seat of the scornful. Believe it, till you embrace the Redeemer by a true faith and devote yourselves to his service, you recede from the path of life, and forsake your own mercies. Multitudes of mankind become confirmed infidels through negligence, and stupid inattention to the high claims and impressive calls of the gospel. They indulge their dreams of a more convenient season to become religious; they tamper with the remonstrances of conscience; listen to the maxims of the ungodly, and linger about the haunts of sinners, till the long insulted Spirit of grace leaves them to fill up the measure of their iniquity; and then is brought to pass the saying that is written, "Ephraim is joined to his idols; let him alone!"

THE GOOD OLD WAY.

Thus saith the Lord: Stand ye in the ways and see, and ask for the
old paths, where is the good way, and walk therein, and ye shall
find rest for your souls.—JEREMIAH vi. 16.

MANKIND are very apt to be captivated with new
things, or ingenious discoveries. Indeed, the love of
novelty is a constituent principle of the human mind;
and, while restricted to its proper province, it is not
only innocent, but useful. It prompts to industrious
enterprise, and prevents that morbid and inglorious
listlessness which makes man a burden to himself and
a nuisance to society. It has also the effect of reconciling us, in some degree, to the vicissitudes of life by
the hope which it inspires, that, in every change of
circumstances, there will be something pleasant, because there will be something new. But this passion,
like every other, when indulged beyond its legitimate
extent, produces serious evils. It, not unfrequently,
makes people discontented with the situation in which
Providence has placed them, creates a hankering
after new occupations, prompts to hazardous experi-
ments, overlooks the common bounties of Heaven,
18

and often produces a disrelish for the sober and daily duties of our station. On the subject of religion, the indulgence of a passion for novelty is attended with extreme danger. God's method of saving sinners is the same now as it ever has been, and ever will be. As in his nature, so in his plans and purposes "there is no variableness nor shadow of turning." But God's way of salvation is humbling to the pride of our hearts. It lays man in the dust before it raises him to glory. It cuts up, by the root, our self-will and self-dependence, stops the mouth of boasting, and puts the crown on the head of the Redeemer. To human vanity this is unacceptable and repulsive; hence men are perpetually striking out new inventions, eager to find some scheme of religion which will better accord with their natural propensities, prejudices, and habits. Hence that guilty and hopeless class of men, characterized by an apostle as "ever learning, but never able to come to the knowledge of the truth." 2 Tim. iii. 7. This evil disease had deeply infected the tribes of Israel in the days of Jeremiah. The Holy Land, at this time, swarmed with teachers, self-commissioned prophets, who "prophesied by Baal, and walked after things of no profit," a sort of spiritual quacks, who healed the hurt of the daughter of God's people slightly; saying, Peace, peace, when there was no peace. Their doctrines were new; they were innovators on the established rites of worship, setters-forth of strange gods. The people, seduced by the charms of novelty, embraced their doctrines, and walked in their ways.

The consequences were shame and inquietude, corruption of manners and idolatry. To remedy these evils, the Lord, by the mouth of his prophet, addressed to them the advice in our text. It is couched in figurative language, taken, probably from the conduct of a wise and prudent traveller, who, anxious to make progress, and avoid the painful toil of retracing his mistaken steps, inquires carefully for the right way: "Stand ye in the ways and see, and ask for the old paths, where is the good way, and walk therein, and ye shall find rest for your souls."

The passage presents us with several interesting and important ideas. It teaches,

First, that there is a good and safe way to heaven.

Secondly, that it is an old way, and that, as we would find it, we should apply to those sources of information that have been proved to be faithful and authentic by travellers who have gone before us.

Thirdly, that having once ascertained the right way, we should walk in it; and, to encourage our diligence in so doing, a promise is added of "rest for souls." A brief and practical illustration of these points, is all that we propose in this discourse.

First, there is a good and safe way to heaven and eternal glory. This consoling truth might be fairly deduced from the fact, that our race was not consigned to ruin immediately on our apostasy from God. The rebel angels were cast down from the heights of heaven, and reserved in chains to the judgment of the great day. They were allowed no respite, so far as we know, because no redemption was designed for them. But man is spared; the race is continued; one generation passeth away, and another cometh. Why this forbearance? Why this opportunity for the propagation of evil, if the Creator did not intend to repair the ruins of the fall; if he did not mean to provide and reveal a way in which we might be saved and regain his blissful favour? He waits, not to aggravate our guilt, but to be gracious. Accordingly mankind, though conscious of sin, and subject to sore tribulation, are, nevertheless, subjects of hope. All are eager in the pursuit of happiness. Even the libertine, who believes in no future state, whose heaven lies within the contracted limits of this short life, and whose maxim is, "Let us eat, and drink, and be merry, for to morrow we die," has frequent misgivings of mind and twinges of conscience. "The fool hath said in his heart, There is no God." It is not his deliberate belief and sober conviction, but the wish of his heart; he tries to hope there is none, because he fears to meet him in judgment. So the man of flesh, and the slave of sensual appetite, is sometimes agitated by emotions which tell him he has a soul, and that it is destined for other worlds, and capable of far other pleasures than those which are common to man and beast.

But all who have not advanced so far in the career of practical impiety as to make it their interest that there should be no hereafter, do long for immortality, and for a happiness that shall endure through eternal ages. This sentiment is so prevalent, that it may be regarded as one of the distinguishing characteristics of man. These things afford strong presumptive evidence, that our existence does not terminate with the dissolution of the body. But whatever darkness rested on the subject previous to the Christian revelation, the New Testament puts it beyond a doubt. Life and immortality have been brought to light through the gospel; and as there is a future life, the strong and unconquerable desire which every human being feels for happiness, indicates that there is some way in which he may attain to such a kind and degree of felicity as suits his immortal nature. For satisfactory evidence that God provided such a way, we are wholly indebted to the sacred oracles. Let us then inquire for this way, and endeavour to ascertain where and what it is.

Second, this is the main duty enjoined in our text. "Stand ye in the ways, and see, and ask for the old paths, where is the good way." We are not to proceed heedlessly along the journey of life. We are to ponder our path, and consider well whither it will conduct us. Like a wise traveller, we are at the outset to stand, to contemplate results, and to ask; lest we waste our time, exhaust our strength, and miss our aim. Ways and paths being mentioned here in the plural number, do not warrant us to believe that there are more ways than one to heaven. There is one good way specified. For this we are to inquire. "It is an high way," says the prophet, "and it shall be called the way of holiness; the unclean shall not pass over it, but the redeemed shall walk there;" and it is so plain, "that wayfaring men, though fools,

18*

shall not err therein." Isa. xxxv. 8. Most of you
have, no doubt, observed winding by-paths in the
neighbourhood of some public roads, and which lead
the traveller, though through some inconveniences,
to the same place, as would the high-way by a safer
and more direct route. These paths in the bush,
stretching along now at a less and then at a greater
distance from the main road, may help us to distinguish between the good way and those other ways
and paths mentioned in our text. The example of
good men seems to be alluded to. But the best of
men are not perfect in this world. Even the patriarchs and prophets, whose names are recorded on the
sacred pages, and whose faith and predominant spirit
we are called upon to imitate, did not walk uniformly
in "the way of holiness." Their paths, however, lay
not very remotely from the good way, and they may
be of great use to those who are desirous of finding
it. As you would find the good way to heaven and
eternal glory, observe the old paths, and consult the
old travellers who have passed the wilderness before
you. Antiquity, other things being equal, is fairly
entitled to our reverence and respect. Modern refine-
ments, and ingenious novelties, should be admitted
with great caution. There is often in them more of
the curious, than of the useful; more of the pride of
learning, than of the sobriety of wisdom; more of the
glare of philosophy, falsely so called, than of that
fear of the Lord which is the beginning of knowledge.

If you wish to know how you should conduct
in the various stations and changing scenes of life,

look at those pious men of whom the world was not worthy. Go forth by the footsteps of the flock, and be followers of them who, through faith and patience inherit the promises. See Enoch; "he walked with God; and he was not; for God took him." See Noah, a preacher of righteousness, who, admonished of God, prepared an ark to the saving of his house; and who, on becoming the father of the new world, embraced the first opportunity of presenting his thanksgiving to the great Author and Preserver of life. See Abraham, quitting his country and kindred at the command of God. His route was marked with altars, and sacred memorials of the Divine munificence and mercy. See Joseph holding fast his integrity in the midst of corruption, flattery, and splendor. See Moses, preferring the society and afflictions of the people of God, to all the luxuries and honours of Pharaoh's court. See David, the beloved king, amid the cares of royalty, delighting in the devotional exercises of the sanctuary, esteeming "the statutes of the Lord more than gold, yea, than much fine gold; sweeter, also, than honey and the honeycomb." But why need we increase the catalogue? These, and a cloud of other witnesses for the truth, "all died in faith, not having received the promises, but having seen them afar off, and were persuaded of them, and embraced them, and confessed that they were strangers and pilgrims on the earth." These all walked in the old paths of righteousness, faith, and piety, "desiring a better country, that is, an heavenly; wherefore God is not ashamed to be called

their God; for he hath prepared for them a city."
Heb. xi. 13—16.

But what is that "good way" by which sinful men
are conducted to the holy city of the living God?
Take an answer to this question from the New Testament: "Thomas saith unto him, Lord, we know not
whither thou goest; and how can we know the way?
Jesus saith unto him, I am the way, and the truth,
and the life: no man cometh unto the Father, but by
me." John xiv. 5, 6. When man became a sinner, he
was expelled from the garden of Eden, the emblem of
heaven; and a flaming sword, which turned every
way, was placed at its entrance, to keep the way of
the tree of life. That delightful communion with his
Maker, to which he had been accustomed, in a state
of innocence, was interrupted, and he was driven
forth, a wretched outcast from the presence of the
Lord. And had he been abandoned in this fallen
state, his case must have been for ever hopeless. He
had violated the covenant, and subjected himself to
the penalty of the law. Acceptance, on the ground
of his own obedience, now became impossible. God
is holy; and holiness can have no fellowship with sin.
To effect a reconciliation, to satisfy the rightful claims
of justice, and open a way whereby the rebel might be
restored to his allegiance, his duty, and his happiness,
the Lord Jesus Christ assumed the office of Mediator;
and in this character he is "the way, the truth, and
the life;"—"the way" to heaven, by the sacrifice of
his blood, by the purity of his doctrine, the energy of
his Spirit, and the attractive influence of his high and

holy example;—"the truth," or substance and end of the typical system of things, persons, and offerings, as well as the completion of prophesy, and the end of the law;—"the life"—the restorer and supporter of spiritual communion with the Father of spirits, the true bread which came down from heaven, to give life unto the world. This doctrine pervades the Bible, and is to be found, either directly or indirectly, on almost all its hallowed pages. "Other foundation can no man lay," says Paul, "than that is laid, which is Jesus Christ." 1 Cor. iii. 11. "This is the stone," says Peter, addressing the Jewish rulers, "which was set at nought of you builders, which is become the head of the corner. Neither is there salvation in any other; for there is none other name under heaven, given among men, whereby we must be saved." Acts iv. 11, 12.

It is needless to multiply quotations. The merits and mediation of Jesus Christ is, unquestionably, according to the Scriptures, the way in which God justifies and saves sinners of the human race. To him give all the prophets witness; to him the patriarchal and Mosaic rites and ceremonies point, as to one common centre. "This is the good way;" a way marked and consecrated by redeeming blood. It is an old and well-tried way; it has been travelled by thousands of thousands, ever since the apostacy of man. It is a way of holiness; the unclean shall not pass over it. But it is a highway—the highway to glory, honour, and immortality, provided by the great King of heaven and earth; and all his rebellious subjects may travel in it freely, who are disposed to return to their rightful Sovereign, and are anxious to regain his propitious smiles and paternal guardianship.

Thus we have arrived at the third particular in our text: "Walk therein." To walk in Christ, implies,

1. An unqualified reliance on him, and an entire confidence in him, as the Lord our righteousness and strength. This reliance and confidence in him we are warranted to exercise, by the testimony of God's word, and by the experience of his people in all ages of the world—Jesus Christ, "the same yesterday, to-day, and for ever." He is the Saviour of all men, especially of them that believe. He was the hope, the strength, the joy of the patriarchs, the prophets, and the apostles. In him the blessed martyrs walked, and walked safe and happy, even while their bodies were wrapped in flames, or torn in pieces by ferocious beasts of prey. And in him may you trust, with the most perfect and undivided confidence. He is the Messenger and Mediator of the covenant—the King of Zion, the Redeemer of Israel, and the hope of the Gentiles; the root and the offspring of David, the bright and morning star; the Prince and Saviour, exalted to the third heavens, to give repentance and remission of sins. In one word, he has all power in heaven and on earth; and he is able to save to the uttermost all that come to God by him.

2. We are to walk in this "good way" by faith. That faith, which is the substance of things hoped for, and the evidence of things not seen, is the divinely con-

stituted medium through which you are to draw, from the Redeemer's fulness, all needful grace, strength, and comfort, in your journey to the skies. You remember how closely his little family of disciples adhered to his person during his visible continuance on earth. How often and how kindly he quieted their fears, solved their doubts, and cheered their hearts by the gracious benediction, "Peace be unto you." By faith you may enjoy the same benefits. "Where two or three are gathered together in my name, there am I in the midst of them." These are his own words. Let them be engraven on your hearts; and let the truth which they convey, induce those who fear the Lord, and think upon his name, to speak often one to another, and pour forth, at the throne of grace, their joint supplications, with thanksgiving. And when, in your individual capacity, you are struggling against the enemies of your salvation, remember he is a Friend near at hand, and mighty to save. And what he once said to Paul, by a voice from heaven, he says to you, from the volume of inspiration: "My grace is sufficient for thee—my strength is made perfect in weakness." Let the lives which you now live in the flesh, be by the faith of the Son of God.

3. "Walk in this good way," by an open profession of your dependence on Christ, and a conscientious and affectionate attendance on all the ordinances which he has appointed for your spiritual nourishment and growth in grace. Seek no by-paths; take the highway, the way of holy obedience; congregate with the

little flock, and feed in their pastures. Why, in the name of Heaven! should any one, whose entire hope is in the Rock of Ages, be ashamed to acknowledge the truth before men? To be ashamed of Him who died for us; who ever liveth to intercede for us: of him whom angels delight to honour; of him who holds the keys of heaven and hell; who is to decide our destinies in the day of judgment—is the folly and reproach of our nature! Many of you have acted thus, alas! too long. Do no more so wickedly. The time is short; life and privileges are precarious. "Whatsoever thy hand findeth to do, do it with thy might." Walk in the good way, by filial confidence, faith, and affectionate obedience; and the promise is sure and unequivocal.

4. "Ye shall find rest for your souls." The Saviour has interpreted this promise, and has applied it in a manner which precludes all doubtful disputation: "Come unto me all ye that labour and are heavy laden, and I will give you rest." Who will accept this gracious invitation? It is given in view of our restless and unhappy condition as sinners. It is given as much in truth and earnestness as if the incarnate Son of God were standing visibly before you. Who, then, will accept it? The Saviour and Judge of the world asks you, through lips of clay. What say you, awakened souls, who begin to feel weary and heavy laden with the burden of your sin? Why will you not come to Jesus, and repose your weary head on the bosom of infinite power, and all-sufficient grace? Here is an open fountain, the true

Bethesda, in which you may wash and be clean. Here is a munition of rocks, where you may take shelter from the flaming sword of incensed and inflexible justice. "Christ is the end of the law for righteousness to every one that believeth, and his blood cleanseth from all sin."

What say ye, amiable worldlings, who are trying to keep ignorant of the malady of your nature, by a perpetual round of business and pleasure? I know you have not found that kind of rest which suits the vast desires of your immortal souls. And try as you may to keep far from you the thought of death and judgment, yet a little while, and you will die: your sources of earthly happiness will fail you. Suppose the king of terrors should find you uninterested in redeeming mercy. How will you dare to send your spirit from this gospel land, back to God who gave it, in all its unpardoned sin and moral defilement? How will you feel, when about to enter the lonely grave, unconscious of an interest in Him who is the resurrection and the life? Will you not be greatly solicitous to know what is to become of you, upon quitting this transient world of sense? Yes, you will, if you be not deprived of reason, or cursed with a scared conscience. Would it not be desirable, to be able to say, with Paul the apostle, "I know whom I have believed"? "For me to live is Christ, and to die is gain"? Come to Jesus, then, that you may find rest to your souls. You may make out to dispense with his holy supports, during the short term of your prosperity; but remember the days of darkness, for

19

they shall be many. If you live in impenitence and sin, you will probably die so; and if you die Christ-less, you will be "cast into outer darkness; there shall be weeping and gnashing of teeth."

What say you, my young friends? You are going abroad, on life's troubled ocean. You need a Divine guide. Your minds are full of schemes for worldly honours, pleasures, and distinctions. But, know that the world is a mocker. If you want a friend who will stand by you in all the exigencies of life and death, come to Christ. He only can give you genuine rest; and *now* is the best time to accept his kind offer. To-morrow may be too late!

THE GLORY AND MAJESTY OF GOD.

I saw also the Lord sitting upon a throne, high and lifted up, and his train filled the temple. Above it stood the seraphims: each ono had six wings; with twain he covered his face, and with twain he covered his feet, and with twain he did fly. And ono cried unto another, and said, Holy, holy, holy, is the Lord of hosts: the whole earth is full of his glory. And the posts of the door moved at the voice of him that cried, and the house was filled with smoke. Then said I, Wo is me! for I am undone; because I am a man of uncleau lips, and I dwell in the midst of a people of uncleau lips: for mine eyes have seen the King, the Lord of hosts. Then flew one of the seraphims unto me, having a live coal in his hand, which he had taken with the tongs from off the altar: and he laid it upon my mouth, and said, Lo, this hath touched thy lips; and thine iniquity is taken away, and thy sin purged.—ISAIAH vi. 1—7.

WE have here a most sublime and impressive representation of the glory and majesty of the God we worship. The whole is a vision, or symbolical exhibition. This was one of the modes in which God was wont formerly to reveal himself, and make known his will to men. The immediate design of this vision seems to have been to animate the prophet with zeal and faithfulness in discharging the arduous duties of his office. The effect which it had upon him is very observable in his readiness to bear that tremendous message of Jehovah to a guilty people, recorded in the ninth and tenth verses of the chapter before us. He hears the voice of the Lord inquiring for a messenger: "Whom shall I send; and who will go for us?" With promptitude and pious firmness he replies, "Here am I, send me." The passage is instructive, and will afford us matter for several devout and useful reflections.

"I saw the Lord," says the prophet, "sitting upon a throne, high and lifted up, and his train filled the temple." This august view of the Divine glory was exhibited in the temple—that holy place in which God delights to meet with his people; where he is used to instruct inquirers and comfort mourners with the consolations of his grace. This appearance, like all others of the Diving Being, in human form, was in the person of Immanuel, God-with-us, the second person in the adorable Trinity. The Evangelist John, in the twelfth chapter of his gospel, alludes to this vision of the prophet, and says, expressly, "These things said Isaias when he saw the glory of Christ and spake of him." Verse 41. "No man hath seen God at any time," i. e., as an absolute God; "the only begotten Son, he hath declared him." "It was the unanimous sense of the ancient church," says Bishop South, "that all the Divine appearances in the Old Testament were made by the Son of God, by whom all the affairs of the church were ordered from the beginning." It was the Divine Saviour, then, that Isaiah calls Lord, or Jehovah. It was Jesus that the prophet saw, in mystic vision, "sitting upon a

throne, high and lifted up;" Jesus whom the prophet
Daniel saw, on another occasion, and describes as the
ancient of days, "whose garment was white as snow,
and the hair of his head like the pure wool. A fiery
stream issued and came forth from before him; thousand thousands ministered unto him; and ten thousand times ten thousand stood before him." Dan. vii.
9, 10. What an exalted idea do these prophetic
visions afford us of the Lord Jesus! By him the prophets were inspired, his messages they delivered to
the world, and of his person, offices, and kingdom, they
spake in strains of holy rapture. Isaiah here saw
him "sitting upon a throne, high and lifted up;"
striking emblem of that throne, on which, at the
great day, he will judge the quick and the dead;
when every eye shall see him, and they who pierced,
and they who despise him, will be covered with shame
and overwhelmed with terror.

"And above it," *i. e.*, above and round about the
throne on which Jehovah sat, "stood the seraphim."
These are believed to be the first and most glorious
order of angelic spirits. They are called seraphim,
i. e., fiery beings, probably in allusion to the purity of
their nature, and the power and rapidity with which
they execute the commands of the Almighty. They
stand before . him, ever ready to do his pleasure.
More than twelve legions of these flaming ministers
would have flown to the relief of the Saviour, when
betrayed into the hands of sinners, had he but given
command. But he neither needed nor wished their
assistance, on that occasion, for he had power to lay

19*

down his life, and he had power to take it again. These glorious beings are furnished each with six wings. "With twain," says the prophet, "he covered his face." So resplendent is the glory of God, so pure his nature, and so august his majesty, that even the spotless seraphim in heaven dare not approach him but with veiled faces, in token of profoundest humility. From hence let us sinful mortals, who dwell in houses of clay, encompassed with infirmity, learn to draw near the mercy-seat of our God, in his earthly courts, with the deepest self-abasement, encouraged by the intercession and covered with the righteousness of Him who is our shield and our hope.

"And with twain he covered his feet." This seems to have been intended as a mark of reverence due to the infinite majesty of heaven and earth. And unquestionably every species of levity and indecorum is unseemly and criminal in the presence of God. Let it be remembered, then, that God is specially present and jealous of his honour, in houses and places consecrated to his solemn worship. Let the sentiments of the holy patriarch be deeply impressed on your minds whenever you enter these hallowed courts of the Lord's house: "Surely God is in this place, and I knew it not; for this is none other than the house of God, and the gate of heaven." "The Lord will be had in reverence of all them that are round about him." In this temple he sits upon his throne of mercy and grace, high and lifted up; his train fills the house, and his eye observes every attendant—nor thought, nor secret purpose escapes his notice. He marks with infinite abhorrence the hypocrite, the caviller, the careless, and the contemptuous sleeper. If you would be benefitted by your attendance, or accepted in your sanctuary services, lay aside the defilement contracted by your contact with the world; put off, as concerning the former conversation, the old man and his deeds; cover your feet in renunciation of your own works; wash you; make you clean in the blood of sprinkling; for the place whereon you stand is holy ground; drive out the buyers and sellers; clear your hearts of all earthly cares and impure desires; this house is the house of prayer. When you enter it, therefore, salute him that dwelleth therein, by devout ejaculation, and address yourselves with attention and seriousness to his service. It is the presence-chamber of the King of kings and Lord of lords. Here your Maker speaks to you in the sweet accents of grace, and permits you to speak to him with the voice of prayer and praise. "Jehovah is in his holy temple, let all the earth keep silence before him."

"And with twain he did fly." This intimates to us the prompt alacrity with which these exalted spirits obey the orders and perform the will of their Almighty Creator. They glory in acting as the ministering servants of the Most High. His service is their freedom and their delight. Those who revolted from the rightful authority of their Maker, fell in the vain attempt to become independent, and shake off their allegiance to the Sovereign of the universe. To be safe and happy, all intelligent creatures, angels as well as men, must be subject to the control and obedient to the commands of their Creator. Those angelic spirits which kept their first estate kept it by obedience, and they are represented as standing before the throne of Jehovah, ready to fly at his command to all parts of his immense dominion. Let us go, and do likewise. We, too, are the servants of God: if we refuse obedience, we prove ourselves rebels, and shall certainly fall under sentence of eternal condemnation. He has made known to us his will in the Holy Scriptures; we are to fulfil his commandment by hearkening to the voice of his word. In imitation of the seraphim, let our obedience be universal, prompt, and cordial. The law of our duty is made so plain in the New Testament that he who runs may read. "Christ is the end of the law for righteousness to every one that believeth; we have redemption through his blood; neither is there salvation in any other." This is the message which he now delivers to you from the oracles of truth. Receive the good tidings thankfully; lay hold of the hope set before you. Receive the atonement; accept the righteousness which is received by faith in the Son of God. Why should any refuse to obey and be blessed? Why turn a deaf ear to the voice of mercy, which cries, "Turn ye, turn ye, for why will ye die?" To believe in Him who came to seek and to save that which was lost, is to do the work which God requires, and secure the good part that shall never be taken from us. Set your hearts to this work. "It is not a vain thing, because it is your life."

"And one cried unto another, and said, Holy, holy,

holy, is the Lord of hosts; the whole earth is full of his glory." Observe the delightful employment of these happy spirits. They are so filled with a sense of the Divine glory that they cannot refrain from pouring themselves forth in strains of the highest praise. This threefold repetition of the epithet Holy, is considered by most commentators, and, I think, justly, as containing an allusion to the three persons in the Godhead. Angels admire the work of man's redemption. They admire the holiness of the eternal Father in requiring satisfaction to injured justice; the holiness of the incarnate Son in redeeming his people from their sins, at the expense of his own blood; the holiness of the Spirit in creating them anew in Christ Jesus unto good works, and fitting them, by sanctification, for the holy employments of a holy heaven.

"Lord of hosts." This is one of the distinguishing titles of the Divine Being. It is emphatically expressive of his authority over, and right to 'the homage of all creatures in heaven and earth. Angels form a part of his hosts. They are all ministering spirits; all employed at his pleasure on errands either of vengeance or of mercy. The stars, and all the celestial orbs, make another part of God's hosts. "He bringeth out their host by number," says the prophet; "he calleth them all by their names; through the greatness of his might and the strength of his power, not one of them faileth." Isaiah xl. 26. All the powers of nature, all the phenomena of this lower world, may be regarded as the servants of the Lord of hosts. The hearts of princes and people, of good men and bad men, are under his control, and subject to his power, when he sees fit to exert it. He maketh the wrath of man to praise him, and the remainder of wrath he restrains. Hell trembles, and heaven rejoices at his matchless power. Let sinners know assuredly, it is a fearful thing to fall into the hands of this holy Lord of hosts. And let saints below join saints and angels above, saying, "Thy kingdom come," till the whole earth shall be filled with his glory.

"And the posts of the door moved at the voice of him that cried, and the house was filled with smoke." What an affecting display of Divine power! At every response of the seraphim the pillars of the temple were shaken, and at length the holy place was filled with smoke. This part of the vision seems to have been designed to impress on the prophet's mind an awful sense of the majesty and glory of God; that, in the comparison, he might see his own vileness, and inefficiency, without Divine assistance, for the work in which he was engaged: at any rate, the whole representation had a powerful effect upon him. We find him in the next verse acknowledging his own sinfulness, and that of the people among whom he laboured, in the humblest terms of contrition and self-abasement.

"Then, said I, woe is me! for I am undone; because I am a man of unclean lips, and I dwell in the midst of a people of unclean lips: for mine eyes have seen the King, the Lord of hosts." He had now been contemplating the glory of the Lord; he had listened to the profound adoration of the seraphim; he had seen the posts of the door shaken, and the temple filled with smoke. He was convinced that a God of such spotless purity, transcendent glory and power, ought to be worshipped and served in the beauties of holiness. This conviction, accompanied with a pungent sense of his own deficiency, humbled him in the dust. The case of the prophet is not a singular one. Just views of the character and laws of God invariably produce humility. This is the test by which we may distinguish Divine illumination from that unsanctified knowledge that puffeth up. Job, in the heat of controversy, labouring to repel the charges brought against him by his vexatious friends, was left to make use of some rash and irreverent expressions respecting the dispensations of Providence. But when Jehovah speaks to him from the whirlwind, and reveals his power and glory, Job falls before him in lowly prostration of soul, and we hear him exclaiming, "Behold, I am vile; what shall I answer thee? I will lay my hand upon my mouth. Once have I spoken, but I will not answer; yea, twice, but I will proceed no farther. I have heard of thee by the hearing of the ear; but now mine eye seeth thee: wherefore I abhor myself, and repent in dust and ashes." So, when Peter beheld the power and authority of his Master displayed in the extraordinary draught of fishes, he fell at his feet, and cried out, "Depart from me, for I am a sinful man, O Lord!" So, when any sinner gets a glimpse of the beauty of the Lord, and the purity and spirituality of that law which he has transgressed, and then turns his eye inward upon his own heart, he cannot but cry out, with fear and trembling, "Woe is me, for I am undone!"

Who can view sin in the light of God's word, and not blush and be confounded for having indulged it? Who can view it in the light of the cross of Christ, and not mourn and be in bitterness, as one that mourns for a first-born, or an only son? Hence it is that persons of unimpeachable moral character, under deep and serious impressions, are brought to consider themselves as the chief of sinners, and can hardly be persuaded that there is any hope in their case. Their good lives, which they once reflected on with complacency, are no longer viewed as affording the least ground of dependence. They see that in all things they have offended and come short of the glory of God. Judging their hearts and conduct by the law, and the testimony of God, they are forced to give sentence against themselves. The heart is found to be deceitful above all things, and desperately wicked. Sins are discovered, and evil propensities felt, which words cannot tell. Formerly, the same sins, the same failures, the same evil thoughts, passed unobserved. Now the light of Divine truth shines upon them, they are seen in their genuine deformity, and seem to set themselves in array against the penitent, as if to overwhelm him in utter despair. Thus we hear St. Paul acknowledging, "The law is holy, just, and good; but I am carnal, sold under sin." And again, "I was alive without the law once, but

when the commandment came, sin revived, and I
died." Once he had entertained favourable thoughts
of his moral conduct and religious character; but
when his mind was enlightened to behold the glory
of God, in the face of Jesus Christ, he condemned
himself as the chief of sinners! nay, after all his
attainments, and abundant labours in the cause of
his Lord and Master, he accounts himself less than
the least of all saints. But, humble penitent, while
you view, with dismay and terror, the enormity of
your sin, look by faith to the altar of sacrifice, and
the blood of sprinkling. While the prophet lies
humbled under a sense of his vileness, a seraph is
commissioned to raise him up, and put a new song in
his mouth.

"Then flew one of the seraphims unto me, having a
live coal in his hand, which he had taken with the
tongs from off the altar, and he laid it upon my mouth,
and said, Lo, this hath touched thy lips, and thine
iniquity is taken away, and thy sin purged!" It is
well remarked by a pious commentator, "that, as the
scene of this vision was the temple, the altar of burnt
offering was full in view, on which the daily sacrifices
were consuming by the fire that came down from
heaven. The blood of innocent victims shed in sacrifice, and their bodies consumed to ashes, that guilty
men might be pardoned and blessed, were constant
declarations that sinners deserve to die, and that
deliverance could be obtained only by faith in the
promised Redeemer—'the Lamb slain from the foundation of the world.' From this altar one of the

20

seraphims took a live coal, and applied it to the prophet's lips, assuring him at the same time, that his iniquity was taken away, and his sin purged." A welcome message, indeed, to a sinner sinking under the pressure of his sins. We may observe, here, the way in which gospel relief is administered to the penitent. Not by persuading him that his sins are small, and that God will not require satisfaction: but by leading the soul, laden with guilt, to the fountain opened for sin and defilement. No attempt was made to persuade the prophet that he thought too unfavourably of himself; on the other hand, the seraph seemed to admit that he was, indeed, a man of unclean lips, but assured him that his iniquity was forgiven, and his sin purged, through faith in the Lamb of God.

Let us hence learn to go ourselves, and lead others, under a sense of guilt, directly to the purifying blood of the Redeemer. If we obtain peace from any other quarter, it will prove fallacious. Come, then, awakened and trembling sinner, try the efficacy of the great gospel propitiation. Renounce every other dependence. Confess that you have ruined yourself, and, without Divine help, are utterly undone. Repair to the atoning blood of Christ— cast yourself into the arms of his mercy, believing that he is both able and willing to save all that come to God by him, and you will soon rise above your desponding fears, and obtain a good hope through grace. Behold the Lamb of God, who taketh away the sin of the world! He is the author and the finisher of faith. Believe his word; trust his grace;

lay hold on the skirts of his garment. "Ask, and ye shall receive; seek, and ye shall find; knock, and it shall be opened unto you." While the infinite power and majesty of Jehovah fill your soul with awe and reverence, let his grace and condescension comfort your heart, and secure your confidence. He is the Lord God, merciful and gracious, slow to anger, and of great kindness. There is forgiveness with him, that he may be feared. "Now, then, we are ambassadors for Christ, as though God did beseech you by us, we pray you, in Christ's stead, be ye reconciled to God, for he hath made him to be sin for us, who knew no sin, that we might be made the righteousness of God in him." Amen!

CONVERSION OF SAUL OF TARSUS.

And Saul, yet breathing out threatenings and slaughter against the disciples of the Lord, went unto the high-priest, and desired of him letters to Damascus to the synagogues, that if he found any of this way, whether they were men or women, he might bring them bound unto Jerusalem. And as he journeyed, he came near Damascus: and suddenly there shined round about him a light from heaven: and he fell to the earth, and heard a voice saying unto him, Saul, Saul, why persecutest thou me? And he said, Who art thou, Lord? And the Lord said, I am Jesus whom thou persecutest. It is hard for thee to kick against the pricks. And he trembling, and astonished, said, Lord, what wilt thou have me to do? And the Lord said unto him, Arise, and go into the city, and it shall be told thee what thou must do.—ACTS ix. 1—6.

EVERYTHING in the life of St. Paul is interesting and instructive. He was a person of great natural endowments, highly improved by the advantages of education. He seems to have been formed by nature to take an active and decided part in whatever cause he espoused. Tarsus, a city in the province of Cilicia, was the place of his nativity. His parents, who were Jews, sent him to Jerusalem, probably at an early period of life, that he might enjoy the instructions of Gamaliel, the celebrated Jewish doctor.

Here, by the force of habit, the influence of his tutor, and his connection with the sect of the Pharisees, he contracted a strong attachment to the Mosaic institutions. And as he could not bear to hear of the abolition or insufficiency of the ritual observances, he imbibed with the first rudiments of his education a spirit of inveterate opposition to Christianity. "He verily thought," as he himself expresses it, "that he ought to do many things contrary to the name of Jesus of Nazareth." Accordingly, his first appearance in the sacred story is in the character of a persecutor. When Stephen, the first Christian martyr, was put to death, Saul consented to the murder, and kept the clothes of those who stoned him. After this we are told, "he made havoc of the church, entering into every house, and haling men and women, committed them to prison." He confesses that he imprisoned and beat in every synagogue them that believed. He appears, in short, to have been set upon the total extirpation of the poor afflicted followers of Christ. He went great lengths in this nefarious work, before it pleased God to interpose and show him the madness of his conduct. But he was a chosen vessel. In the eternal counsels of God, it had been determined that he should bear the unsearchable riches of Christ to the Gentiles. His call to the apostleship was long delayed; but at last it is revealed and made effectual.

In the passage of sacred history before us, we see this gross offender, in the height of his destructive career, arrested, humbled, and laid low at the feet

20*

of Jesus. His case, duly considered, will give us occasion to blush for the corruption of human nature; to admire the sovereignty of Divine grace; and acknowledge the salutary effects of this grace upon the converted sinner. After a brief illustration of the several verses which constitute our text, we shall close the discourse with a few practical reflections.

I. "And Saul, yet breathing out threatenings and slaughter against the disciples of the Lord, went unto the high-priest, and desired of him letters to Damascus to the synagogues, that if he found any of this way"—*i. e.*, of the Christian faith and profession—"whether they were men or women, he might bring them bound unto Jerusalem." How furious the rage, how cruel the designs of this enemy of the cross! Such was his bitterness against the Saviour and his followers, that with every breath he poured forth the virulence of his heart in menaces of slaughter and death. One can hardly help asking, What had the disciples of Christ done to excite the hatred of this polished pupil of Gamaliel? The answer is at hand. He was a proud, self-confident sinner, who, ignorant of God's righteousness, went about to establish one of his own. The gospel scheme, if true, proved his expectations to be vain. In order, therefore, to check the progress of a system so humiliating to the pride of a Pharisee, its adherents must be harassed, and, if possible, exterminated from the earth. To accomplish this end, the champion of the Mosaic ritual comes forth in all his vengeance. Not content that his efforts should be confined to Jerusalem and its neighbourhood, he volunteers his services abroad. Learning that some of the disciples of the Lord had found their way to Damascus, the capital of Syria, and were there propagating their tenets, he resolved to pursue them, "even to strange cities." And that nothing may be wanting to give effect to his infamous design, he applies to the high-priest, who acted as president of the Jewish Sanhedrim, for letters to the rulers of the synagogues in Damascus, commanding them to take measures to apprehend all, both men and women, without regard to age or sex, who avowed their attachment to the despised Nazarene, that they might be brought bound to Jerusalem, for condign punishment. The project, no doubt, met the cordial approbation of the high-priest and the grand council of which he was the head.

Saul, we may suppose, was furnished with the desired credentials; and that he might execute his commission with the greater confidence and promptitude, a band of armed soldiers accompanied him. But we pause, and ask, For what is this extraordinary apparatus? Is an enemy approaching? or are they convicted criminals who have escaped from public justice, that are to be pursued? Ah! who would not blush for human nature, on contemplating these preparations, when he considers that they are directed against the mercy and grace of God, displayed to a perishing, guilty world! It is the Gospel, which contains everything that is honourable to God, and precious to the sinner! It is the Gospel, which reveals the only Saviour of fallen man, and the only effica-

cious sacrifice for sin! It is the Gospel, which publishes good tidings of great joy unto all people, that
these combined efforts of Saul and the high-priest,
the Sanhedrim and the soldiers, are intended to arrest
and destroy, to extirpate from the earth.

But how foolish and impotent are the most vigorous exertions, and the best laid schemes of mortals,
when opposed to the counsels of the Almighty! Poor,
trembling disciples, you may dismiss your fears; for
the Captain of your salvation is mighty to save. He
can, in a thousand different ways, disconcert the most
artful plots of your enemies, and effect your deliverance
from the most appalling dangers. Of this consoling
fact you are now called to behold an illustrious veri-
fication.

Saul and his company had come near the place of
their destination, no doubt elated with sanguine hopes
of the success of their mission, when an extraordinary
occurrence completely blasted their expectations and
covered them with shame. "And, as he journeyed,
he came near Damascus; and suddenly there shined
round about him a light from heaven; and he fell to
the earth, and heard a voice saying unto him, Saul,
Saul, why persecutest thou me?"

We do not stop here to notice the various opinions
that have been advanced respecting this light which
dazzled the eyes of the persecutor, and caused him to
fall prostrate on the ground. We would only observe
that as the event took place at noonday, a circum-
stance not noticed here by the historian, but mentioned afterwards by Saul himself, and as an articu-

late voice proceeded from the midst of the light, it is surely absurd to suppose, as some do, that it was merely a flash of lightning. We are astonished, indeed, that it was not lightning, charged with a thunderbolt of death. We wonder that the eyes of this notorious sinner were ever opened again, but to see himself encircled by the flames of Tophet. But he was a chosen vessel, soon to be prepared for the Master's use. Without hesitation, we believe it was a miraculous light, and that it proceeded immediately from the glorified body of Jesus Christ, whose countenance St. John describes by the brightest emblem in the universe, "The sun shining in his strength." But hark! from that effulgent, overwhelming light, there issues a voice; and it is the voice of mercy— "Saul, Saul, why persecutest thou me?" What a penetrating question! Every syllable is emphatic; the energy that accompanies it is omnipotent. It pierces the obdurate heart of the haughty Pharisee, and forces from the flinty rock the waters of penitence. And who is this, that looking from the heavens, sees all that is done upon earth? Who, but the Omniscient Redeemer—the Angel of the Covenant that appeared to Moses, first in the burning bush, and afterwards on Mount Sinai, in the midst of supernatural thunder and lightning? He that speaks from the clouds, and calls the persecutor by name, must be a Divine personage. Of this Saul, himself, seems to have been fully convinced; though it had not yet entered his mind that Jesus of Nazareth was the speaker. Him he had long been accustomed to consider an impostor, had loaded his name with obloquy, and was now endeavouring to rid the world of his deluded disciples. But how must he have been surprised when, to the anxious question, "Who art thou, Lord?" he received for answer, "I am Jesus, whom thou persecutest"! As if the insulted Saviour had said, "I, who appear before thee with such undeniable marks of dignity, am no other than the despised Nazarene against whom thy rage is ultimately aimed; for I consider the insults and oppression inflicted on my faithful disciples as offered to myself." A solemn warning this, to all who reproach the pious, disturb their devotions, or oppose their attention to the ordinances of the gospel.

Christ is touched with a sense of the ill-treatment, as well as with a feeling of the infirmities of his people. The union between him and them is intimate. He is the vine; they are the branches. He is the head; they are the members of his body—the church. Though himself in heaven, far beyond the reach of the destroyer, he is not unmindful of his followers, who are making their way to him through great tribulation. He is their sun and shield—their sun, to enlighten their path, and warm their souls in the dark and stormy day—their shield, to cover them from the shafts of malice, and fend off the fiery darts of the wicked one. Trust in the Lord, therefore, ye righteous, and rejoice in your union with Christ. They are his own words; "Because I live, ye shall live also." Your enemies may prove as thorns in your sides, to try your faith, and make you long for the heavenly rest; but your souls they cannot injure, your crown no one taketh from you. "Your life is hid with Christ, in God." Let those who take counsel together, and set themselves against the Lord and his anointed, know assuredly that their efforts are vain. Their own feet will be taken in the net which they are spreading for others. The blows which they aim at Christ and his cause, like the arrows which the foolish Scythians shot at the sun, will recoil upon their own heads with redoubled violence.

"It is hard for thee to kick against the pricks." This is a proverbial saying, taken from a well-known custom of applying goads to oxen, for the purpose of urging them on to the draught; which, if they resist, they only wound themselves. The case is the same with sinners who oppose the gospel, and resist the means that are used for their conviction and conversion from the paths of the destroyer. The pricks which Saul resisted, were, in general, the testimony of the prophets, the miracles wrought by Christ in proof of his Divine mission, and all the evidences that attended the first introduction of Christianity into the world; but, particularly, the preaching, the admonitions, the patience, the meekness, and dying testimony of St. Stephen. O, how many pricks and goads have gospel-despisers of our own times to resist before they can fill up the measure of their iniquity, and make their way to hell! The religious instructions received in childhood, the alluring example of the pious, the threatenings and promises of the Bible, the dispensations of Providence, the crosses, the pains, and sicknesses which themselves experience; the deaths of their relations and acquaintances, the preaching of the gospel, the warnings and invitations delivered from the pulpit, the prayers and intercessions offered at the throne of mercy in their behalf, the admonitions, and occasional forebodings of conscience, and the strivings of the Holy Spirit, with which they are sometimes indulged, are all intended to stimulate them to duty, and rouse their attention to the things which belong to their everlasting peace. But these means of grace they resist, and, in so doing, treasure up for themselves wrath against the day of wrath, and the revelation of the righteous judgment of God." O, may the compassionate Redeemer speak to our hearts, with an energy like that which accompanied his address to Saul! that, like Saul, we may bow to his authority, and throw ourselves into the arms of sovereign mercy!

"And he, trembling and astonished, said, Lord, what wilt thou have me to do? And the Lord said unto him, Arise, and go into the city, and it shall be told thee what thou must do." Wonderful, indeed, was the condescension of the Lord, in thus reasoning with one whose heart was enmity and bitterness against him. It was owing to the Saviour's merciful long suffering that he did not "make bare his arm," to destroy the persecutor, and leave him a monument of his righteous vengeance. But so it is; he spoke in mercy; his word was with power, and the call was effectual. Saul immediately submitted, with deep repentance, not presuming to offer a syllable, by way of apology for his outrageous conduct. An awful sense of his guilt, accompanied by a view of the glory of Jesus, whom he had so daringly insulted, at first overwhelmed him with grief, and almost drove him to despair. But to whom could he apply, with any hope of relief, but to Him, who, he was now convinced, is mighty to save? He resolved, therefore, to try the efficacy of an humble petition. Self-condemned, self-diffident, and sensible of his perishing need of Divine teaching, he cries out, in the language of entire submission, "Lord, what wilt thou have me to do?" Thus resigning himself unreservedly to the grace and disposal of the Almighty Redeemer, he obtained forgiveness, and was directed to go into Damascus, to be further instructed in his duty, by one of those very disciples of the Lord, whom he had intended to carry bound to Jerusalem.

Behold here the invariable effect of Divine grace upon the converted sinner. The language of Saul is the language of every real convert. "Lord, what wilt thou have me to do?" His first concern is to get a clear and satisfactory view of the way in which pardoning mercy can be extended to the penitent, returning rebel. Next the claims of gratitude are felt and acknowledged. Since this gracious Saviour has bought me with his blood, and has an indisputable right to my undivided service, how would he have me employed? How can I honour him? What can I do to promote his cause? By what means can I contribute my mite to diffuse around me, and send abroad in the earth the sweet savour of his name,

21

which has become to me "precious as ointment poured forth"? Are my present habits of life, the business in which I am engaged, the order of my family, the company I keep, and the manner in which I spend my leisure hours, and dispose of my possessions, such as comport with the precepts of his gospel? Are all my pursuits, my connections, my dealings with mankind, my speculations, and plans for enhancing my fortune, such as warrant me to expect the blessing of my Lord and Saviour on everything I do? Will the manner in which I now live and act afford me a pleasing retrospect on the bed of death? Lord, assist me in these inquiries; enable me to rectify whatever is wrong, either in my conduct or temper, and show me what thou wouldest have me to do. These and the like questions claim the attention, not only of young converts, but of every professor of the Christian religion.

In Saul's being directed to go into the city to be instructed fully in the doctrines of the gospel, and the principles of duty, we see the honour which Christ confers on his own institutions. This poor, convicted Pharisee, who had now become as a little child, that he might be made wise unto salvation, was conducted into Damascus blind, a striking emblem of the darkness of his understanding in Divine things. After three days' blindness, spent in fasting and prayer, a disciple of the Lord was sent by express commission to restore his sight, and confirm him in the Christian faith. Ananias, a minister of the gospel, was commissioned to teach this disciple of

Gamaliel, what were the first principles of the oracles of God. Under his ministry Saul was enlightened, comforted, filled with the Holy Ghost, furnished with miraculous powers, and recognized as a member of Christ's church, by receiving the ordinance of baptism. Let none, then, despise or neglect the instituted means of religious instruction. Let all attend on the preaching of the gospel, and the dispensation of its other ordinances, with seriousness, and docility of mind. "Then shall ye know, if ye follow on to know the Lord," in the way of his appointment.

But to return to the case of Saul. We have seen him, with the torch of persecution in one hand, and the death-warrant of the Lord's disciples in the other, with a band of armed soldiery in his train, leaving Jerusalem like a man of blood, breathing forth threatenings and death. We have followed him, with mingled emotions of pity and indignation, to the suburbs of Damascus, the intended scene of slaughter. There we have beheld him suddenly and unexpectedly arrested, humbled, convicted, and led into the city, as a captive of sovereign grace. And now, to our utter astonishment, and contrary to all human calculation, we behold him, with the temper of a little child, in his right mind, sitting at the feet of Jesus!

And here we might close this discourse, in devout admiration of the power and grace of the Son of God, displayed in producing such a marvellous change in such a marvellous sinner! Who is this that prays? Is Saul also among them that call on the name of the

Lord Jesus? What is become of his bloody designs against the disciples at Damascus? Where is the fury of the persecutor? Surely the prophet spoke as he was moved by the Holy Ghost; for here we see, "the wolf dwells with the lamb, and the leopard lies down with the kid," no longer seeking to hurt or destroy. Could this effect be produced by natural causes? As well might you attempt to convince me that the waters of yonder river can be made to flow backward in its channel; that the tornado can be arrested in its furious progress by the resistance of a straw; or that the sun can be obstructed in his course without the miraculous interposition of Divine power. "It is the Lord's doing; and it is marvellous in our eyes." "Blessed be the Lord God, the God of Israel, who only doeth wondrous things: and blessed be his glorious name for ever." Ps. lxxii. 18, 19.

We will close the discourse with a few practical reflections.

First, what a convincing proof does the conversion of Saul afford us of the truth and Divine original of our holy religion! Perhaps no single argument has given infidels more uneasiness than this. They never have been able, and we are confident they never will be able to dispose of it, even to their own satisfaction. The only way in which they can get rid of it, is to pronounce the whole of the history which relates to the case a cunningly devised fable. But this is manifestly unfair and foolish. With men of common sense and a sound mind, assertion will not pass for reasoning, nor will a stroke of profane wit frighten them out of their religion, or sweep away the pillar of their best hopes.

I regret that time will not allow me to place this argument in that impressive shape of which it is susceptible. All that I can say upon it, at present, must be condensed within a very small compass. When I consider Saul's education, the strength of his mind, and the force of his reasoning apparent in his writings; when I take into view his pharisaical prepossessions, his firm attachment to the Mosaic rites, his prospects of preferment among. his own nation, his early and inveterate opposition to the gospel; when I look at him leaving Jerusalem, and bending his course towards Damascus, with the deliberate determination of destroying the disciples of the Lord; when I see him, on his way, smitten to the earth by an overpowering light beaming from the heavens, and hear the voice of Jesus addressing him from the midst of that light; when I see him conquered, and hear him acknowledge the conquest; when I see him changed, and totally changed, led by the hand into the city, blind, humble, and penitent; when I look at him receiving instruction from Ananias, with the meekness of a child; when I keep my eye upon him till his sight is restored, till I see him baptized in the name of Jesus, filled with the Holy Ghost, armed with miraculous powers, going forth under the banner of the cross, proving to all, both Jews and Gentiles, that Jesus is the Christ, preaching the faith which he so

21*

lately laboured to destroy; when I follow him from town to town, from province to province, from Asia into Europe, and from Europe back again to Asia, enduring every conceivable privation, accounting all things but loss for the excellency of the knowledge of Christ, glorying in his cross, and esteeming it an honour to suffer reproach and persecution for his name, and at last, scaling his testimony with his blood, the argument drawn from his case, in confirmation of the Christian faith is, to me, absolutely irresistible and conclusive. If Paul be regarded as an honest and intelligent man, his declarations prove, incontestably, that our religion is Divine. He affirms that he received it by inspiration of God, and not by human teaching. He preached it with zeal and success before he had any communication with the other apostles; and yet he and they coincided substantially in their account, both of facts and doctrines. Now to what shall we ascribe this exact agreement, but to the influence of Heaven? Will it be said that Paul was an impostor? By what motives could he have have been induced to leave his party and form such a scheme of deception? Did he seek wealth, honour, power, or sensual gratification? No; these were not among Christians. Was he an enthusiast? No; none farther from it. He felt and manifested a noble ardour which arose from a consciousness of truth and rectitude.

But perhaps he was deceived by others. By whom? Not surely by the disciples of Christ. With them he had had no communications, and had left

Jerusalem on purpose to harass and destroy them. Nor by his former associates; for they would have put him to death for deserting their cause. The circumstances of the case leave no room for collusion. The only rational conclusion, then, is that he was constituted an apostle by the Lord Jesus Christ, and that the doctrine which he preached is a revelation from heaven, worthy of God, and suitable for man.

A second reflection is the sovereignty of God in providing for the exigencies of his people. The prospects of the Church have seldom been more unpromising than when Saul set out for Damascus. The disciples were oppressed, and harassed beyond measure. Their number was small; and as to wealth and talent, they had neither. The spirit of persecution threatened to carry all before it. But, behold, how easily Jehovah can blast the hopes, and baffle the designs of his enemies! We see here the champion of Judaism, and the avowed enemy of the cross, not only checked and defeated, but completely changed; and the whole force of his great mind directed to build up the cause, which till now he had been assiduously labouring to destroy. In view of this fact, let the friends of Christ and his gospel take fresh courage. The Church of God is bought with precious blood. She is founded on a rock, and the gates of hell shall not prevail against her. The anointed Son of the Most High sits upon God's holy mountain. Blessed and safe are all those who put their trust in him.

Thirdly, learn from this subject the freeness and efficacy of Divine grace. Let the conscience smitten penitent, who trembles under a sense of his guilt, have immediate recourse to that blood which cleanseth from all sin. Let him listen to the testimony of this same Saul, speaking from experience, and under the inspiration of God; and let him be no longer faithless, but believing: "This is a faithful saying, and worthy of all acceptation, that Christ Jesus came into the world to save sinners; of whom I am chief. Howbeit, for this cause I obtained mercy, that in me first Jesus Christ might show forth all long-suffering, for a pattern to them which should hereafter believe on him to life everlasting." 1 Tim. i. 15, 16.

CHOOSE WHOM YE WILL SERVE.

And if it seem evil unto you to serve the Lord, choose you this day
whom ye will serve.—JOSHUA xxiv. 15.

THESE words form part of the valedictory address of
Joshua to the people of Israel. About to resign his
post as their leader, and foreseeing the danger to
which they were exposed from the idolatry of the
nations among whom they were now settled, he
assembled all the tribes, with their religious and civil
officers, at Shechem. Here, after recounting to them
the wonders which God had wrought in their behalf,
he gives them a most solemn charge to pay a strict
regard to the statutes of the Lord, and abstain from
every form of idolatrous worship; warning them, at
the same time, of the consequences of a revolt from
their rightful sovereign, and pressing upon them the
necessity of an immediate and decided choice of the
God whom they will serve. "And if it seem evil
unto you to serve the Lord, choose you this day
whom ye will serve." "All Scripture is given by
inspiration of God, and is profitable for doctrine, for

reproof, for correction, and for instruction in righteousness." The passage which we have chosen as the foundation of the present exercise, appears to me, when taken in its general application, to reprove those persons who are halting between two opinions; those hesitating characters to whom the service of God seems evil, *i. e.*, hard and unreasonable, but who are yet afraid openly to renounce his claims to their obedience. If this be the case with any of you, attend, if you please, while I endeavour to influence your decision on this interesting and momentous subject. The text suggests to us three particulars, to which your attention is now requested.

I. We must serve some master.

II. We ought to serve God, rather than any other.

III. We should choose whom we will serve without delay.

I. We must serve some master. If we refuse allegiance to our lawful sovereign, we unavoidably become the slaves of some tyrannical usurper. This is proved from Scripture, and from the nature and constitution of man. The Scriptures uniformly divide mankind into two classes—the servants of God, and the servants of sin; and they teach us that a revolt from God is always followed by a more abject subjugation to some other master. Thus, says the apostle, "while they promise them liberty, they themselves are the servants of corruption; for of whom a man is overcome, of the same is he brought into bondage. Know ye not that to whom ye yield yourselves servants to obey, his servants ye are whom ye obey, whether of sin unto death, or of obedience unto righteousness?" To the same effect is the language of God to the Israelites: "Because thou servedst not the Lord thy God with joyfulness, and with gladness of heart, for the abundance of all things; therefore shalt thou serve thine enemies, which the Lord shall send against thee, in hunger, and in thirst, and in nakedness, and in want of all things; and he shall put a yoke of iron upon thy neck until he have destroyed thee." Is not all this verified in the unhappy experience of sinners? Are not those persons who take the most pains to make proselytes to impiety, and who promise their followers a complete deliverance from the trammels of education, and the scruples of conscience, themselves the most pitiable drudges of Satan? Yes; they have performed his service, and worn his fetters, till they are become insensible of their bondage; till mistaking the shadow for the substance, they glory in their imaginary liberty. These men resemble the Jews, who boasted to our Saviour that they were Abraham's children, and were never in bondage to any man; while they forgot Egypt and Babylon, and felt not the yoke of Cæsar, which was then pressing upon them.

A slight acquaintance with our own constitution will convince us that we were not formed for independence. We must pay homage; we must worship something as God. Man is an active being, and his exertions will be directed to some end. He is dependent, and must have some support, either real or imaginary, on which to rest. He is insufficient for his own happiness, and will seek it in something external. He has a soul of vast desires, and having forsaken the fountain of living waters, he will hew out for himself broken cisterns, which can hold no water. In a word, his affections must be placed supremely on some object; and it is the very nature of love to subject us, in some degree, to the object beloved. And whatever engrosses our affections, and is the object of our main pursuit, assumes, in our estimation, the place of God, and becomes our idol. It is unquestionable—if you do not serve the Lord who made, and who governs all things, you must serve some of his enemies. If you be not the servant of Jesus Christ, you are the slave of some unhallowed passion. If you be not the subject of humility, you are the abject vassal of pride. Let a man once yield himself to the dominion of any inordinate passion, and where is his boasted liberty? See the avaricious man; his money is his God: and what sacrifices is he not obliged to make to it! To it are consecrated his early and his late hours. His love of gain forbids him all that luxury which the liberal man enjoys in relieving the wants of the needy. It denies him even the necessaries and conveniences of life; he lives poor and despised, and dies unnoticed and unlamented.

The votaries of sensual pleasure and libertinism complain that the service of Jesus Christ requires too much self-denial; while they, at the same time, submit to laws the most arbitrary and unreasonable. The laws of the gospel, which require us to love God, to do unto others as we would they should do unto us; which require us to keep ourselves unspotted from the world, studying to preserve a conscience void of offence towards God and man, appear to many persons altogether intolerable, while they yield an implicit and cheerful obedience to the laws of opinion, of extravagance, and of folly. Did the service of my Master make it necessary for me to renounce any of the endearing relations, or rational enjoyments of life; if it required me to adopt expensive modes of living, which would involve myself and connections in wretchedness and want; if it required me to sacrifice all that is easy and natural in my manners, to forms and ceremonies which are studied and artificial; if it required me to hazard my own life, and the life of my neighbour, for an offence given, perhaps, inadvertently; if it denied me the pleasure of overcoming evil with good; then, indeed, I should consider it irksome; then would I sigh for deliverance from obedience to laws so harsh and despotic. "But we have not so learned Christ." These are the requirements of *your* master, O ye men of the world; these are the self-denials, these the low services which the world imposes on all its subjects. Since, therefore, you cannot remain neutral; since you must obey some master, we plead for God, and entreat you to engage in his service freely and cordially. We come to the second division of our subject.

II. We ought to serve God rather than any other being. His commandments are not grievous, but joy-

22

ous. He will give grace and glory; and no "good thing will the Lord withhold from them that walk uprightly." "My yoke is easy, and my burden is light," says the blessed Redeemer. But I blush for human nature, when I consider that arguments are necessary to induce men to engage in the reasonable and delightful service of their God and Saviour. Hear, O heavens, and be astonished; give ear, O earth, and tremble; for the Lord hath spoken: I have nourished and brought up children, and they have rebelled against me!   .

I am at a loss, not for motives, but to know what motives to select and propose to you. Consider, in the first place, the obligations which you are under to God. Creating goodness, providing munificence, and redeeming love, bind you by the most sacred ties to serve the Lord. But a few years ago you had no place in existence. Who gave you, not only a being, but so high and so honourable a grade in the scale of being? The answer is obvious. You have a soul susceptible of the purest enjoyment, and which is endued with immortality. Who thus distinguished you from the beasts of the field, and the fowls of the air? In whom do you live and move? Whose air do you breathe, whose sun warms you, whose bounty feeds you, whose earth supports you? Who preserves your health, while others are sick? Who prolongs your life, and gives you space for repentance, while others die around you? Who sent his Son to seek and to save you, when lost, and guilty, and helpless? In the hour of death, when heart and flesh shall fail, who do you expect will be the strength of your soul, and your portion for ever? From whose mercy do you hope for pardon and salvation? and in whose heaven do you hope to spend an eternity of bliss? The answer to these queries is plain and indubitable. If then there is such a thing as justice, and if it consists in rendering to every one his due, be just, and you must serve God. If there is such a thing as gratitude, and if it consists in a readiness to make a suitable return for favours received, be grateful, and you must be religious. Consider who is the Author of your life, your happiness, and your hopes; and let me "beseech you, therefore, brethren, by the mercies of God, that you present your bodies a living sacrifice, holy and acceptable unto God, which is your reasonable service."

Consider, also, the end for which God employs you in his service. The devil and the world would enlist you in their service, from interested and selfish views. But in this respect, who is a God like unto the Lord? Does he wish to display his grandeur, and reap advantage from the increase of his subjects? "Can a man be profitable unto God, as he that is wise may be profitable unto himself?" "Is it any pleasure to the Almighty that thou art righteous; or gain to the Most High that thou makest thy way perfect?" No, no; he stands in no need of you, but he knows that you stand in perishing need of him. "O," says he, "that there were such a heart in them, that they would fear me, and keep all my commandments always, that it might be well with

them, and with their children for ever." Our Heavenly
Father wishes you to serve him here, that you may
be fitted to enjoy him hereafter. By the humble
forms of worship which he has established in his
Church militant, he intends to prepare you for taking
part in the more exalted services of his everlasting
temple above. He does not require you to obey
him that he may derive advantage from your obedience, but that he may bestow upon you innumerable
blessings under the idea of a reward. And by what
strong and lively images do the Scriptures describe
the reward which remains for the righteous! It is
a house not made with hands, eternal in the heavens;
it is a city which hath foundations, whose builder
and maker is God; it is a kingdom which cannot
be shaken; it is a crown of glory which fadeth not
away. He has given you exceeding great and precious promises, to engage and encourage you in his
service; and these promises are yea, and amen, in
Christ Jesus. "Therefore, thus saith the Lord God,
Behold, my servants shall eat, but ye shall be hun-
gry; behold, my servants shall drink, but ye shall
be thirsty; behold, my servants shall rejoice, but ye
shall be ashamed; behold, my servants shall sing for
joy of heart, but ye shall cry for sorrow of heart,
and shall howl for vexation of spirit." "Even the
youths shall faint and be weary, and the young men
shall utterly fail; but they that wait upon the Lord
shall renew their strength; they shall mount up with
wings as eagles; they shall run and not be weary,
and they shall walk and not faint." And does not

the experience of God's real servants, attest his faithfulness to these engagements? If not, why do they persevere in his service? Why do they not return to the country whence they came? Ask them, and they will tell you, that having tasted of the grapes of Eshcol, they no longer sigh for the leeks and onions of Egypt. It is true, they will acknowledge to you, We have often to mourn and lament; the service of our Master, however, is not the cause of our grief, but our want of perfect conformity to his will, is what pains us. We are nevertheless cheered with the hope, that our sorrow shall be turned into joy. When the world frowns, we are not dismayed; for our Saviour has forewarned us, that in the world we shall have tribulation. Our God sometimes smiles upon us, and in our darkest seasons, he orders our lot, and makes all things work together for our greatest good. "Heaven," says one, "will more than make amends for these troubles of the way thither." And when told that his happiness was all future, "No," he replies, "I have now foretastes and earnests of my heavenly inheritance. I feel a peace which passeth all understanding; and sometimes I rejoice with joy unspeakable and full of glory. In his earthly sanctuary, I behold his power and his glory. In my closet, I find it good to draw near my God. His statutes are my song in the house of my pilgrimage, and I rejoice in his word, as one that findeth great spoil. Once I thought like you. I supposed if I began a religious course, I should never have another happy day; but I never had a happy

22*

day before. I have found nothing of the fetters and bondage of which I had heard, and by which I had been disgusted. His service has been perfect freedom; and none of his commands are grievous. And O could I now lay open my soul! could I make you see as I see, and feel as I feel! O taste and see that the Lord is good; blessed is the man that trusteth in him."

And now having shown you that it is more reasonable, and more advantageous for you to serve God than any other master, let me press upon you the necessity of an immediate and decided choice.

III. We should without delay choose whom we will serve. "If it seem evil unto you to serve the Lord, choose you this day whom ye will serve." Remember the time is fast approaching, and may now be much nearer than we imagine, when a marked distinction will be made between him that serveth God, and him that serveth him not. I am the more urgent on this point, because I believe that could you be brought to make a decisive choice, you would choose the good part, which shall never be taken from you. The world is filled with almost-Christians, and there is awful reason to fear that many who are now halting between two opinions, will at last strive to enter in, and shall not be able, because they did not engage in the service of God with full purpose of heart. Are you in some measure convinced that it is your duty to serve the Lord? Why not enter upon his service with all your hearts now, without farther delay? Are you discouraged by the obstacles which lie in the way? But when will these obstacles diminish? Are you afraid to encounter the frowns of the world? But when will the world, which lieth in wickedness, be favourably disposed to real godliness? Do you fear the difficulty of changing your manner of living, or the mode of your family government? Be assured this difficulty is every day increasing. But still you wish a little more time to consider on the subject. Pray, when will you determine? The next year, the next month, to-morrow? We have nothing to do with to-morrow. We know not what a day may bring forth. Choose you *this day.* " To-day, if ye will hear his voice, harden not your hearts." While you are hesitating, God may say of you, "None of these men who were bidden, shall taste of my supper." The arrows of death fly thick on every side of you, and have you made a covenant with death? are you at an agreement with hell? Perhaps the feet of them who have buried thy neighbour are at the door to carry thee out. "Awake, thou that sleepest; arise from the dead, and Christ shall give thee light." Will none of you realize that pleasing prophecy which has for many ages excited the prayers, and encouraged the hopes of the pious? "One shall say, I am the Lord's; and another shall call himself by the name of Jacob; and another shall subscribe with his hand unto the Lord, and surname himself by the name of Israel."

It is high time for us to awake out of sleep; the night is far spent, the day is at hand. Many of us, it is to be feared, have been serving the flesh and the lusts thereof all our days. Surely it is now time that we begin to serve the Lord who made us. The time of our probation may be much nearer a close than we imagine; and nothing is more certain, nothing is more reasonable, than that he who refuses to serve God here, should be excluded from his presence and enjoyment hereafter. But perhaps you are ready to say to me, as the people of Israel said to Joshua, "God forbid that we should forsake the Lord, to serve other gods." Would to Heaven this were the firm purpose of your souls! I do not suppose that any of you bow down to idols made with men's hands; but I nevertheless fear that many of you are justly chargeable with a species of idolatry no less dangerous. "No man," says our Saviour, "can serve two masters; for either he will hate the one and love the other, or else he will hold to the one and despise the other. Ye cannot serve God and mammon." From this declaration, it is plain that you may serve mammon to the neglect of God; for both together cannot be obeyed. Wealth, power, honour, fame, sensual pleasure, gay amusement, constitute what we usually express by the term *mammon*, or the world, when opposed to religion. Here then are the two masters that claim dominion over us—God and the world. One of them we must serve, both we cannot; because their dispositions and their commands are diametrically opposite to one another. The world invites us to indulge all our appetites without control; to entangle ourselves in the cares and distractions of business; or to give ourselves up entirely to pleasure, amusement, and every kind of luxurious indulgence. These are the services which one master requires. But there is another Master, whose injunctions are of a very different nature. That other Master is God; and his commands are, to give him our hearts; to love him with all our heart, soul, mind, and strength; to be temperate in all things; to make our moderation known unto all men; to fix our affections on things above; to have our conversation in heaven; to cast all our cares upon him, and to take up our cross, and follow Christ.

You see, then, it is impossible to obey two masters, whose orders are so contradictory. Now, whether you should serve a world which lieth in sin and ignorance, rather than your Maker and Redeemer, let reason and common-sense decide. Our Creator expects to reign absolute in our hearts. He will not be served by halves; he will not accept of a divided empire; he will not suffer us to halt between two opinions; we must make a choice, and cleave to the one side or the other. Therefore, "if the Lord be God, follow him; but if Baal, then follow him."

DIVINE GUIDANCE.

And I will bring the blind by a way that they knew not; I will
lead them in paths that they have not known: I will make darkness light before them, and crooked things straight. These things
will I do unto them, and not forsake them.—ISAIAH xlii. 16.

SPIRITUAL blindness is one of the sad effects of our
apostasy from God. We were formed, originally, in
the image of our Maker, and that image consisted
partly in knowledge—a true and correct knowledge
of Him who made us, of the duty which we owed him,
and of the happiness to be enjoyed in his favour and
service. But, ever since our first parents ate "the
fruit of that forbidden tree, whose mortal taste
brought death into the world, and all our woes,"
"darkness has covered the earth, and gross darkness
the people." "The God of this world hath blinded
the minds of them which believe not, lest the light of
the glorious gospel of Christ, who is the image of God,
should shine unto them." 2 Cor. iv. 4. And what
renders our case the more deplorable is, that we naturally "love darkness rather than light." We are
willing to remain ignorant of our duty, because we
have no disposition to perform it. And were the
Father of lights to leave us to follow the bias of our

depraved hearts, our ignorance must inevitably issue in the shades of eternal death. But, blessed be God, who, in tender mercy, hath caused the day-spring from on high to visit us, to give light to them that sit in darkness and in the shadow of death, to guide our feet into the way of peace! O how much to be admired is the condescension of the high and lofty One in the conduct of his redeeming grace! Self-moved and unsolicited, he comes, by his Holy Spirit, to recover us from the ruins of the fall. He finds us not only lost to all sense of duty and gratitude, but utterly unacquainted with the malignity of our disease and the process by which an effectual cure may be expected. He graciously undertakes to heal our maladies, to reclaim our wanderings, to impart to us the light of life and the joys of salvation. "I will bring the blind by a way that they knew not; I will lead them in paths that they have not known." This saying is verified,

I. In the conversion of sinners. Here God's ways are not as our ways, nor his thoughts as our thoughts. Persons generally expect to be translated from darkness to light, and from the power of Satan unto God, by a sudden and sensible, but joyous and delightful operation of Divine grace upon their minds. They fancy that the change will be attended with such strong marks and evidences as shall afford them an assurance of their interest in the Redeemer, and inspire them at once with joy unspeakable and full of glory. But, in this instance, God moves in a mysterious way. He brings them to himself in a way which they knew not. He wounds to heal, and humbles to exalt. He apprizes men of their danger, and then presents them with a suitable remedy. He gives them a view of the corruption of their nature, and fills them with shame and sorrow for their sin. He shows them the purity and majesty of his law, and by setting their iniquities in array before them, makes them sensible that they deserve to be punished. He charges home guilt upon the conscience and makes them feel the plague of their own hearts. He presses upon their minds the obligations of duty, and, at the same time, convinces them of their insufficiency to perform one holy act, or put forth one right desire. When they would do good, evil is present; when they attempt to pray, they find it a strange work; their doubts and fears, with the remembrance of their past neglect of God, drive them back from the throne of grace. Satan assails them with his fiery darts, their attention is diverted, their minds are harassed with evil thoughts, and they are sometimes ready to yield to despair and turn back to perdition. Yet an awakened conscience will not permit them to live easy in the neglect of known duty. They are straitened in their own bowels, their understandings are enveloped in darkness, their wills are obstinate, their souls cleave to the dust, and they are often constrained to cry out, with fear and trembling, "What shall I do to be saved?"

Thus they are conducted "in a way which they knew not." But this is the way in which God ordinarily brings back the blind to the Shepherd and

Bishop of their souls. The three thousand, who were pricked in their hearts, on the day of Pentecost, probably did not regard their conviction of sin as a token of the Lord's mercy. But it so turned out. "They who gladly received the word were baptized; and, continuing daily, with one accord, in the temple, and breaking bread from house to house, did eat their meat with gladness and singleness of heart; praising God, and having favour with all the people." The jailor at Philippi, under his first awakening impressions, was tempted to destroy himself; but, in due time, he was made to rejoice, "believing in God, with all his house."

II. This saying is verified in the experience of the pious. They are conducted, by the providence of God, in paths which they have not known. The life of Christians is far from being a life of uninterrupted joy and peace. They who expect the crown of righteousness without contending for it, will find themselves in a mistake. It is true, "the ways of wisdom are ways of pleasantness, and all her paths are peace;" but the most eminently pious still bear about with them a body of sin and death. Here is a source of great trouble and solicitude. The depth of iniquity in the heart is not discovered all at once, and every new discovery gives fresh uneasiness; and God often permits his people to be in heaviness through manifold temptations. The heart is treacherous; and the world, with its painted pleasures, is constantly opposing their growth in grace. The streams of depravity flow in all directions; and, though persons whose dispositions are congenial to the spirit of a world that lieth in wickedness, sustain no conflict, experience no trial from this quarter, yet those who are born of God, and are breathing after holiness, are deeply affected with the opposition, and realize the Saviour's declaration: "In the world ye shall have tribulation."

By the dispensations of his providence, also, God often leads his people in paths which they have not known. How mysterious his conduct towards Israel! He had taken them under his special care. He was their Ruler, their Protector, and Guide; yet they were allowed to wander amid dangers and discouragements for forty years in the wilderness. How distressing the case of Job! How complicated and overwhelming his afflictions! Verily he was led in paths which he had not known; and the difficulty of reconciling providences with promises, impelled him, on several occasions, to charge God foolishly. "Is it good unto thee that thou shouldest oppress, that thou shouldest despise the work of thy hands, and shine upon the counsel of the wicked?" Job x. 3. "If I be wicked, woe unto me; and if I be righteous, yet will I not lift up my head. I am full of confusion; therefore see thou mine affliction, for it increaseth. Thou huntest me as a fierce lion: and again thou showest thyself marvellous upon me." Job x. 15, 16. The result proved the blindness of Job, and illustrated the Divine goodness: "The Lord blessed the latter end of Job more than his beginning." St. James's decision in the case, is full of piety and useful instruction: "Behold, we count them happy which endure: ye have heard of the patience of Job, and have seen the end of the Lord; that the Lord is very pitiful, and of tender mercy." James v. 11. The experience of Joseph is also in point. God intended, from the beginning, to make him ruler over his brethren; but antecedent to his exaltation, he permitted him to be greatly afflicted and depressed. He fell a victim to fraternal jealousy; was sold by his own brethren, and dragged into Egypt as a slave, and was there cast into prison on a false accusation. He languished for years, a stranger in a strange land; but in due time the purpose of Heaven was developed, when it became evident that the path·in which this good man had been led, though covered with clouds and darkness, was, nevertheless, the right way.

Not to mention other instances, the Saviour himself was a man of sorrows, and acquainted with grief. In bringing many sons to glory, he was made perfect, through suffering. In short, the subjects of Divine grace find themselves, from first to last, conducted in a way which they knew not, and in paths which they have not known. In regeneration, all things become new; and, during the progress of sanctification, many things in the conduct of Providence appear dark and mysterious. But the next clause of our text contains a promise, at once animating and consolatory:

III. "I will make darkness light before them, and crooked things straight." The convinced sinner, and the young convert may take encouragement from this promise. It seems intended to induce such to give all diligence to make their calling and election sure. "Then shall ye know, if ye follow on to know the Lord." The good work may have been begun, where it is, yet, far from being completed. The dawn of the morning preeedes the full blaze of noon-day. The light is the same in kind, but inferior in degree. All that are born of God are influeneed by the same spirit, and are impelled by similar hopes and desires; but all may not have arrived to the same stature, or possess equal light and strength. The Scriptures speak of little ehildren, young men, and fathers in Christ. They who have but just begun to breathe in the new world, eannot eomprehend all the wonders with which they are surrounded. The infant arrives by progressive steps to the maturity of manhood. The heavens and the earth might have been ereated in an instant by the Almighty; but he saw fit to spend six days in doing what he eould have aecomplished, by the word of his power, in a single moment. The designs of Providenee are unfolded gradually. Several ages were oceupied in completing the work of redemption. Let not the young Christian, then, be diseouraged, if he does not attain suddenly to the stature of a perfect man in Christ. However defieient in knowledge and emper you may now be, if the Spirit of the Lord has become your Teacher, he will make you wise unto salvation. In the mean time, be doeile, be diligent, seareh the Scriptures, be often at the throne of grace. Let not your minds be distraeted by intrieate and abstruse points in religion. A speeulating and disputatious spirit is extremely unfavourable to your profieieney in the Divine life. You should direct the whole foree of your mind to the plain doctrines and duties of the gospel. Look narrowly into your own bosoms. "Examine yourselves, whether ye be in the faith." Try to ascertain what spirit you are of. Rest not easy, waste not your time on other subjects, till you find drawn upon your souls those features which mark the new man, in Christ Jesus. Contemplate the law of God in its purity, spirituality, and awful sanctions. Consider what sin is: the transgression of the law, or any want of conformity to it; ingratitude to your most bountiful Benefactor; disobedience to your Heavenly Father; treason against the Great King of heaven and earth. Meditate much and deeply on the love of God, as it is manifested in the gift of a Saviour. Fix your attention closely on the mediatorial character of Jesus Christ. He is "the end of the law for righteousness to every one that believeth"—make him your righteousness. He is our wisdom—let his word dwell in you richly. He is the propitiation for our sins—his blood cleanseth from all sin; go, wash in this fountain, it is the true Bethesda. In one word, "He is the way, the truth, and the life." Commit yourselves to him in well-doing; prove your respect for his authority by keeping his sayings, and he will give you the light of life, and you shall not be confounded, world without end. "I will make darkness light before them, and crooked things straight."

Yes, Christians, though clouds and darkness, difficulties and dangers lie along the path to heaven, these clouds shall be dispersed, and all your trials shall conduce to your peace and comfort in the issue. Even in this vale of tears, you have frequently occasion to acknowledge that it is good for you to be afflicted. And what you know not now, you shall know hereafter. The light of glory, reflected back on those mysterious paths in which you are now travelling, will constrain you to acknowledge the goodness of God, and to sing through eternal ages, "Just and true are all thy ways, thou King of saints!" If your Heavenly Father permits you to fall into divers temptations now, it is for the trial of your faith, and for the display of his power and grace in rescuing you from the snares of the adversary. He regards you as trees of his own planting; and, if he prune you, it is that you may be the more fruitful. All the paths of the Lord are mercy and truth, to such as keep his covenant, and do his commandments. They shall realize the promise, "I will make darkness light before them, and crooked things straight."

But, perhaps, you are sometimes fearful that God may yet leave you to perish. Dismiss the unworthy suspicion. God will not despise the work of his own hand, neither will he leave it unfinished. His kindly regards for his people are permanent and unalterable. Hear how he speaks in the conclusion of our text: "These things will I do unto them and not forsake them." He may, indeed, seem to forsake them for a season; but he will never utterly abandon them. He says, "For a small moment have I forsaken thee; but with great mercies will I gather thee. In a little wrath I hid my face from thee for a moment, but with everlasting kindness will I have mercy on thee; saith the Lord, thy Redeemer." Isa. liv. 7, 8. The Lord will not suffer the soul of the righteous to perish.

Paul says, "I am persuaded that neither death, nor

life, nor angels, nor principalities, nor powers, nor things present, nor things to come, nor height, nor depth, nor any other creature, shall be able to separate us from the love of .God, which is in Christ Jesus our Lord." Rom. viii. 38, 39.

If God had meant to leave you to die in your sins and perish, he would not have convinced you of your depravity, and filled your minds with those anxious desires to glorify and enjoy him. Contrition of soul, solicitude to know your duty, and a relish for the things of religion, are not the fruits of nature, neither are they the productions of Satan. He who hath wrought these dispositions in you, is God; and he does nothing in vain. He cannot deny himself; he will cherish the seed which he has sown, and gratify the holy longings which he has imparted to the soul. "Be not faithless, then, but believing." Be strong in the Lord Jesus Christ, and hope unto the end. The path in which God is leading you is not strewed with flowers; but it has been trodden by thousands, who are now walking the golden streets, and rejoicing in the light of heaven. It is one which, though beset with thorns, and sometimes enveloped in darkness, leads to glory, honour, and immortal felicity. Yet a little while, and your faith shall give place to vision, and your mourning be turned into joy unspeakable and full of glory. He who hath begun the good work in you, will perform it till the day of Jesus Christ; till that happy day to be followed by no night, when you shall join the triumph of angels and the spirits of the just made perfect.

Finally, if the view which we have taken of this

subject be correct, it is plain that those persons who are still walking in the old beaten path of depraved nature, are strangers to a work of grace on their hearts, and have not yet taken one step heavenward. "If any man be in Christ, he is a new creature." God conducts his people in a way which they have not known. This conquest of redeeming mercy is not achieved without a struggle between the flesh and the Spirit. The truth is fully established by the testimony of holy writ, and by the experience of the pious in all ages of the world. "Examine yourselves, whether ye be in the faith." If you are in religious matters now what you have always been, you have fearful reason to conclude that you are in the gall of bitterness and in the bond of iniquity. I know that the Scriptures speak of some who were "sanctified from the womb;" but the meaning is that they were designed and raised up by Providence for some special service in the church, not that they were so pure and blameless as not to need the renewing grace of God, which turns men from darkness to light, and conducts them to glory in a way to which they are by nature strangers.

THE END.

www.ingramcontent.com/pod-product-compliance
Lightning Source LLC
Chambersburg PA
CBHW021057030726
47496CB00006B/1876